THE FIXER ..ER

PHOEBE MACLEOD

Boldwood

First published in Great Britain in 2024 by Boldwood Books Ltd.

Cover Design by Head Design Ltd

Cover Photography: Shutterstock

A CIP catalogue record for this book is available from the British Library.

Paperback ISBN 978-1-83751-438-0

Large Print ISBN 978-1-83751-439-7

Hardback ISBN 978-1-83751-437-3

Ebook ISBN 978-1-83751-440-3

Kindle ISBN 978-1-83751-441-0

Audio CD ISBN 978-1-83751-432-8

MP3 CD ISBN 978-1-83751-433-5

Digital audio download ISBN 978-1-83751-436-6

Boldwood Books Ltd
23 Bowerdean Street
London SW6 3TN
www.boldwoodbooks.com

To Sarah and Phoebe. Thank you for your encouragement and support.

1

'I'm telling you, it's perfect, Em. Just what we've been looking for. Two bedrooms and a five-minute walk to the station for you, possibly even less.' I'm barely able to contain my excitement, but I can tell that my best friend still has doubts.

'It's Sevenoaks though, Alex. We can't afford that, can we?'

'It's only a hundred a month each more than we agreed. If we economise a bit, I reckon we can do it. Plus, the person in the flat opposite is moving out as well and the landlord is listing it with us, so I'll even be able to choose our neighbours.'

'Alexandra Griffiths!' Emma exclaims, using my full name to emphasise her disapproval. 'You can't do that! Surely that's against some law of estate agency? Anyway, if both flats are falling vacant at the same time, that's an alarm bell, isn't it? Why does everyone suddenly want to leave?'

'It's nothing to worry about,' I reassure her. 'The woman who lives in our flat is marrying the bloke in the flat opposite and they're buying a house together. A very nice house, actually. I took them on the viewings.'

Emma sighs. 'You're really sold on this place, aren't you?'

'I am a little,' I admit. 'We can continue looking if you want, but I think we'll be hard pushed to find anything better. I can even vouch for the landlord. He owns the photographic studio underneath and has been a customer of ours ever since he first let the flat out.'

Emma laughs. 'You do know that you referred to it as "our" flat just now, don't you? That kind of gives you away as more than "just a little" sold on it. Here's a question though: if the landlord is only downstairs, how do we know he's not going to keep "just popping up" at inconvenient moments? Morgan at work was telling me about this flat she rented where she was convinced the landlord had hidden cameras installed, because he always arrived to fix or check things when she was in her dressing gown.'

'He's not going to be perving at us. Apart from anything else, I've met his wife and she's not someone who would put up with him eyeing up other women. So, what do you say?'

The silence from the other end of the phone indicates that my pitch hasn't quite worked yet so, after a few seconds, I continue. 'Think about it: no more having to justify your comings and goings to your parents, a much shorter commute for your glamorous marketing job, and you get to share a flat with your best friend.'

'Huh. It doesn't feel very glamorous at the moment. I'm working on a campaign for dog food, did I tell you? Anyway, do I get to see it before I make my mind up?'

And this is where I'm going to have to really turn my saleswoman's charm up to the max.

'It's not on the market yet,' I explain. 'The landlord only confirmed that he's looking to let it again on Monday and I went over to take pictures this afternoon. Roxanne, my boss, knows I'm interested, but she's also made it clear that she's not going to stall putting it on the open market because of me. A flat as nice as this isn't going to hang around, especially given how close it is to the station, so I don't think we can wait until the weekend. I can send you pictures though.'

'We can always go for the other flat if we miss this one, can't we?'

'It's not as nice.'

'Oh, for goodness' sake! You're impossible to negotiate with when you're like this. How long do I have to make my mind up?'

'I need to know by close of play tomorrow. Sorry, Em. You won't regret it, trust me.'

'I do. You are supposed to be the property expert, after all. But it's a big thing to sign up for a flat without even seeing it. Send me the pictures and I'll have a look at them tonight.'

'Will do. And look on the bright side.'

'Which is?'

'If we were looking in London, we would probably have to pounce without even seeing pictures. I've heard flats there go within minutes of being listed.'

'Just as well we aren't, then. I'll catch you later, yeah?'

As soon as I hang up the phone, I open a new email, attach the pictures of the flat, pausing once again to admire the sleek kitchen units, large living space and the two decent sized bedrooms. I particularly like the main bedroom, which has a lovely en-suite bathroom, and I can't help seeing myself in it, even though I know I may have to let Emma have it as a concession for the flat being more expensive than we'd budgeted. I'm just reviewing them one final time, trying to second guess how she will feel when she sees them, when I hear my name being called.

'Alex!' Roxanne calls. 'You need to get going if you're going to get to the Chevening viewing before the Robertsons.'

'Shit. Sorry, Roxanne.' I hastily check that I've attached all the photos to the email and click send, before grabbing my bag, the

details of the house I'm showing the Robertsons, and dashing out
of the back door to my car.

Mr and Mrs Robertson are a lovely couple, looking to downsize
now that their children have flown the nest. They've accepted a
substantial seven-figure offer on their current home in Kippington,
but nothing they've viewed so far has hit the mark. The fact that
they don't really know what they want makes it particularly difficult to choose which properties to show them. I know they're registered with pretty much all the estate agents in Sevenoaks, and
Roxanne has made it clear that I should see it as a personal chal-
lenge to find them their dream home and secure the business.
However, we're eight properties down so far without so much as a
flicker of excitement. I'm showing them an oast house today,
hoping that they'll be captivated by its individuality.

'I'm so sorry I'm late!' I exclaim as I pull up behind them and
practically throw myself out of the car.

'Don't worry, Alex,' Mrs Robertson soothes. 'We were early
because George wanted to spend some time getting a feel for the
area.'

'What do you think?' I ask him.

'I like it. A village feel, but not too remote. I've driven past it a
number of times but I've never been into the village itself.'

I switch seamlessly into sales mode. 'You're right. You've got the
best of both worlds here because you're away from the main road
so you get the village feel, but you've still got everything you're
used to in Sevenoaks pretty much on your doorstep.'

'I'm just not sure an oast house is us,' Mrs Robertson says
uncertainly. 'I've never understood how you order fitted carpet for
a round room.'

'Why don't I show you inside and then you can get a better
impression,' I tell her as I unlock the door. The truth is that I don't
have any idea how you order carpet for a round room either, but

I'm hoping that the general standard of fit and finish in here will deflect her. 'The current owners have done a lot of work,' I explain as we step into the hallway, 'but it's very sympathetic to the character of the house. So you've got all the mod cons, but tastefully done.'

Half an hour later, I'm cautiously optimistic as I wave them goodbye. Mrs Robertson's concern about the round room was immediately silenced when she saw the elaborate parquet floor with underfloor heating that the current owners had laid in the oast, and they were both very taken with the garden. Mr Robertson was even working out where he'd put his new garden office, which I took as a very good sign.

'How did you get on?' Roxanne asks as I breeze back into the office just after four.

'I don't want to jinx anything, but they liked it. This might be the one,' I tell her.

'That would be a relief. One in the eye for Sarah too. She was convinced they were going to buy that revolting new build she's got on her books.'

Roxanne's rivalry with Sarah Hungerford, who runs one of the other estate agencies in Sevenoaks, is both long-standing and fierce. The weird thing is that they're also close friends, meeting up after work most Fridays for a drink and often socialising at weekends with their families. I have no idea how they square the two sides of their relationship, but they seem to manage. Roxanne's latest jibe does make me smile though; she couldn't talk highly enough of the new build when she was the one pitching to sell it. She was practically drooling over the double height hallway and the acres of glass that flood the house with natural light, but as soon as Sarah snatched it from under her nose, it was downgraded to little more than a disgusting hovel.

I unlock my computer and check my emails and I'm surprised

to see that Emma has come back to me already. I open her mail and read.

Which bedroom do I get?
E x

I consider carefully for a few moments. The fact that she's asked means it's not a done deal and I could potentially wangle the bigger bedroom, maybe citing it as part of my finder's reward, but I can't do that to my best friend. Instead, I tap the reply button and type:

Toss a coin? Rock paper scissors? Best of three?
A x

I'm flat out for the rest of the afternoon, giving updates to customers and chasing solicitors, but I keep a careful eye on my inbox and, just before five, the reply comes in.

Are the bedrooms next to each other? I don't want to listen to you and Thomas having sex.
E x

She's unbelievable. I start banging out a reply about our ability to have sex surprisingly quietly before realising that this is totally inappropriate content for an email from my work account. Deleting my original rant, I reply more tactfully.

There is a bathroom between the two bedrooms. You can be assured of my discretion and I will trust you to return the favour. I'm about to leave work so suggest you contact me on my phone if there's anything else you need.

A x

A few seconds later my phone pings with a message from her.

'Assured of my discretion'? LMAO! Sounds creepy as fuck. We're renting a flat, not burying a body. Plus, what have I got to be discreet about? Chance would be a fine thing.

Emma wears her singleness like a badge of shame, but the reality is that she'd have no trouble getting a boyfriend if she wasn't paranoid about still living at home with her parents at the age of twenty-seven. As she puts it, 'It would be a hell of a passion killer if Mum knocked on the door asking if we wanted a cup of tea when we were in the middle of getting it on'. I understand where she's coming from, but this is one of the reasons why moving in together is going to be so good for both of us. I get to leave behind my room in the grotty terraced house I share with two slobby boys in Tonbridge and she gets her longed-for freedom. I smile as I type out a message to her.

For all you know, the man of your dreams is somewhere in Sevenoaks waiting for you. Are you a howler BTW? I need to know in case there's something in the rent agreement about excess noise.

As suspected, she comes back straight away.

Is that an actual thing that would be in the agreement??

I smile as I type my reply.

Can you imagine? 'No sex above fifty decibels.' Maybe we should add it. You'd be amazed about the number of noisy sex complaints people

make in flats. 'In order to secure your letting, please submit a recording
of you having sex so we can assess the noise level'... ROFL x

She must be on her way to the station to catch her train home,
because I can see she hasn't read it. I quickly bash out a couple of
replies to enquiry emails before shutting down my computer and
setting off for home. When I get there, the two bikes clogging up
the hallway tell me that my housemates, Damian and Gareth, are
obviously home already. I don't know what it is about bicycles, but
they seem determined either to impale you with something sharp
as you pass or ensure that a handlebar snags on some part of your
clothing, causing them to lose their precarious balance and
collapse in a heap on the floor. I won't miss the bikes, that's for
sure. I stick my head around the sitting room door, but they're
deeply engrossed in some shoot-em-up game on the PlayStation,
so I file through to the kitchen to make a cup of tea to take up to
my room. Our kitchen is a bit of a shithole at the best of times, but
it's reached a whole new level today. There are dirty dishes piled
up in the sink and on the side, as well as a smear of what looks like
butter on the edge of the worktop where one of them obviously
wiped a knife.

'Guys, what the bloody hell?' I shout at the top of my voice as I
survey the carnage.

'Don't worry, we're going to clear it up as soon as we've finished
this,' Damian replies from the other room.

There are so many things I am not going to miss about living
here, I think as I fill the kettle and try to decontaminate a tiny
space to make my cup of tea. My phone vibrates in my pocket; it's a
message from Emma.

It's been so long since I had sex that I can't remember what noises I
make, let alone whether they're above fifty decibels. How loud is that

anyway? I really need to get away from Mum and Dad. I just hope this flat is as good as you say it is. It looks very nice in the photos. I've even checked the ticket prices and Sevenoaks to London is over £100 cheaper per month than Tunbridge Wells, so I'm quids in!

I smile as I reply.

I'm sure the odd ladylike whimper will be fine, just keep it down, OK? Are we taking it then?

Her answer comes straight back.

You bet we are! What are we going to do about furniture though?

I've already thought of this.

If you like the look of the furniture that's already there, I think Sophie, the current tenant, is open to offers. I'm happy to buy her bed off her, if you're happy to bring yours.

I've carried my tea up to my room and I'm changing out of my work clothes when her final message comes in.

If you think I'm bringing my tragic single bed to my new life, you've got another thing coming. The gorgeous man you've promised me will take one look at it and run a mile. I will be bed shopping on Saturday.

I glance down at my own single bed, where Thomas and I have spent a number of very uncomfortable nights, and imagine myself sinking into the sumptuous double that awaits me. I can't wait to move in.

2

'I know I said this last time we came in here, but this is even better than it looked in the photos,' Emma remarks as we unlock the door and walk into the flat laden with supermarket bags on our first day. 'Are you sure you don't mind having the smaller bedroom?'

'You won fair and square,' I tell her, plastering on a smile. Of course I would have preferred the bigger bedroom, but the other one is still nice, and it's a small price to pay in the grand scheme of things. It took a bit of pushing and shoving to manoeuvre the bed that Sophie left behind into the second bedroom to make way for the massive double bed that Emma has bought, but I was comforted to see that there's still plenty of space in the smaller bedroom, so I don't feel like I've been too short-changed. Also, I'm expecting to spend my evenings in the sitting room watching TV, reading and chatting with Emma, rather than hiding in my bedroom like I used to in Tonbridge, so I really will just be using my room to sleep in. I brush my hand over the immaculate worktop in the kitchen and sigh with contentment.

'Tell me about the people in the flat opposite,' she demands as we're unpacking the grocery shopping. We decided to go halves on our first shop; a move I'm already regretting as Emma patently has no concept of living on a budget, lobbing random products into the trolley 'just in case' or because 'it's a store cupboard staple'. I don't know in which parallel universe anchovies and artichoke hearts are store cupboard staples, but I'm so happy to be in this beautiful flat that I'm prepared to overlook this particular quirk for now.

'I don't know much about them,' I tell her. 'I didn't handle the letting in the end. It's two men and they're moving in in a couple of weeks, that's all I know.'

'Two men as in a couple, or two men as in a flat share like us?'

'No idea. Does it matter?'

'Of course not. I was just curious, that's all.'

'If you wanted, we could be good neighbours and invite them round for a drink or something. What do you think?'

'I don't know, Alex. What if they're really boring and we can't get rid of them, and then they invite us back and we get sucked into having to be friendly with the dullest people on the planet?'

'Bit pessimistic, but I take your point.'

'Why don't I go round there with a packet of biscuits or something when they're moving in and get the lie of the land instead? That way we can find out what they're like without committing to being pally.'

'Good idea. I like that,' I agree.

'Talking of men, when's Thomas coming to stay?' Emma reaches into the bag she's unpacking and pulls out a packet of earplugs, waving them suggestively at me. At least I know what they're for now, I suppose.

'We haven't set anything yet. He's focused on his exhibition at the moment. It's only a couple of weeks away now, so he's a bit stressed.'

'Is this the local art group one, in the village hall?'

'Yes, but you'd think it was a top London gallery from the way he talks about it.'

'Are you going?'

'Of course. I've promised his mum that I'll help her with the refreshments. She's got this whole bee in her bonnet about serving wine and canapés like art galleries do when they have exhibitions, bless her.'

'She's not going to do that for the whole weekend, is she? It'll bankrupt her!'

'No, just the preview evening on the Friday, thankfully. From what she's told me, it will be the people who have pieces in the exhibition, their hangers-on and a few other specially invited guests. Thomas only has three paintings in the show; the rest of the exhibition is stuff from other local artists. Apparently, there's been a bit of controversy because one of the local groups has been doing a series on life drawing, and the parish council were worried about obscene content.'

'Hang on, let me get this straight,' Emma remarks when we've finished sniggering. 'Are you telling me that Thomas's mum is splashing out on wine and canapés for all these people when her son only has three paintings in the show? Isn't anyone else contributing?'

'I think she's trying to curry favour. According to Thomas, a couple of the other exhibitors weren't completely happy about him taking part when he's not a member of a recognised group or society.'

'She's buying them off then.'

'Yup, that's pretty much exactly what she's doing.'

'Wow. I wish my mum would do things like that for me.'

'Yeah, me too. But he's her only child and she dotes on him, especially since the divorce. If I'm honest, I think she's a bit lonely, so she's compensating by living vicariously through him.'

'Doesn't that worry you?'

'In what way?'

'If he's the focus of her life, she's going to make it difficult for him to move out to live with you when the time comes, isn't she?'

'Thomas has promised me he'll move out as soon as she either meets someone or he thinks she's ready to be on her own.'

'And how long will that be?'

'Are you worried I'm going to abandon you in this lovely flat? I won't, I promise.'

'The thought did cross my mind,' she admits. 'Is he good, by the way?'

I'm glad I don't have anything in my mouth, as I'd undoubtedly spit it everywhere.

'What kind of question is that?' I ask incredulously.

'I meant, is Thomas any good as a painter?' Emma clarifies once we've stopped giggling.

'Ah. You're asking the wrong person, I'm afraid. I know sod all about art, but he's been passionate about it in various different forms for as long as I've known him.'

'What do you mean?'

'Well, for example, he was really into poetry when we first started going out. Don't you remember?'

'Not really. Did he write you love sonnets?' she giggles again.

'No, thankfully. His stuff was more about challenging what he saw as the "excessive interpretation of the written word".'

'The what?'

'That's pretty much what I said. Basically it means reading more into a piece of text than the author ever intended to put there. Do you know the Stevie Smith poem, "Aloft in the Loft"?'

'No.'

'Neither did I, but it basically goes "Aloft, in the loft, sits Croft; he is soft."'

'Is that it?'

'Yup. It's a really famous poem, allegedly. Thomas told me they had to do a literary criticism of it at school, answering questions such as "Who is Croft?", "What might the author be describing when she talks about him being soft?" and "Why is Croft in the loft? Is he hiding? Discuss with reference to the rise of Hitler and the Third Reich".'

'All that, from a tiny verse?'

'Exactly. It wound him right up, he said, so he wrote an answering poem and set of questions as his essay.'

'This I have to hear.'

I cast my mind back, trying to remember. I can clearly picture Thomas telling me the story; we were sitting in a pub early in our relationship, and I was mesmerised by the reflection of the flames from the open fireplace in his dark brown eyes. We went to bed for the first time later that evening, and I'm momentarily lost in the memory of it.

'Alex?' Emma's voice punctures the daydream.

'Sorry, I was trying to remember. "The cat sat on the mat; he is fat." That's what he wrote, along with some questions about whether the cat was a metaphor for the Nazis, or whether the cat was fat because it had eaten Croft, stuff like that.'

'That's kind of cool. I've never seen him as the rebellious type.'

'Oh, he has his moments. Unsurprisingly, his teacher didn't see the funny side and he got a shedload of detention. But it sowed a seed, and he got quite into writing poetry for a while, parodying other famous poems. He used to submit them to competitions and his mum kept encouraging him to send them into publishers. He didn't get anywhere though, and eventually he lost interest and moved on to photography.'

'I remember that one. Didn't he ask you to pose for him?'

'Only once. It ended in a bit of a row. He's such a gentle person normally, but he was really snappy with me when I didn't pose exactly as he wanted, and then he got arsey when he wanted me to do a fine art set for him and I said no.'

'Why did you say no?'

'Because what he meant by fine art involved me posing in the buff! He assured me it would all be very discreet and tasteful, but can you imagine if, say, Roxanne saw it? Or one of the guys from work?'

'Has he ever asked to paint you nude?'

'No. He doesn't really paint people.'

'What's his bag then, landscapes?'

'He describes his style as "neo-cubist impressionism".'

'And what the hell is that, when it's at home?'

'Honestly? I have no idea,' I laugh. 'It seems to involve lots of geometric shapes made up of tiny dots of paint. It's really not my kind of thing, but it makes him happy, and he'll be even happier if he actually sells one at this exhibition. Now, are you cooking tonight or am I?'

'How is the new flat?' Thomas's mother asks me. It's the first night of the exhibition and I'm carefully pouring prosecco into the glasses she's borrowed from one of the local supermarkets.

'It's lovely, thanks Claire. Such an improvement on where I was before.' While broadly true, living with Emma hasn't proved to be quite the plain sailing that I'd hoped. The kindest way to describe it is that there are certain life skills she hasn't had the opportunity to learn while living at home with her parents. Washing up was the first hurdle we had to navigate. To begin with, she genuinely didn't seem to understand why the plates in the dishwasher were still dirty the morning after she'd loaded them in, so I had to show her where to put the tablet and how to turn it on. Her mother evidently did all the laundry too; that one is still a work in progress. Although I explained to her about separating whites from colours, she was convinced that was an old wives' tale and she could get away with putting them all in together. The two pinky-grey blouses that came out at the end of the cycle, along with some once-white knickers in the same shade, have expensively proved her wrong.

Even though I came here straight from work, I haven't seen Thomas, or even any of the exhibition, yet. Claire was waiting for me and ushered me straight into the kitchen, where I've been ever since. She's really pushed the boat out, even buying a canapé book specially for the occasion. Unfortunately, although she's done as much advance preparation as she could, most of the recipes seem to require at least an element of last-minute assembly, so we've been operating a production line for the last couple of hours. The buzz of conversation outside the serving hatch tells me that the guests have arrived for the preview evening, and we're just putting the final touches to everything before we take it out to hand round.

'Ready?' Claire asks me as I lift the tray of drinks, and I can't help but notice that her eyes are glistening.

'Are you OK?' I ask her.

'I'm just nervous. It's such a big thing for Thomas and I want it to be perfect for him, I suppose.'

'It will be. I'm sure he appreciates how much you've put into this.'

'I know. It's just that, well, some of the other people were so snooty because he isn't a member of one of the art groups. It feels like he's got ground to make up.'

'Come on. Let's get some drinks and food inside them. People are always nicer when you're feeding them and giving them free booze.'

'I hope so. I really do.'

It takes me a few moments to spot Thomas in the hall because it's so busy. The conversation is much louder now we're out of the kitchen, and it's punctuated by the occasional braying laugh that makes me jump. Thankfully, I manage not to spill any of the drinks, but poor Thomas looks so nervous I think he might actually throw up.

'How's it going?' I ask once I've managed to manoeuvre my way over to his corner. 'Sold anything yet?'

'No,' he replies miserably.

'Ah well, you've got the whole weekend.'

'I think this was a mistake,' he murmurs.

'Why?'

'See that man over there?' He discreetly points towards the sculpture area, where a red-faced gentleman is engaged in animated conversation with a waspishly thin woman.

'Yes?'

'He's the chair of the watercolour society, you know, the ones who've been doing the life drawings.'

'What about him?'

'He came by earlier, so I thought it would be polite to introduce myself. He completely blanked me, looked at my paintings like they were dog turds and then said, "Explain to me, boy, how is this art?".'

'That's unbelievably rude!'

'Yeah, but what if he's right?'

'Of course he isn't right. He's entitled to his view, but art isn't black and white, is it? Remind me why you don't go to the National Gallery?'

'Because it makes me angry.'

'And why is that?'

'Because I don't understand who gets to decide which paintings are fine art and belong in a museum, and which don't. Art is about the eye of the beholder and, if you see something and perceive it as beautiful, then it is.'

'Exactly. You've got just as much right to be here as him. Remember that.'

I keep my eyes on the man as I continue circulating with trays of drinks and canapés. As an exhibitor, he's wearing a name badge, but it takes me a couple of circuits to get close enough to him to read it and then find his entry, which turns out to be a female nude leaning against what looks like a doorframe with one arm stretched over her head. The colours are generally fairly muted, but he's used a darker colour to accentuate her pubic hair, areolae and a thick mat of armpit hair as well as the hair on her head.

'What do you think?' The man has obviously noticed me looking and is now standing next to me. 'Pretty good likeness, wouldn't you say?'

'I can't comment on that, having not seen the original subject,' I remark blandly as vengeful inspiration strikes, 'but it seems to me that there is a lot of rage in this image.' Oh yes, Mr Tell Me How This Is Art, you're not the only one who can play this game.

'What makes you say that?' I can see him looking me up and down, trying to work out whether I'm just a waitress or whether I might actually know something about watercolours. I don't, but I can spin convincing bullshit when I need to, as he's about to find out.

'Look how the pubic area is rendered,' I observe, waving my hand at it vaguely. 'From the pattern of the brushstrokes, it looks like the artist created the effect of individual hairs by placing the brush directly onto the page and pressing down to spread the bristles. It's symbolic, don't you see? The brush is his penis, and he's jabbing the page with it, as if he's trying to penetrate her but is unable to. This image is all about the artist's frustration with his own sexual impotence.'

'How do you know it was painted by a man?' He's sounding a good deal less certain of himself all of a sudden. Good.

'Because it says so underneath. *Nude in Doorway* by Arthur Bellis.' I give him a wink, like we're co-conspirators, ignoring the badge that tells me I'm talking to the artist himself. 'Let's hope his luck changes soon, poor guy.'

As I move away, I can't help noticing that Arthur Bellis's face is puce, either with anger or embarrassment. Thomas is staring at me from his corner, obviously trying to work out what has happened, so I give him a quick grin and a wink. That'll teach you to mess with my man, Arthur.

3

'What are you smiling about?' I ask Thomas. My operation to cheer him up culminated in him staying over last night for the first time since I moved in and, because I'm not working today, we're enjoying a Saturday lie-in after (quietly) christening my new bed.

He rolls onto his side and I see the twinkle of mischief in his eyes. 'I still can't believe you told the chair of the watercolour society he basically had an erectile disorder,' he says.

'He shouldn't have been such an arse then, should he? He was quick enough to accept your mum's hospitality, so the least he could do was be civil to you. Even after our little chat, I don't think there was a single time I passed him when he didn't take something off the tray.'

Thomas's smile widens. 'Do you know if that café in the row of shops underneath is any good?'

'I've never been in, but it always looks busy. Why?'

'I thought I might buy you breakfast to say thank you for standing up for me.'

'Hm. I've got a dilemma now.'

'What?'

I wriggle further under the duvet. 'Breakfast sounds lovely, but it means getting out of bed and I'm very comfortable here.'

'Tough decision,' he murmurs, placing his hand over my belly button and slowly starting to inch lower. I'm just about to lean over and kiss him when there's a crash from the kitchen, followed by loud swearing.

'Are you all right?' I call.

'No! I dropped the fucking frying pan, and now there's omelette all over the floor and I think I've burned myself,' Emma's muffled voice shouts back.

With a sigh, I detach myself from Thomas and throw on a dressing gown to go and investigate her latest mishap. Cooking is another area where Emma's knowledge is decidedly patchy. When I reach the kitchen, it's pretty much as she described. Hastily, I turn on the cold tap and grab her hand, shoving it under the flow.

'Don't move,' I tell her. 'What happened?'

'It's my own fault. I put the pan under the grill to cook the top and stupidly didn't realise the handle would heat up. Luckily, it was only the bit nearest the pan that was really hot and I have quick reflexes so I don't think it's as bad as it could have been, but I've made a bit of a mess, sorry.'

'Don't worry. You keep that hand under the cold water and I'll sort this.' I turn off the grill and carefully lift the frying pan into the sink using an oven glove, before wiping up the egg mess from the floor and a couple of the cupboard doors.

'I'm not sure omelettes are my thing,' Emma declares ruefully as I scrape the last bits into the bin. 'I just fancied something a bit more interesting than cereal as it's the weekend.'

'Alex and I were thinking of going down to the café for breakfast,' Thomas remarks. He's pulled on his T-shirt and boxers and is standing in the doorway, calmly observing the fallout from Emma's omelette disaster. 'Why don't you come with us?'

'Thank you, Thomas, but I wouldn't want to play gooseberry to you two lovebirds.' Emma shoots me a meaningful look as she says the last word and I blush slightly, wondering whether perhaps we weren't as discreet as I thought we'd been.

'No, come,' I add. While I love her and enjoy spending time with her, my main reason for jumping on Thomas's invitation is that I genuinely worry she might do herself a serious injury or burn the flat down if she's left in the kitchen unsupervised. Thankfully, she doesn't seem to pick up on my concern as her face lights up.

'Only if you're sure,' she says, but the hope in her eyes is almost comical.

'Of course we are. Why don't we get showered and dressed, and we'll all meet back here in half an hour?' Thomas suggests.

Having retrieved her hand from under the tap and ascertained that she hasn't done herself any lasting damage, Emma skips off into her bedroom to get ready.

'Thank you,' I say to Thomas. 'That was really kind, and it obviously means a lot to her.'

'It's nothing. I think she might be finding this a bit harder than she was expecting,' he remarks. 'And, of course, she's moved to a strange town, so she doesn't know anyone.'

'I've moved to a strange town too!' I exclaim.

'Hardly,' he laughs. 'You may not have lived here before, but you've worked here for years, haven't you. You've probably sold half the houses here. Plus, you were living independently before. It's a big thing, moving away from your parents for the first time.'

'Says the man who still lives with his mum.'

'That's different,' he retorts. 'You know how Dad's affair and then the whole divorce thing knocked the wind out of Mum. I like to hope having me around gives her something other than her own problems to focus on.'

'Plus she waits on you hand and foot.'

He sighs. This is a well-worn argument that we've been round many times. Thomas likes to see himself as Mr Independent, but the reality is he's completely mollycoddled by his mother.

'I told you. I'll move out when the time is right. I want us to move in together as much as you do, but I need to be sure she's OK first.'

'Do you honestly think she'll meet someone?'

'I hope so.'

'What if she gets a toyboy who's even younger than you? That would be weird, don't you think?'

He scrunches his face in disgust. 'You're putting me off my breakfast. It's bad enough with Dad and New.'

'Remind me what her proper name is?'

'Michelle, but she'll always be New to me. At least she hasn't asked me to call her Mum, I suppose.'

'What's the age gap between you and her?'

'She's five years older than me. I try very hard not to think about it when I see her and Dad together.'

It was his parents' divorce that brought Thomas and me together, in a roundabout way. Jack, Thomas's dad, describes himself as an entrepreneur in the beauty industry. What this means in practice, Thomas informed me some time ago, is that he owns a number of fairly grotty nail bars that are regularly raided by the police checking for evidence of modern slavery, as well as a couple of hairdressing salons and waxing parlours. He was heavily into those places you used to see a few years ago where people went to have their feet nibbled by fish, but congratulates himself for selling those on just before the bottom fell out of that market. Michelle is a hair stylist who used to work for him, but has apparently embraced the life of leisure since they moved in together. I first met Thomas when he accompanied his mother to a viewing of the house she now lives in, and we started going out a month or so later. I've never met the legendary Jack or Michelle, but I hear plenty about them from Thomas – none of it good.

The café is absolutely rammed when we get down there, so we have to wait a while for a table. My first instinct is to suggest we go somewhere else, but Thomas is practically drooling as he watches a full English breakfast being delivered to a nearby customer, so I don't think he's going to be receptive to that idea. Thankfully, it's not long before a table falls vacant and we settle ourselves at it.

'How's work, Thomas?' Emma asks him once we've placed our orders. He's gone for a full English, unsurprisingly, and Emma and I have both ordered omelettes.

'Same old conveyor belt,' he tells her. 'Babies come into the nursery at one end, and we spit out supposedly school-ready children at the other. We're so busy now that parents are having to sign up for a place before their children are even born if they want to get them into the nursery.'

'And which age group are you working with at the moment?'

'Dawn, the manager, likes to move me about. I reckon she sees a male member of staff as something of a trophy, and she thinks it's good for all the children to have regular exposure to a male voice. I prefer working in the pre-school, because the children are more interesting and active, but the babies can be very sweet too. In fact...'

Thomas tails off because it's suddenly clear that Emma isn't listening to him any more. Her eyes are fixed on two men who have just come through the door and are gazing around, looking for a table.

'Well, hello there,' she mumbles under her breath, suggestively.

'Everything all right there, Emma?' I ask, trying not to giggle.

'Very much so. Have you seen the hunk in the rugby shirt?'

I cast my gaze back towards the door as subtly as I can. Emma's eyes are practically out on stalks, so I'm not sure why I'm bothering, but thankfully they don't seem to have noticed her or her blatant ogling yet. The first man is probably around six feet tall, with wavy blonde hair that is just slightly too long at the front so it partially covers one of his eyes. The second is shorter, with an unruly mop of dark curly hair and wire-framed glasses that don't really suit him. No prizes for guessing which one Emma is staring at. As I watch, the blonde one obviously spots Emma staring, because the corners of his mouth lift into the barest hint of a smile.

'Oh, fuck. Hormone meltdown,' Emma whispers.

'Really?'

'What do you mean? Look at him!'

'He's good looking, I grant you, but he's not that special, is he? Plus, he might be in a committed long-term relationship with the one in the glasses.'

'Noo!' she wails. 'I'd already gone to some seriously dirty places in my fantasy world, don't spoil it.'

'We need to get you a boyfriend, and fast,' I observe. 'You're a danger to yourself and others in this state. Now, didn't your mother tell you it's rude to stare?'

She drags her eyes back to me with a sigh. 'You're right. Distract me. Tell me about the exhibition.'

Thankfully, the story of my interaction with Arthur Bellis is stimulating enough to keep her entertained until the food arrives. I do notice her stealing the occasional look at the man in the rugby shirt from time to time, but they've found a table and he's sitting with his back to her so is unaware of her ongoing admiration.

We're just finishing our drinks when Thomas's phone pings with a message. His whole face lights up when he reads it and he even does a little fist pump, which amuses me as it's totally out of character for him.

'Good news?' I ask.

'I've just had a text from Mum. She's popped into the exhibition and one of my paintings has a red sticker on it. I've sold something!'

'That's brilliant, congratulations!' I exclaim, leaning over the table to give him a kiss. 'Maybe Arthur Bellis came to his senses and realised there's more to art than watercolours of naked women.'

'I don't care who bought it. Well, I do, obviously, and I hope they'll be very happy with it. The point is that I'm now a proper artist. You know what this means, don't you?'

'Umm, you're the new Van Gogh and I can give up the day job?'

'No. Although I'm technically just as commercially successful as him at this point.'

'Umm, Thomas. I don't want to prick your balloon, but Van Gogh is literally one of the world's most famous painters,' Emma tells him. 'I think you might be over-reaching a little there.'

'I'm not, actually. Did you know he only sold one painting in his entire life?'

'You're winding me up.'

'It's true. He might be famous now, but he wasn't when he was alive. He would often trade paintings for food or painting supplies, but the only one he ever sold was the *Red Vineyard*, which he got about sixteen quid for. Anyway, that's not what this is about. What this means is that I now meet the criteria to apply to the San Francisco College of Artistic Expression.'

'The *what*?' I ask. This is news to me.

'I'm sure I told you about it. It's this incredible school, well, community really, set up by a guy called Jorge Henriksen. I read about it online, and they do these residential courses that promise to take your art to the next level. They have regular exhibitions with a curated celebrity guest list, and it's not unheard of for paintings and other works of art to sell for thousands. It could be the making of me.'

'And this place is in San Francisco, as in America?'

'Where else would it be?' He's looking puzzled.

'How long would you be away for?'

'They do courses of different lengths, but they recommend at least a month to fully immerse yourself and get the best out of it.'

'But what about your job?' I ask, just about managing to resist adding 'and what about me?'

'I'll talk to Dawn if I get accepted. I'm sure we'll be able to figure something out.' He obviously spots the concern in my face, because he adopts a more conciliatory tone.

'Look. The website says that it's heavily oversubscribed, so there's only a tiny chance I'll get in. But if I do, by some miracle, I'd be mad not to do it, wouldn't I? This is the opportunity of a lifetime. Maybe you could come out for a week as well and we could tour around a bit.'

Much as I don't like the idea of Thomas possibly disappearing off to the States for a whole month, I have always wanted to go to California, and San Francisco in particular. I imagine myself riding the cable car like a local, zipping up and down the hills with Thomas beside me. The scene in my mind cuts to us enjoying a glass of wine as the sun sets over the Golden Gate Bridge.

It's not as filthy as the fantasy that Emma seems to have slipped back into, if the expression on her face is anything to go by, but it's not bad. I realise I've been acting a little churlish, so I turn to Thomas and smile.

'I'm so proud of you,' I tell him.

4

'Oh, it's you.' Emma's voice is dripping with disappointment when she walks out onto the landing as I'm climbing the stairs. Thomas was so excited about selling a painting that I felt I had to go back to the village and admire his red sticker with him. Unfortunately for me, he's so hyped up about this art school that our planned trip to the cinema this afternoon has been summarily cancelled so he can start work on his application.

'Nice to see you too,' I remark, wondering what's flipped her mood so completely since this morning.

'I didn't mean it like that,' she says, grabbing my elbow and dragging me through the door into the flat.

'What are you doing?' I ask as she closes the door behind us. 'I thought you were going out.'

'Shh. I'll tell you in a minute.' I watch with mounting incredulity as she carefully reopens the door just a crack and places a folded piece of what looks like kitchen roll underneath it.

'I need to be able to hear. The wedge is to stop the door moving until I'm ready,' she explains in a whisper, leaving me even more confused.

'To hear what? What's going on?'

'Keep your voice down. Do you remember the gorgeous guy from the café?'

'I remember a guy you were very keen on,' I reply. 'Recollections vary about his level of gorgeousness.'

'You've stolen that phrase from the Queen, God rest her soul.'

'It's such a brilliant line though, isn't it? Anyway, yes, I remember the guy.'

'When did you say our new neighbours were moving in?'

'What's that got to do with anything?' I think for a moment. 'It must be about now, I reckon.'

'It is now, and I've only gone and discovered that Mr Hot-As-Fuck and his friend are, in fact, our new neighbours.' She does a little excited dance. 'I heard voices in the hallway, so I stuck my head out to see who it was and there they were, bringing their stuff up from a van.'

'So what did you find out about them? Beyond the fact that the tall one seems to send you into a sexual frenzy every time you see him, obviously.'

She sighs. 'I didn't find anything out. I was so surprised to see *him* again that I was momentarily lost for words. I think I made a bit of a tit of myself, if I'm honest.'

'Oh dear. What did you do?'

'I'm so embarrassed. Picture the scene. There's Mr Hot-As-Fuck looking even hotter than he did in the café because he'd pushed his sleeves up and I could see the muscles in his forearms – there's a whole world waiting to be discovered there, let me tell you – and the other one, a chest of drawers and me. "Hello," says Mr Hot-As. "I think I saw you in the café earlier, didn't I?"'

'So far, so normal,' I remark.

'Yes, but I panicked. I mean, I was so surprised to see him again, and that he remembered me from earlier, that I didn't know what to say. So I burbled something like "Hello, sorry, I've got something in the oven I need to check," and slammed the door.'

It takes me a while to stop laughing. 'You have got it bad, haven't you?'

'It's not funny.'

'Umm. It really is.'

'Stop it, Alex. I've never been so embarrassed. After that, there was no way I could go back out there to try to fix it, but I watched them out of the window and, after a few trips bringing things in, they got in the van and drove away. I've been thinking about what to do since they left, and I have a plan. With the door positioned just as it is, it looks closed, but I'll be able to hear when they come back. All I have to do then is saunter out nonchalantly, pretending I'm going to the shops or something, and then I can say hello properly.'

'How long have you been waiting?'

She glances at her watch. 'Two and a half hours so far.'

'That's a long time to wait for someone you know absolutely nothing about. Where do you think they've gone?'

'To get more furniture, obviously. They're bound to be back soon.'

'More likely they've gone straight round to our office to demand a refund, because there's no way they're living opposite the crazy woman who stared at them all the way through their breakfast and then blurted total gibberish at them on the landing before slamming the door in their faces.'

Her face falls. 'Was it that bad, do you think? Can you ring the office and check whether they've been in?'

'Pull yourself together. I was joking, for goodness' sake. I know he's good looking and everything, and that he's doing frankly bizarre things to you, but he is just a man and there are lots more like him out there. Men are like houses: you rarely buy the first one you view.'

'Sign me up for a viewing then,' she sniggers. 'You'd better book a double appointment, because I'm going to be checking out every feature in considerable detail. Oh yes. I will want to run my hands over *all* the surfaces to check for, erm, dust.'

'You're starting to make me feel ill. Do you need a cold shower?'

'It's all right for you! You have Thomas at your beck and call. I've got years of pent-up sexuality waiting to be unleashed on a lucky recipient, and Mr Hot-As is in the spotlight. Shh. I think I can hear something.'

Sure enough, the sound of the door at the bottom of the stairs accompanied by the friendly back-and-forth of two male voices indicates that our new neighbours have returned. Emma sits up so straight, she reminds me of a meerkat who's spotted danger. She gets up and tiptoes over to the door, listening intently, obviously waiting for the perfect moment to strike. When it sounds like the voices have reached the landing, she throws open the door and marches out.

'Hello again,' I hear one of the men say. 'Did you sort whatever was in the oven?'

'What?' Emma replies blankly, before she evidently remembers her previous excuse. 'Oh yes, all sorted, thank you. So, you're our new neighbours?'

'It would seem that way,' the voice replies. 'I'm Mark, and this is Callum.'

'Pleased to meet you, Mark. I'm Emma, and my flatmate is Alex. Short for Alexandra, in case you were wondering. She's a girl Alex, not a boy Alex, haha.'

Oh Lord, this is unbelievably awkward. I'm just about to go out and rescue her when she continues.

'I'd introduce you to her but she's out at the moment. Which is where I'm going, actually. I was just popping out to the shops for, umm, ingredients.'

'Well, don't let us hold you up. It was lovely to meet you, Emma.'

'And you. I'm sure we'll be seeing much more of each other, once you're settled in and everything. If you need anything, just knock, OK?'

'That's very kind.'

'I mean it. OK, I'll, umm, let you get on.' Our front door closes and Emma reappears, looking triumphant.

'I think that went rather well,' she declares.

'Brilliant,' I remark, trying to stifle the giggles bubbling up inside me.

'What? What's so funny?'

'If they didn't think you were a lunatic before, they're going to be in no doubt now.' I can barely get the words out as the laughter explodes from me.

'What do you mean? I told them who we were and found out their names. I reckon that's progress.'

'Let's see. "She's a girl Alex, not a boy Alex, haha." Let's start there.'

Her face drops. 'Shit, I said that, didn't I.'

'Yup. Along with "I'm sure we'll be seeing *much* more of each other."'

'I didn't say it like that!'

'You so did, but it doesn't matter, because it was eclipsed by your crowning glory, the *pièce de resistance*.'

She looks at me warily, waiting for me to continue.

'It's a tiny thing,' I explain as the laughter threatens to overwhelm me again, 'but when people say they're going out, it's normal for them to, you know, actually go out.'

'Oh, shit.'

'Other than that, you were brilliant, honest. I'm sure they didn't notice a thing.'

'Piss off. I'm going into my room and I'll be staying there for the next thirty years.'

* * *

'I have good news,' I tell Roxanne after I've hung up the phone. It's Monday morning and, while Emma hasn't been quite as good as her word, she certainly kept a very low profile for the rest of the weekend. I've tried to persuade her that it's not the end of the world, but she was still mortified when she left the flat to go to work this morning. Hopefully, she'll forget all about it once she's back in the office and focused on her latest marketing campaign; some kind of recipe box, if I remember correctly.

'Oh yes?' Roxanne lifts her eyes from her screen and waits for me to continue.

'That was the Robertsons. They want a second viewing of the oast in Chevening. I've provisionally booked it for this afternoon so they don't have time to change their minds. I just need to check with the vendor.'

'That's excellent, well done. Sarah's accepted an offer on the revolting new build, so I need something to take the wind out of her sails a bit. Tell them we've had lots of interest; that will hopefully push them into making an offer.'

'Will do. I've also had a call from a Mr and Mrs Jennings, wanting a valuation of a property on The Drive. I've put it in your calendar for Wednesday morning. I hope that's OK.'

'Fine. Thank you.' Although we all do valuations, there are certain streets where Roxanne likes to do them herself, and The Drive is one of them.

As I turn my attention to my stack of emails and paperwork, my mind drifts back to yesterday. Thomas came round and I cooked the three of us a roast, but it was like they had both checked out. Emma was still fretting over the mess she'd made of saying hello to our new neighbours, and all Thomas could talk about was the art school in California. I tried not to tune him out as he explained the entry criteria about having to have had your work exhibited and having to have sold at least one piece, but I nearly dropped the tin of roast potatoes when he mentioned the six-thousand-dollar course fee.

'Bloody hell, Thomas, that's a fortune!' I'd exclaimed.

'It's not cheap, but I can cover it with my savings. What's the phrase? "You get what you pay for."'

'Are these the same savings that you were planning to put towards our house?' I had asked, ashamed to hear the note of petulance in my voice.

'It will set things back a little,' he'd replied, trying to sound conciliatory but coming off closer to patronising. 'But sharing this lovely flat with Emma for a bit longer isn't much of a price to pay, is it? This is my big chance, Alex.'

'I'm sorry. You're right,' I'd said. I do want him to be happy, and if this is going to be the springboard his career needs, then it might actually put us in a better position.

'For that kind of money, I'd want to sell several paintings for astronomical prices to someone incredibly famous,' Emma had remarked, catching me by surprise. I thought she was lost in her own world of misery. 'Do they give you any indication of which celebrities are on their "curated guest list"?'

'Of course not,' Thomas had told her. 'Nobody who works with celebrities ever reveals the names. It's an unwritten rule.'

'I think I'd want to know that we were talking A list,' she'd continued thoughtfully. 'I'd be pretty pissed off if I forked out all that cash and the only celebrities I saw were the kind of Z listers who hawk themselves round the reality shows, desperately trying to revive their faded careers.'

'It's fine. I've done my research and the reviews are superb. Anyway, I haven't been accepted yet, and there's only a tiny chance that I will be. It says on their website that they get over a hundred applications for each place on the course.'

After lunch, while Emma was huffing and puffing her way through loading the dishwasher and clearing up, Thomas had shown me the website. I still think it's an awful lot of money to pay for a one-month course, even if it does include accommodation and two meals a day, but I have to admit that the website is slick and they do look like a professional outfit. There are carefully posed pictures of Jorge Henriksen on most of the pages, interacting with students, appraising a canvas or sharing a joke. He looks exactly like I expected him to look, with long grey hair tied back in a ponytail, bright blue eyes and a long beard. He's tall but slightly rotund, like a paint spattered Father Christmas figure. As well as painters, the course accepts ceramicists and sculptors. There's even a picture of one of the fabled exhibitions, although I can't see any celebrities in it, even when I zoom in to examine the guests' faces closely.

I'm still feeling a bit mixed about it, but I think that's probably just me being selfish and not wanting Thomas to disappear to the other side of the world for a month. For a few minutes, I let my mind wander onto the idea of me flying out and spending some time there with him. I probably won't do it, as that will eat even more into our reserves, but it's nice to enjoy the fantasy. In the meantime, I've got project 'persuade our neighbours that they're not living next to a pair of certifiable madwomen' to crack on with.

If I can help Emma to show Mark she's actually quite normal most of the time, it will hopefully lift her mood out of the doldrums and give me something to take my mind off Thomas's plans.

With a renewed sense of purpose, I turn my attention back to the screen.

5

Even though her mood has improved, I've decided not to say anything to Emma about my plan to re-habilitate her with our neighbours. The plan itself is pretty simple: I'm going to knock on their door and invite them over for beer and pizza (or wine and pizza in my case; beer makes me terribly gassy) one night this weekend. Everyone loves pizza, I reckon, so it should be pretty safe. My reasons for not telling her are also pretty simple. Since her disastrous encounters with Mark on the landing, she's obsessed over him, either beating herself up for making such a fool of herself or inventing ever more ludicrous fantasies about him and sharing them with me. If I hear her say 'Can you say Mark without saying Mmmm' one more time, it's likely that something bad will happen to her, and it will be my fault.

One of the good things about my plan is that I always leave after her in the morning and get home a good hour before she does, so I have opportunities at both ends of the day to knock on Mark and Callum's door without her being around. The weakness is that her continuing obsession with Mark means that we have to tiptoe around and speak in whispers until she hears him come home from work, so I know for a fact that he doesn't get in until after she does. Which leaves either knocking in the morning and hoping that he hasn't already left, or talking to Callum.

Callum appears to be something of an enigma. We don't hear him coming and going at all, which either means his job involves irregular hours or he works from home. As Emma isn't remotely interested in Callum and I'm honestly not that fussed about either of them, it's not a mystery either of us have put any effort into solving. We've noticed it, put it down as unexplained, and left it.

What this means is that I have no idea what the best time is to knock on their door. I don't want to disturb Callum if he works shifts, as he's much less likely to accept my invitation if he's in a bad mood because I've woken him up. And I badly need him to accept so that Emma can get over herself and reduce the chances of me accidentally murdering her with the kitchen scissors. After a lot of pondering, happily interrupted by the Robertsons ringing to put in an offer on the oast at Chevening, I decide six o'clock in the evening is the perfect time to strike. It's at least half an hour before Emma gets home, which allows for a bit of chitchat before I spring the invitation. Also, if Callum's job does involve night shifts, he should be getting up to get ready for work, so I hopefully won't be getting him out of bed. To make my plan foolproof, however, I decide I need a gift, so I take advantage of Roxanne's delight at getting an offer out of the Robertsons to slip away from the office before the shops shut.

I quickly learn that buying a gift for people you don't know is surprisingly hard. Flowers are obviously not suitable as there are too many ways in which they can misread the gesture, and I swiftly rule out any kind of home accessory as well. As I pass the Italian deli, I'm briefly inspired to make them a mini hamper of cured meats and cheeses with a bottle of wine to help wash it down, but by the time I've stepped inside I've managed to convince myself that they're teetotal vegetarians who are also allergic to lactose. Everyone loves posh biscuits, I think, before the possibility of gluten intolerance rears its head. This also puts the whole pizza plan at risk, I realise, and my earlier optimism starts to nosedive. Eventually, I reluctantly settle on jars of different antipasti on the basis that they can always give them away if they don't like them. After all, it's the thought that counts, and this supposedly simple expedition has already taken way more thought than I anticipated.

Things go from bad to worse when I knock gently on the door of their flat and nobody answers. After thirty seconds or so, I give the door a decent bang just to be sure. After all, if the flat is genuinely empty, I'm not going to be disturbing anyone with my hammering. I'm now paralysed with indecision. I could leave the basket of goodies with a note explaining that it's a gift to say welcome, but then I won't get the opportunity to convince Callum we're not mad and invite them both over, which is the whole point of this increasingly stressful exercise. I could take the basket back to our flat and try another time, but how do I explain it if Emma finds it? She has no concept of privacy, and regularly goes through my wardrobe looking for things to 'borrow', even though we're different sizes.

'Are you OK there?' the voice snaps me out of the spiral of doom in my head and I turn to see that the door has silently opened and Callum is standing on the threshold, watching me quizzically.

'Oh, hi!' I exclaim, my surprise making my voice sound weirdly squeaky. 'You're Callum, right?'

'That's me.'

'I'm Alex. I think you met my flatmate, Emma, at the weekend?'

A flicker of a smile crosses his face. 'Yes. Is she OK? I'm not very knowledgeable about these things, but Mark thought she seemed a little flustered.'

'She's fine,' I assure him. 'Anyway, I thought I'd come over and bring you a little something to say welcome.' As I hold out the basket of goodies, my eyes are drawn downwards, and I can't help noticing the enormous pair of fluffy dinosaur slippers on his feet.

'Don't read anything into them,' Callum tells me, having obviously spotted my look of surprise. 'They were a joke present from Mark and it just so happens that they're very comfortable.'

'Hey, no judgement from me,' I reply. Of course I've judged him. What kind of grown man wears novelty slippers?

'These are lovely, thank you,' he continues, reading the labels on the jars. This feels incredibly awkward for some reason. He's obviously waiting for me to say something, and it's a few moments before I remember the main purpose of this mission. I swear those bloody slippers are putting me off my game; even though I'm trying not to look at them, I'm acutely aware of them.

'Emma and I have only been here a couple of weeks ourselves, actually,' I say to fill the silence while I work out how to segue seamlessly into an invitation for the weekend.

'I see.'

'So I was wondering,' I continue when it's clear that's all he has to say, 'whether you and Mark would like to come round for pizza or something on Saturday, so we can get to know each other.'

'Do we need to get to know each other?' His tone is curious rather than hostile, but I'm seriously beginning to wonder whether he's being deliberately curt to wind me up.

'No, of course not. I just thought it would be nice, as we're neighbours and are likely to bump into each other from time to time.'

'I'm not a particularly sociable person, I'm afraid.' The phrase 'No shit, Sherlock' forms in my mind but I just manage to avoid saying it out loud. It's clear that my brilliant plan has failed, and

I'm just trying to work out the politest way to disengage when I realise he's speaking again.

'However, it's a very kind thought. Let me have a chat with Mark to make sure he hasn't got any plans. Shall I get him to bang on your door?'

That is the last thing I want to happen, because Emma will have a full-on meltdown if she gets to the door before I do and finds Mark standing there. I need to handle her carefully, giving her just the right amount of time to prepare.

'Umm, no.' Come on, Alex, think of a plausible excuse. 'Emma is sensitive to sudden noises after a trauma she suffered as a child. That's why she appeared flustered the other day; the sound of you bringing stuff in triggered her. Let me give you my number and he can call me on that. Is that OK?' None of that is true, but it sounds believable.

'I'll just grab a pen and some paper.'

'You did *what*?' Emma shrieks when I break the news to her on Saturday afternoon. Mark phoned later the same evening to thank me for my gift and accept the invitation, and I was delighted to discover that he's much easier to talk to than Callum. I've waited until a couple of hours before they're due to arrive before telling Emma; she would only have obsessed constantly if I'd said anything earlier, but equally I want to give her a bit of time to prepare so she doesn't start blurting nonsense at him again.

'I invited them over for pizza. It seemed a neighbourly thing to do.'

'Why didn't you tell me before?'

'Sorry. I got distracted and forgot all about it. I've only just remembered.'

'Bullshit. Oh, bloody hell, what am I going to wear?' She dashes into her room and, after a few moments, I follow. Emma's room is as chaotic as everything else about her. There are piles of clothes on the floor and on the chair, but she's currently rifling through the built-in wardrobe, muttering to herself and occasionally flinging a piece of clothing on the bed.

'Emma?' I prompt, carefully picking up a dress from the new pile and holding it up.

'What?'

'It's takeaway pizza on a Saturday night. Don't you think this is a bit over the top?'

She stops what she's doing and stares at me blankly for a moment, as if she's forgotten who I am.

'What are you wearing then?' she asks.

'Just my jeans and a hoodie or something. The whole point is that this is supposed to be a casual thing. If you dress up to the nines, it'll look a bit weird, don't you think?'

'I guess so,' she admits reluctantly. 'But I want to look nice, otherwise he might not notice me.'

'Em, there are only going to be four of us. How is he not going to notice you?'

By the time Mark calls me to let me know they're coming over, I've managed to talk her down as far as a pair of jeans, a fitted top and subtle make-up to cover her freckles. I think they suit her, but she always complains about them, as if they were an unwanted side-effect of being a redhead. Although she's washed and blow-dried her hair, I also managed to persuade her to leave it in a simple ponytail rather than anything elaborate. It's been a full-time job creating a look that she's happy with but doesn't look like she's gone overboard, so I haven't even had time for a shower.

'You must be Alex,' Mark says as I open the door. 'Pleased to meet you in person at last.'

'You too,' I reply as I step aside to let him and Callum come in. 'I think you know Emma?'

'We met on the landing. I'm sorry about the amount of noise we made.' He smiles at her and I notice her ears have flushed scarlet. There's an agonising pause while I wait to see whether her nerves are going to overwhelm her again but, to my relief, she simply steps forward and holds out her hand for him to shake.

'We brought booze,' Callum tells me, handing over a plastic bag.

'Thank you.' I glance down at the trainers on his feet. 'No dinosaurs today?'

'Not today,' he replies without a flicker of a smile.

'Right. Let's get this party started!' Emma exclaims, seemingly oblivious to the difficult atmosphere between Callum and me. 'What would you boys like to drink?'

Any hope that a bit of alcohol will loosen Callum up quickly proves misplaced. While an evidently much happier Emma turns her charm levels up to dazzling with a seemingly appreciative Mark, I do my best with Callum but it honestly feels like pushing water uphill.

'How did you and Mark meet?' I ask him, after one of his long silences.

'Through a website. I was looking for someone to share a flat with and so was he.'

'And were you living together before you moved here?'

'Yes.'

'Where was that?'

'Sidcup.'

'I see. And what prompted you to move here?' I take a large mouthful of wine to numb the pain of this conversation. I'm starting to wonder if the silence was actually better.

'Mark. He wanted to live somewhere with more green space, but still within easy reach of London.'

'Well, there's plenty of green space here. You should check out Knole park, for starters. It's a lovely place for a walk.'

'Thank you for the recommendation.'

'And what about you? Do you have an office you need to get to?'

'Yes, but I don't go there very often, so it doesn't matter so much for me. I work mainly from home.'

'What is it that you do, if you don't mind me asking?'

'Not at all. I'm in IT.'

'Right. I'm going to get a top-up. Would you like something?'

'I'm fine, thank you.'

This is purgatory, I think as I make my way to the kitchen. I just hope it turns out to be worth it for Emma.

6

'I think I'm in love,' Emma declares as we're clearing up.

'Steady, tiger. You've only just met him, and several years on a sexual starvation diet might be affecting your judgement just a little bit,' I reply with a smile. I'm so relieved that my plan worked and Emma is back to her normal self.

'You've seen him, right?'

'Yes. He's good looking. You also appeared to be getting on very well, which is a good sign. All I'm saying is that he's also the first man who's caught your eye since you escaped from your parents, so you don't need to rush in. Do you think he feels the same way about you?'

'He's invited me to the cinema tomorrow. I don't think he would do that if he wasn't into me too, would he? I gave him some pretty strong hints, so he can't be in any doubt about how I feel.'

'That's certainly true,' I laugh. 'If you'd been sitting any closer to him you would have been in his lap.'

'He didn't seem to mind.'

'So what are you going to see?'

'That was a bit weird actually. We looked up what was showing on his phone, and there's a Daniel Craig film I quite liked the look of.'

'Because you generally quite like the look of Daniel Craig. You know he's nearly old enough to be your dad, don't you?'

'Pah. Every woman needs a dad crush. It's a fact. Anyway, I thought it would be a good film for him too, because there are lots of action sequences and stuff blowing up to keep him entertained while lovely Daniel entertains me, but he said he thought it might be too noisy. Of course it's bloody noisy, that's what you go to the cinema for! Anyway, he ended up suggesting we see some cheesy-looking romcom instead. What's that about? I don't mind, I quite like romcoms, but I can't imagine it's his thing.'

I can feel myself beginning to blush. 'I, umm, might know something about that.'

'Uh-oh. What did you do?'

'When I went over there to invite them round, Mark wasn't in so I had to talk to Callum. God, that man is hard work. Anyway, he said he'd get Mark to bang on our door to let us know if he could make it. I couldn't let that happen, so I made up a story about you being triggered by sudden noises.'

'You *what*? Why would you do that?'

'I was worried that you might have another of your episodes if he did that and you answered the door.'

'What episodes? I have no idea what you're talking about.'

'She's a girl Alex, not a boy Alex,' I remind her. 'I'm on my way out to get ingredients for the imaginary thing in the oven that I told you about last time I burst out of this door spouting complete crap, only I'm actually not going to go anywhere. That kind of episode.'

'Fuck off. I hate you.'

'No you don't. You love me because I have just endured a whole evening trying to make conversation with the most monosyllabic man in the world, all so you could rub thighs and make puppy-eyes at Mark.'

'Fine. I love you. Was Callum that bad?'

'Yup. You know how most men love to talk about themselves and don't ask you any questions?'

'Yeah.'

'He didn't ask me any questions, and made it pretty clear he didn't want to talk about himself either. Where do you go with someone like that?'

'I'm sorry. I should have looked out for you and shared the load. I haven't been a very good friend tonight, have I?'

'It's fine. You were busy, and the whole purpose of the evening was to give you the opportunity to show Mark there's actually a normal person underneath the complete lunatic he met on the day he moved in. Let's not do it again for a while though.'

'Fine with me. But how am I going to explain that I'm not actually bothered by loud noises?'

'I don't know. That one is on you. Goodnight.'

'Night. And Alex?'

'Yes?'

'Thank you.'

* * *

'Bloody hell, Alex. Look at this!' Thomas strides into the kitchen holding out his phone.

I'm bent over with my head in the fridge, engaged in a seemingly fruitless search for breakfast ingredients, and I'm surprised to see that he's completely naked when I close the fridge door and turn to face him.

'Thomas, I know Emma isn't here, but nudity in the kitchen

isn't really my vibe,' I admonish him. 'We aren't starting a naturist colony, so would you mind popping a pair of boxers on at least?'

After explaining that she didn't have a problem with loud noises at all, Emma and Mark had a very happy time watching the Daniel Craig film, although neither of them seemed to be able to remember that much about it when I asked, so I suspect they were a little distracted. They've been dating for just over a month now, and I'm happy for her; he seems a genuinely nice guy and they're absolutely besotted with each other, but I prefer it when she stays the night in his flat, which is where she is now. It's not so much about noisy sex, although I did hear them once when I came out of my room to grab a glass of water late one night. Let's just say they were being a lot less discreet than I like to think Thomas and I are, and there are some things you definitely don't want to hear your best friend shouting in the throes of passion. The issue is more around food.

I don't know whether sex makes them hungry or Mark just eats a lot, but the contents of the fridge take a serious hit every time he stays over and, because they both have to be out early during the week, there have been a few times where I've got up to find the dishwasher still full and their dirty breakfast things abandoned on the counter. Emma is always very apologetic when I mention it, and promises to replenish everything and clear up, but it keeps happening. Abandoning the search for milk, eggs and bacon, I turn to the cupboard and find that the jar of Nutella that I only bought on Tuesday also seems to have staged a vanishing act, not that there appears to be any bread to put it on, and my mood sinks further when I realise that the café downstairs isn't even an option because it's Sunday and it will be closed.

'This is more important than boxer shorts,' he says, his voice practically quivering with excitement. 'You'll never believe it. I'm in!'

'In what?' Although I'm partly engaged in the conversation, most of my mind is occupied with trying to come up with a viable option for breakfast. There's another café at the top of the High Street that I'm pretty sure is open on Sundays, but I have a feeling it's more of an avocado on sourdough sort of place than somewhere we'd be able to get Thomas his beloved full English.

'The San Francisco College of Artistic Expression, of course! They emailed overnight to say that my application has been successful. Look.'

That's enough to focus me, and I take the phone off him.

'Read it out loud,' he urges. 'I still can't quite believe it's real.'

'"Dear Mr Walsh",' I begin. '"Thank you for submitting an application to study at the San Francisco College of Artistic Expression. I'm sure you are aware that our courses are held in extremely high regard, both within the United States and internationally. An accreditation from SFCoAE confers opportunities on the holder that cannot be obtained anywhere else, and this is just one reason why our courses are so heavily over-subscribed. SFCoAE graduates are also evangelical about our uniquely immersive learning environment, often saying that they could not have gained the understanding and passion that has launched many stratospheric careers without the intensive mentoring and support that SFCoAE provided them during their time with us." They're very pleased with themselves, aren't they?'

'They have every right to be.'

'Hmm.' I turn my attention back to the text. '"It will come as no surprise, therefore, that our candidate selection process is rigorous. We only accept candidates of the highest calibre, who we believe will benefit from our unique teaching methods and will thrive in our collegiate community. Those accepted to study with us have to be prepared to immerse themselves fully in the course. SFCoAE has no concept of 'the working week'; our students are regularly to be found in the studio at night and during weekends. This is one reason why we only accept artists who have already established a track record by exhibiting and selling their work." Thomas, I don't want to be rude, but do they know you've only been in one exhibition and sold one painting?'

'I may have, umm, exaggerated that very slightly.'

I try to give him a disapproving look, but it's very difficult when he's almost dancing with excitement and has no clothes on.

'I can't do this with you like that. I'm not reading another word until you stop waving your willy at me and put some boxers on.'

He sighs expressively. 'Fine.'

'Right, tell me how you "exaggerated slightly",' I demand when he reappears looking slightly more decent.

'The form didn't ask me to specify *how many* paintings I'd sold, or *how many* exhibitions I'd been in. It just asked me to attach pictures of works that had been completed, exhibited and sold. Everything I've finished fits one of those categories, so I attached pictures of the lot.'

'But that's misleading! It's obvious that they want pictures of works that satisfy all three criteria, not just one.'

'They should have worded the question better then, shouldn't they?'

'What happens if you get found out? Have you thought about that?'

'I won't be.'

'How do you know? I don't want to burst your bubble, but this is a very expensive course, and if you find yourself floundering and out of your depth—'

'Are you saying I'm not good enough?' he cuts in. Thomas and I don't argue that often, but I can recognise the tone of voice that tells me this is where we're heading.

'No, of course I'm not,' I backtrack. 'I just want you to be sure that it's right for you, that's all. I'd hate for you to go there and be miserable, or be chucked out after the first week when they find out you're not quite as established as you implied you were.'

'It'll be fine. Read the rest of the mail.'

'"As part of the course, students are expected to submit works to be displayed in our regular exhibitions. These are held every two weeks in our own gallery and are open by ticketed invitation only. Our guest list is carefully curated and includes leading figures from the arts world, as well as high-profile collectors, many of whom have considerable worldwide influence. These exhibitions provide a unique opportunity for our students to showcase their talents to the very people who have the means to launch their careers on the international stage, as has happened for many of our alumni." Do you know any of their famous alumni?'

'No. They do have some names and quotes from past students on their website, but I suppose they're mainly people who are better known in America than here.'

'I guess that makes sense.' I turn back to the email. '"While we expect the very best from our students, we also recognise our responsibility to provide superlative teaching and mentorship. It would be easy for us to lower our standards and expand, but we know that it is the exclusive access to our renowned college principal and head tutor, Jorge Henriksen, that is at the heart of our success. This is why we continue to zealously restrict our intake, to ensure our students get the very best experience that we can offer." Talk about labouring the point. We get it, you're exclusive and everything you do is unique. Jeez. What do you know about this Jorge Henriksen guy?'

'There's a long bio of him on the website. He's been all over the world, learning skills and working with different materials. Get this: at one point, he spent a month with a tribe in the Amazon rainforest, just so he could learn how they make their pigments. He's also the leading authority on ancient Maori ceramics.'

'Sounds a bit niche.'

'That's the point. They have tutors who know all about mainstream artists, but Jorge is the main draw because he's got all this next-level experience.'

'Let's hope he doesn't leave then.'

'He won't. He founded the College to share his learning. It's his baby.'

Thankfully, my questions seem to have put Thomas off the idea of me reading the entire email out loud, and I skim through the rest of it, which is filled with the same self-congratulatory guff, until I get to the part where they offer him a place.

'It's next month!' I exclaim. 'Surely that won't give you long enough to sort out work, will it?'

'I'll talk to Dawn tomorrow, but I don't think it will be a problem. I only have to give a month's notice, so I'll resign if push comes to shove.'

'You'd give up your job to do this?'

'Yes, of course. It's a once-in-a-lifetime opportunity.'

'It says here you have to send the entire course fee now, otherwise you'll lose your place.'

'Does it?'

I hand the phone back and show him the relevant text.

'Crap. I'd better get home so I can get onto the computer and make the transfer. You don't mind, do you? I know we normally have breakfast and everything, but—'

'It's fine,' I sigh. 'Go and do what you have to do.'

The flat seems very empty after he leaves, and I'm momentarily tempted to go and knock on Mark's door to demand breakfast as they've cleared out our kitchen again, but he and Emma might still be in bed and I definitely don't want to play gooseberry or end up having another awkward conversation with Callum.

Avocado on toast for one in the posh café it is, then.

7

It's a nice day and I'm not in any particular rush, so I decide to walk up to the posh café. This quickly proves to be a mistake as the hill feels considerably steeper as a pedestrian than it does in the car. By the time I reach the top, I'm out of breath and I'm sure my face is bright pink from the exertion. At least it will be downhill on the way back, I suppose. I decide to call in to the newsagent and buy one of the Sunday broadsheets, the idea being that I'll look like an independent woman who is taking time out of her busy schedule to enjoy a Sunday morning latté, rather than a sad loner whose boyfriend has abandoned her to enrol on an art course for the impossibly smug.

When I finally reach the café, I'm dismayed to see that every table is occupied.

'I'm afraid it's going to be at least a twenty-minute wait for a table if you haven't got a reservation,' the server tells me. I have to swallow the urge to tell her crossly that I've walked halfway up a bloody mountain to get here, and I'm therefore much more deserving of a table than, for example, the beardy bloke sitting by the window who is obviously trying to spite me by cutting his omelette into ridiculously small pieces and savouring each one as if it were nectar from heaven. As my gaze travels around the room, trying to work out if all the people here are, as I now suspect, in on some secret plot to ruin my morning, I spot a face I know. Sitting alone at a table for two, with his nose in a hardback book, is Callum.

My desire for coffee and breakfast quickly overrules any qualms I might have about what I'm letting myself in for, and I turn back to the server and plaster a smile on my face.

'It's OK,' I tell her. 'I'm meeting a friend and I've just spotted him over there.' Before she has a chance to say anything, I wriggle my way through the tables and plonk myself down in the seat opposite Callum. He raises his eyes from the book and looks at me quizzically.

'Hi Callum! I'm *so* sorry I'm late,' I exclaim for the benefit of the server, who I can sense watching me closely for any evidence that I'm trying to cheat the system. As I lean across the table, giving him what I hope looks to the casual observer like a kiss on the cheek, I whisper, 'Please play along. I can explain.'

'Hello, Alex,' he replies. He doesn't sound pleased to see me, but I don't think the server notices as she's grabbed a pad and gone to take an order from one of the other tables. As soon as I'm certain we're not under observation any more I turn back to Callum, who raises his eyebrows to indicate that I should probably tell him what on earth is going on.

'Here's the thing,' I begin. 'I was supposed to be having breakfast with Thomas, but he's skipped off to pay for this poncy art course he's just enrolled on. There's no food in the flat because Emma and Mark are like bloody locusts and the café underneath us is closed, so I thought I'd have a leisurely walk up here, but have you got any idea how steep that sodding hill is? And then, when I finally get here, her ladyship over there tells me I have to wait twenty minutes because the rest of the world has miraculously decided to come here as well, clearly with the sole intention of stopping me having any breakfast and ruining my day. So when I saw you, I told her I was meeting you because I'm honestly starving and I can't wait twenty bloody minutes for a table, watching everyone else eating while I drool like one of Pavlov's dogs. Look, I know you probably don't want to talk to me or anything and that's fine, but if you let me stay and have breakfast, I'll buy yours as well. That's a good deal, isn't it?'

Callum stares at me for what feels like an age.

'Who is Thomas?' he asks eventually.

'My boyfriend,' I reply.

'I see.' He drops his eyes back into the book, which I take as acceptance of my plan, so I turn my attention to the menu. It's just as I suspected; there are omelettes like the one the beardy man is still cutting into nano-bites, incarnations of sourdough bread, avocado and eggs in various forms, but I'm delighted to spot a full English at the bottom of the list. They've zhuzhed it up, naturally; the tomatoes are heritage, the mushroom is organic, the meat comes from a local butcher, and the eggs are not only free-range but also from a particular breed of hen. The price is nearly double what I'd pay down the hill, but beggars can't be choosers I suppose, and I reckon I've earned a decent breakfast after my exertions to get here.

'Are you having your usual, love?' the server asks, making me start. Not only did I not hear her approach, but the easy familiarity with which she addresses Callum is totally at odds with my experience of him.

'Perfect, thank you, Leah,' he replies, giving her a smile. I've never seen Callum smile before, and it's rather unnerving.

'And for you?' she continues, turning to me. Despite my frankly inspired play-acting, I can still hear an undertone of suspicion in her voice.

'I'd like the full English please, and a latté.'

'Eggs?'

'Yes please.'

'I meant how would you like them. Poached, fried or scrambled?' The server sounds slightly triumphant now, as if my misinterpretation of her question is the proof she was looking for that I'm an impostor. To my shame, I can feel the tell-tale heat in my cheeks that means I'm blushing guiltily.

'Oh, um, poached please.'

'Toast?'

'No, thank you.'

'Fine. I'll get that going for you.' Leah stalks off and Callum turns his attention back to his book. It's a thriller of some description, if the cover is anything to go by, and it's encased in one of those transparent plastic wallets that gives it away as a library book. However, I'm burning with curiosity, so his reading will have to wait.

'Your usual, love?' I mimic Leah's voice as best I can. 'You've got a fan there.'

'I've come here every Sunday since we moved in,' he replies without looking up. 'I have the same breakfast every time and Leah always serves on Sundays, so she's picked up on it. Before you ask, I know her name because it's on the badge that she wears and I smile at her because it gets me better service.'

It's obvious that the conversation is over, so I turn my attention to the newspaper. This is another mistake as the damned thing is huge when I start to unfold it. I'm in serious danger of hitting one of the other diners as I wave my arms about trying to get it under control, so in the end I crumple it up and open one of the supplement magazines instead. Callum's nose is still in his book, but I can sense him watching me.

'I'm no expert,' Leah observes drily when she brings our drinks, 'but most friends who meet up in here actually talk to each other.'

'We're, umm, in the same book club,' I bluster. 'So we meet up to read.'

It's very subtle, but I spot the corner of Callum's mouth twitch. He's enjoying my discomfort, the bastard.

'Aren't you supposed to read the same thing? Isn't that the point?' she asks. Bloody hell, she's like a dog with a bone, determined to prove that I'm up to no good.

'You're quite right,' I reply smoothly. 'The thing is that I've already finished the book, so I'm just keeping Callum here company while I wait for him to catch up.'

'Was it good?'

'Was what good?'

'The book. Did you enjoy it? I like a thriller, so I might give it a try if you recommend it.'

'Yes, it was very good.'

'What's it about?' For fuck's sake. What is this, the Spanish Inquisition?

'Oh, you know. Usual thriller stuff.'

'That's not giving me much.'

'Yeah, well, I can't tell you anything because it'll spoil it for Callum.' I have to say that I'm pretty chuffed with how I'm holding up under her interrogation.

'Fair enough.' She turns and walks away, and I heave a sigh of relief.

'She's relentless!' I say to Callum.

'She's on to you,' he replies simply.

'What makes you say that?'

He sighs and looks up from his book. 'Do you know why I got a table and you didn't?'

'You got here before me.'

'Yes, but I also made a reservation. For one.' My face drops in horror as the implications of that sink in.

'She said something about reservations when I arrived, but I wasn't really listening. What kind of café takes bookings?' I whisper.

'This one.'

'Can't you tell her it was a mistake? That you forgot you were meeting me? She's going to give me indigestion at this rate.'

'Why would I do that? It's not my fault that your boyfriend left, or that there isn't any food in your flat. I was sitting here quite harmlessly minding my own business at a table I reserved, and now you want me to take responsibility for your drama?'

I'm staggered, both by his rudeness and the callous, almost surgical way he's summed up my situation and dismissed me. I'm also deeply embarrassed because his description is spot on.

'You're right,' I reply. 'I'll go. Sorry for disturbing you. Enjoy your breakfast.'

I start gathering the various bits of my newspaper together, but my haste to get away is making it even less co-operative than before and a couple of the supplements fall on the floor. As I bend to pick them up, my head hits the side of the table.

'Ow!' I exclaim as tears of pain and humiliation prick my eyes. There is no way I'm giving Callum the satisfaction of seeing me cry, so I pinch the bridge of my nose and squeeze my eyes shut to try to stop them.

'Are you OK?' Callum asks, surprising me with the concern in his voice. 'Look, I was rude. I'm sorry. I told you I'm not good with people. Please, stay and have your breakfast.'

'Why on earth would I do that?' I reply. 'You've made it

perfectly clear that I'm spoiling your precious routine, and Leah is probably going to frogmarch me out in a minute anyway.' As if on cue, Leah appears, setting down cutlery and a mini bucket filled with sachets of different sauces.

'Is everything alright?' she asks, obviously picking up on the tension.

'Yes, thank you,' Callum replies smoothly. 'Alex was just worried because I realised that I forgot she was coming when I made the booking. It's not a problem, is it?'

'It's fine,' she tells him. 'Everything is taking a little while longer because we're so busy this morning, but I'll bring your food out soon.'

'I really am sorry,' Callum says to me once Leah has retreated. 'I didn't mean to sound so harsh. I was just feeling a bit over-whelmed, I suppose, and I lashed out. You didn't deserve it.'

'It's my fault,' I reply. 'I shouldn't have dumped myself on you like that. It hurt to hear it, but your summary was completely accurate. I'll leave you to enjoy your breakfast in peace.'

'I won't be able to enjoy my breakfast if I'm worried about you fainting from hunger halfway down the hill. Look, I know I'm not very good company, but they're probably cooking our food already so it will only go to waste if you don't stay and eat it.'

'I'm not sure I'm hungry any more.' The words are barely out of my mouth before my stomach rumbles loudly. Callum evidently hears it because he raises his eyebrows and the corners of his mouth lift.

'Fine. I'm hungry,' I admit.

'That's settled then.' He picks up his book and I carefully retrieve the supplements from the floor and start flicking through one of them. It has a puzzles section near the back, so I fish in my bag for a pen and start looking at the quick crossword. I'm just filling in the third clue when I become aware that Callum has put down his book and is watching me.

'I can't resist a crossword, especially the cryptic ones,' he says when I look up at him. 'They're so clever, don't you think? It takes a special kind of mind to put them together. I reckon setting crosswords would be my dream job.'

'Would you like the cryptic one?' I ask. 'I can tear it out for you, and I have a spare pen in my bag.'

The look on his face tells me everything I need to know. I carefully tear out the page containing the cryptic crossword and hand it to him, along with my spare biro. I return my gaze to my puzzle, but I'm somewhat distracted by the speed with which Callum is working.

'I can never make head nor tail of those,' I observe as he confidently fills in another clue.

'It's all about the rules,' he explains. 'Once you understand how to read the clues, and which rules to apply, it's actually fairly straightforward. Take this one, for example. "Garment from Pacific country with middle cut out". Four letters.'

'The only garment I can think of with the middle cut out is a poncho, and I'm pretty sure they come from South America,' I tell him after thinking about it for a minute or two.

'It's also more than four letters. What you have to do is work out what the clue is, and what the instructions are for solving it. So, let's start with the country. What Pacific countries are there?'

'Umm, Australia, New Zealand, Fiji. Isn't Hawaii in the Pacific?'

'It is, but it's not a country. It's a US state. The answer you're looking for is Tonga. What happens to Tonga if you cut the middle letter out of it?'

'It becomes Toga.'

'Which is our garment. See?' He fills in the clue with a flourish.

By the time Leah brings our breakfasts, the crossword is

complete but, despite Callum's explanations, I'm no nearer to understanding how cryptic crosswords work. What I have learned, much to my surprise, is that Callum is positively chatty when you give him a subject he's comfortable with. It's just a shame he's so surly and monosyllabic the rest of the time.

8

'Are you OK?' Roxanne asks. 'You seem a little down in the dumps.'
It's a quiet Friday afternoon and I'm sitting at my desk, absent-
mindedly twirling a biro between my fingers.

'Sorry, Roxanne. I was miles away.'

'The boyfriend?'

'Yes. He's flying to San Francisco tomorrow. I'm trying to be
upbeat about it when he's around because he's so excited, but I'm
dreading it really.'

'It's only a month, isn't it? He'll be back before you know it.'

'It's not just the physical separation,' I explain. 'I can deal with
that. It's what this course might do to him. Don't get me wrong. I
like art, but I like the kind where you can tell what the picture is,
not the abstract stuff that he does. I make a point of making
supportive noises while he explains it to me, but I still don't get it
even then, most of the time. I just worry that this course is going to
make that gap bigger.'

'But this is just a hobby, right? Even if you don't connect over
the art, all the other things that make you two work will still be
there.'

'It's not though. If it were just a hobby, as you put it, I wouldn't have a problem with it. But Thomas doesn't do hobbies. What happens is he gets interested in something, and then it quickly turns into a passion that he decides is going to be his ticket to fame and fortune. That's how it was with the photography, and it's exactly the same with the painting. What if this course reinforces that, and he becomes completely obsessed to the exclusion of everything else, including me? Or, more likely given that he was a little creative about his success on the application form, what if he tanks the course and comes back all bitter and resentful?'

'You are in a mess, aren't you? Tell me, are you up to date with all your paperwork?'

'Yes.'

'Good. Why don't you have the rest of the afternoon off and spend some time with him before he goes? It's very quiet, probably because you're putting the punters off with your wet weekend face, so you won't be missed.'

'Are you sure?'

'Of course I am.' She smiles. 'Go, and don't come back until you're nice again.'

I don't need telling twice, and I'm soon in the car on the way to Thomas's mum's house.

'Hello, Alex.' She smiles as she opens the door. 'You timed that well; I've just taken Thomas's last load of laundry up to him and the kettle's on. He's upstairs, putting the finishing touches to his packing. I offered to help, but he's being all macho and independent about it.'

The idea of Thomas being macho is enough to bring a smile to my face. He has many qualities, but macho is definitely not one of them. 'How is he?' I ask.

'It's a bit like being in the house with a five-year-old the night before Christmas. He can't keep still and keeps double-checking things, unpacking and repacking. They threw him a good luck party at the nursery this morning before he left, and Dawn even told him his job would be waiting for him when he gets back. Not many employers will do that these days, will they? I told him it shows how highly they must rate him, but I don't think he was listening.'

'That's a lovely gesture. He'll need it too, after the dent all this is putting in his savings.'

'Ah. Didn't he tell you?'

'What?'

'His dad coughed up the money to pay for it. Flights, course, everything. It's not costing Thomas a penny.'

This is amazing news. 'Really?'

'Yes. I reckon it's probably a guilt offering because of the divorce and New. I can't decide if it's a good thing or not though. On the one hand, it means Thomas's savings are intact, but I can't help wondering whether his father is trying to buy his way back into his good books, and that doesn't sit well with me at all.'

'I need to find someone who is feeling six grand's worth of guilt about me,' I laugh.

'Your parents are still married. That's worth a lot more than six thousand pounds,' she says wistfully.

'Sorry. I didn't mean to be insensitive.'

'You weren't. But, talking of money, can I borrow you for a minute before you go up to see him?'

I follow her into the kitchen and she closes the door behind us. Whatever she wants to say is evidently not for Thomas's ears.

'You know the art school does these exhibitions every two weeks?'

'Yes.'

'I thought I might go along to one and surprise him. He might be feeling lonely all alone in a strange place, so a familiar face might cheer him up.'

'What a fabulous idea.' This is so typical of Claire; it wouldn't surprise me if she sends him food parcels as well.

'That's what I thought,' she continues. 'The thing is, I'm not a particularly confident traveller. Jack always dealt with all that when we were married and Thomas will obviously be away. So, I wondered whether you would like to come with me.'

'Oh, Claire. I'd love to, but I don't think I could get the time off work at such short notice, even if I could afford it.' It is a nice idea, of course it is, but when I checked the cost of a trip to San Francisco, the prices were way out of my league.

'You don't need to worry about the money. It would be my treat.'

'I couldn't possibly let you pay! It must cost a fortune.' I don't want to embarrass either of us by revealing that I know the price. If she finds out I've been looking it up because I wanted to go, she'll feel obliged to take me, I know she will.

'Nonsense. I'm not sure I'd be able to do it on my own, so you'd be doing me a favour.'

A thought comes to me. 'How would you get into the exhibition though? Tickets are for invited guests only and, according to the blurb Thomas read me, the list is heavily curated.'

'I looked them up online and sent an email. They said family are always welcome and sent me two tickets to each of the shows they're holding during his course. Please say you'll come?'

She's not going to let this go, I realise. 'What are the dates?'

'The last exhibition, which the email said is usually the best one to come to, is on the seventeenth of July. That's a Friday. I thought we could fly out on the Thursday and take most of Friday to get over our jetlag before turning up to surprise him at the show in the evening. Then I thought we could spend a couple of days with him before catching the Monday night flight back, arriving home on Tuesday morning. What do you think?'

My resistance crumbles as I realise my dream to ride the cable car and watch the sun setting over the Golden Gate Bridge with a glass of wine might actually come true. A couple of other images involving Thomas and me pop in as well, but they're not ones I'm going to share with Claire.

'It does sound a lot of fun,' I tell her. 'Let me talk to my boss on Monday.'

'Erm,' she falters.

'What?'

'I know I'm being pushy, but do you think you could talk to your boss now? The travel agent said the flights are nearly full already, so I need to book quickly.'

This puts me in a difficult position. Roxanne has already sent me home early, and she may not take kindly to me immediately ringing to ask for more time off. However, Claire will also be mightily pissed off if I make her wait until Monday and she then finds all the flights are full and neither of us can go. I pull my phone out of my bag and wander out into the garden to make the call. I don't want Claire listening in if Roxanne takes it badly and gives me an earful.

'Hi Alex. I'm running late to meet Sarah for our Friday night drinks,' she tells me when the call connects. 'Is it something urgent?'

'Only a quick one. Would it be OK to have a few days off in the middle of July to go to San Francisco?'

'Is this to do with the boyfriend?'

'It's his big exhibition and his mother is flying out to surprise him. She's invited me to go as well. It's a flying visit from Thursday to Tuesday.'

'Of course you must go!' she exclaims. 'Although I'd go for a week if you can. I went to Florida a couple of years ago and the jetlag was horrendous. San Francisco will be even worse. Just make sure you're up to date with everything before you leave and do a handover of your active accounts so we have cover while you're gone. Is that it?'

'Yes, thank you.'

'No problem. I must dash now, but I expect you in on Monday looking a damned sight happier than you were this afternoon, OK?' The call disconnects before I have a chance to reply.

Once I've shared the good news with Claire, I leave her calling the travel agent and head up to Thomas's room, where it looks like his suitcase has exploded. There are clothes everywhere. Given that he's normally one of the neatest people I know, it takes me a moment to acclimatise.

'Hiya, you're early,' he says, coming over to give me a kiss.

'Roxanne gave me the afternoon off to spend with you before you go. What's going on?' I ask him.

'I can't work out what to take. California's, like, proper hot over the summer so I packed T-shirts and shorts, but then I read an article online today that says San Francisco is actually pretty chilly a lot of the time. So now I don't know what to do.'

'Talk about first world problems,' I laugh. 'Here, let me help. Let's start with the essentials. Whatever the weather, you're going to need underwear, right? So bung that in and we'll work up in layers from there.'

It takes nearly an hour, but eventually his case is packed and he has clothing for every eventuality.

'I'm really going to miss you,' he says, taking me in his arms and pressing his lips against my forehead.

'I'm going to miss you like crazy too,' I reply into his chest. 'But it's only a month. That's what we've got to hang on to. Plus, you'll be busy creating all these amazing paintings that the celebs are going to pay fortunes for. I expect you to come back a multi-millionaire, do you understand?'

'It would be nice, wouldn't it? We could march into your office, pick out a house we like and say, "We'll take that one. Don't bother to wrap it."'

'Yeah, and you'll have your own series on TV called something pretentious like *Thomas Talks Art*. Of course, your voice will be a bit muffled because your head will be so far up your arse, but it'll get rave reviews from the critics.'

He laughs and picks up the baseball cap that's sitting on top of his suitcase, putting it on back to front. 'Nobody appears on TV any more, you know that. I'm going to be Tommy, the TikTok artist who's down with the kids.'

'That's actually not a bad idea!' I enthuse. 'There's loads of money in TikTok. Perhaps you should call this place in California and tell them you've had a better offer.'

'Nice try, but I've got six grand invested in this course.'

'It's not technically your money though, is it.'

'Why do you say that?' He's not laughing now; if anything he's looking pissed off.

'Your mum told me that your dad is paying for the course. She reckons it's a guilt offering because of the divorce.'

'She had no business telling you that.'

'Why? What difference does it make? I was joking about brushing them off, for goodness' sake!'

'It makes all the difference. I don't want you thinking that I'm some spoiled little boy whose daddy opens his wallet every time I ask. It makes me feel bad because I know your parents couldn't afford to do something like that.'

'This has nothing to do with me, my parents, or what they can and cannot afford!' I cry, suddenly exasperated. 'Why not just be grateful that your dad is supporting you in this, instead of pulling some fake guilt trip that frankly just makes you sound like a condescending wanker?'

'I'm sorry,' he says. 'I don't want to fight with you, today of all days. Truce?'

'Are you going to stop talking bollocks?'

'I'll try.'

'Fine. Truce.'

'Actually,' he murmurs as our arms slide around each other once more, 'I might have something of a going away present for you.'

'Oh yes?'

'It's something... How can I put it... Personal and intimate, just for you.' He drops his hands onto my backside, pulling me closer against him, and I suddenly realise what he's hinting at.

'Your mother is downstairs!' I hiss.

'We'll just have to be super discreet then, won't we?'

9

'Stop it.'

'Stop what?' Callum asks. Thomas left yesterday, and I woke this morning feeling at a loose end, so I've somehow found my way to the posh café, where I was relieved to find not only Callum at his usual table, but also a much less hostile Leah. Callum has already completed the cryptic crossword that I offered as a bribe for disturbing his Sunday breakfast again, and I'm doing my best with the quick crossword.

'Stop staring at me. You're putting me off.'

'Sorry. If it's any help, three down is "Liegeman".'

'What?'

'The answer to the clue "Vassal". It's "Liegeman".'

'I've never heard of that. Anyway, get off. This is my puzzle, not yours.'

'Not reading today?' Leah asks as she comes to take our order.

'Umm, no,' I reply. 'The book club thing didn't really work out, so we've started a crossword club instead.'

She smiles. 'I prefer the crossword club. At least you two are talking to each other. Let me guess, two full English breakfasts, one with fried eggs and one with poached. No toast. One breakfast tea and one americano coffee. How did I do?'

'You must have a photographic memory,' I tell her.

'Not really. I know this gentleman's order because he's a regular and, although it's been a few weeks since you were last here, you did stand out a bit, so I can remember what you had as well. Ask me what most of the people in here on a Sunday morning have and I wouldn't have a clue.'

'Well, you're spot on with my order,' I say, and Callum also nods.

'Great. I'll go and get these on. We're a bit quieter today so hopefully it won't be much of a wait. Enjoy your crosswords.'

By the time she comes back with our drinks, I've got three clues left, but I'm pretty much stuck. I can almost feel the tension coming off Callum; he's desperate to tell me the answers but also trying very hard not to show it.

'Oh, for goodness' sake!' I exclaim crossly, pushing the paper over to him. 'Go on then, clever clogs.'

He hurriedly fills in the final clues and gives me the puzzle back.

'You've made this up. What on earth is a capybara when it's at home?'

'It's the largest member of the rodent family and it lives in South America. Whenever you get a clue like "large rodent" the answer is almost always capybara.'

I still don't believe him, so I take out my phone and Google it, only for the results to show that he's absolutely right.

'I don't know who set the puzzle today, but someone ought to tell them to stick to words that normal people are likely to know, rather than liegeman and capybara. Honestly.'

'But you'll know them when they come up next time.'

Now that the crosswords are done, we seem to have run out of things to talk about and silence descends. Callum reaches for his book but, having broken through his shell a little, I'm interested to see how far I can push it.

'Tell me something,' I say to him. 'You seem convinced that you're not very sociable and, based on the way you were when Emma and I invited you and Mark over for pizza, I would be inclined to agree. However, shove a crossword in front of you and you suddenly become positively chatty. What is that about?'

He stares at me without speaking for what feels like an age before answering, and I'm starting to wonder if I've massively put my foot in it.

'I'm just not very good at making small talk with people I don't know,' he says eventually. 'I'm acutely aware that most of the things that interest me are not likely to interest anyone else so, rather than be a bore, I stay silent. I will admit that I was in the middle of trying to solve quite a tricky work problem when Mark and I came over for pizza that time, so I was a little preoccupied. I'm sorry if I came across as a bit distant.'

'A bit distant? You were continents away! Anyway, small talk is easy,' I tell him. 'In fact, it's just like your crosswords. If you know the rules, you're most of the way there.'

'There are rules?'

'Oh yes. I ask you a question about you, and then you ask one about me. If you don't feel comfortable talking about yourself, then simply ask the other person more questions. Most people, apart from you it seems, think they're the most fascinating beings on the planet and will happily talk about themselves for hours.'

'It can't be as simple as that.'

'It really is. Let's role play. Hi, I'm Alex, nice to meet you.' I hold out my hand as if we're meeting for the first time and, after a moment's hesitation, he takes it.

'Nice to meet you too. I'm Callum. Now what?'

'You could ask me if I come here regularly, or if I live nearby.'

'Sounds a bit creepy and stalkerish.'

'It doesn't have to. Are you local to the area, Callum?'

'Yes.'

'You need to offer more than that.'

'Such as what? I'm not giving my address to someone I've only just met.'

'You don't have to, but you could say something like "Yes, I live near the station", or "I've only just moved here, so I wouldn't call myself a local yet". The second one is better, because it opens you up for more questions, such as where you lived before. Do you see?'

'Kind of. But that's just you asking me questions. What am I supposed to ask you?'

'You could stick to the same area. Let's try it again. Are you local to the area, Callum?'

'Kind of,' he replies. 'I live in a flat near the station, but I only moved in a couple of months ago so I don't know the area that well yet. What about you?'

'Isn't that interesting? I live near the station as well. Maybe we're neighbours. I haven't lived there long myself, but I've worked in the area for a number of years so I know the town pretty well.'

'What do you do?'

'Good. You picked up on the fact that I mentioned my work and made a question out of it. I'm an estate agent. You?'

'I work in IT.'

'OK, that's too broad. You could literally be anything from a salesperson in PC World to the CEO of Microsoft. Also, your tone of voice as you said it indicated that you were trying to close the subject down.'

'I was trying to close it down, because IT isn't that interesting to most people, and my actual job title doesn't make that much sense if you're not in the industry.'

'Try me.'

'OK. I'm a penetration tester.'

'A what?'

'Exactly.'

'Dare I ask what a penetration tester does? It sounds a bit smutty.'

'It totally isn't. Basically, my role is to try to penetrate the IT security systems of the companies that hire us.'

'Like a hacker?'

He smiles. 'A bit like a hacker, yes. Only what I do is legal and the victims, if you want to put it that way, know I'm coming.'

'Do you know what?' I smile. 'That's actually pretty cool.'

Callum looks like I've just made his day.

* * *

'Where the hell have you been?' Emma demands when I get back to the flat.

'Good morning, Emma, and nice to see you too,' I reply sarcastically.

'Don't take that tone with me, young lady.' She is trying to sound stern but really not doing a very good job of it. 'I left Mark looking frankly edible in his bed because I thought you might be missing Thomas and need cheering up, only to find no sign of you when I get in and not even a note to say where you'd gone. I've been worried.'

'I'm sorry. You don't normally appear until late afternoon on a Sunday, so it didn't occur to me to leave a note.'

'So where were you?'

'I went out for breakfast. I think it's my new Sunday thing.'

'Nice try. The café downstairs doesn't open on a Sunday. Where were you really?'

'Shall I fetch your pipe and violin, Sherlock? There are other cafés in Sevenoaks, you know. There's one up near Waitrose that's open on a Sunday, and that's where I went.'

I can see her trying to figure something out, and after a minute or two she narrows her eyes suspiciously.

'OK. I'll buy that for now. What's it called, this café?'

'Why does that matter?'

'Just answer the question.'

'The Pear Tree, I think.'

'I thought as much. Did you see anyone you know there?'

'What is this, twenty questions? I went to The Pear Tree, I had breakfast, I came home. The end.'

'Then I call bullshit. See, I happen to know that Callum goes there every Sunday morning, regular as clockwork. You would have seen him if you were really there. I'll ask you one more time: where were you?'

She's starting to piss me off now. 'OK. One, you're not my mother and you're pretty much never here on a Sunday, so you can back off with the inquisition. Two, I did see Callum as it happens. We had breakfast together. Three, I don't appreciate your tone.'

Her eyes widen and her mouth drops open, making me wonder for a moment whether I've gone too far.

'You had breakfast with Callum?' she repeats slowly.

'Yes. We did the crossword and had a chat.'

'You had breakfast and a chat... with Callum?' she repeats again. 'Even if we ignore the fact that you're hanging out with another man pretty much before Thomas's side of your bed is even cold, there's so much to unpack there, I barely know where to start. Go back to the very beginning. I need to know everything.'

She listens carefully as I fill her in on the essentials of my two breakfasts with Callum, leaving out my little lesson in social chitchat, but including his excuse for being so surly when he and Mark came over.

'I guess that explains it,' she observes once I've finished. 'I asked Mark about it after you'd told me how difficult Callum was, and he said that he's just very shy and slow to open up to people. Mark said he's actually a really nice person when you get to know him, but it takes a while and you have to be patient and let him go at his own pace. Anyway, what's the plan? Is this crossword club going to be a thing now? What does that mean for Thomas?'

'It doesn't mean anything for Thomas. I'll shut you straight down on that one. Yes, I might wander up the road on a Sunday and take the crossword with me, but that's all that's going to happen. I think Mark's assessment of Callum makes sense, particularly when I think back to how easily they were chatting to each other before you ambushed them on the day they moved in. Talking of which, how is Mark?'

'I think I love him.'

'Woah, that's big. Have you said anything to him?'

'God, no! I mean it though. He's kind and funny, he's great in bed, he has a good job and he's so gorgeous that I could spend all day just staring at him. What's not to love?'

'Should I be Googling wedding hats?'

'Not yet, but it wouldn't surprise me if he's the one. I just get this feeling when I'm around him that everything is going to be great.'

'Have you two argued yet?'

'No, why?'

'It's none of my business, but I'd hold fire on booking the registry office until you've had a few rows. He sounds perfect now, but what if he turns out to be a sulker? Or one of those really annoying people who won't just let something go so you can agree to disagree, but continues to snipe away at you until you're so worn down you tell them they're right just to shut them up?'

'I don't think he's a sulker, and we disagree on lots of things. For example, I like wine and he prefers beer.'

'Hmm. Hardly life or death, is it?'

'We agree on pretty much everything else.' She's sounding a little petulant now.

'I'm sorry. I'm glad you're happy, I really am. And thank you for worrying about me, but I'm just fine, I promise.'

'I still can't believe you had breakfast with Callum. And crossword club! You'll be wearing matching nerdy specs next.'

'Emma?'

'Yes?'

'Piss off.'

She laughs and disappears into her room, humming under her breath. She might think it's funny, but the truth is I could get into crossword club.

10

'Are you nice now?' Roxanne demands as I walk into the office on Monday and settle myself at my desk.

'I'm lovely.' I smile. That isn't a total lie. Yes, I'm missing Thomas, but I had a WhatsApp message from him yesterday evening to say he'd arrived safely. He hasn't met the famous Jorge Henriksen yet, but he's met a few of his course mates and says they're nice. We're going to have a video call next weekend, so that gives me something to look forward to, and Claire is texting me regularly with little updates about our upcoming trip.

'Good. Sad faces don't sell houses. What have you got on today?'

I fire up my computer and check my diary. 'Just the one viewing of the property in The Drive. Mr and Mrs Watkins at ten o'clock. I also need to make an appointment to take photos and measure up at the new listing in Dunton Green, and I've got the usual round of solicitor chase-ups and paperwork.'

'That property in Dunton Green is going to be a nightmare to sell, although I didn't tell the owners as much, obviously. The house is pretty enough, but you have to go down a dreadful track to get to it, you can hear the motorway from the garden and it's got an indoor swimming pool, which will put a lot of buyers off. Do your best to make it look irresistible, will you? You know the drill.'

'Do I have a budget?'

'Fifty quid. That should get you a bottle of wine, some flowers and a few other bits and pieces to jazz the photos up. I'll need a receipt.'

'No problem. Thanks.'

When I pull up on the road outside the house in The Drive, I'm momentarily distracted by the enormous SUV parked on the other side of the road. It's jet black with blacked out windows and the shiniest, most enormous gold wheels I think I've ever seen. The front doors open as I climb out of the car and, if there are any net curtain twitchers in the surrounding houses, I'm sure they'll be goggle-eyed at the occupants. I'm struggling not to do a double take myself.

'Mr and Mrs Watkins?' I ask as they cross the road towards me.

'That's us,' the man replies. 'All right, darlin'? You must be Alex, right?'

The first thing that stands out about Mr and Mrs Watkins is their colour, which is the brightest shade of spray tan orange I've ever seen. You'd be forgiven for thinking that they glow in the dark. However, the more I look at them, the more there is to take in. Mr Watkins's hair is totally jet black and the colour is so unnaturally even that I am sure it either came out of a bottle or he's wearing a wig. Mrs Watkins is the opposite, with long brassy blonde hair that is a stark contrast to her thick, dark eyebrows. As my eyes travel down, I take in chunky gold necklaces and gold bracelets on both of them, as well as an array of large rings on their hands. Mr Watkins is wearing an enormous signet ring set with some kind of stone, one of those gold sovereign rings and a gold thumb ring, in addition to a fairly ostentatious wedding band, but it's her that really draws the eye here, with large sparkling stones on the fingers of each hand. Her leopard print leggings are finished off with matching stilettos that she totters slightly awkwardly in, as if she's had a few drinks. Mr Watkins is fairly casually dressed, with a white shirt open halfway down his chest, black jeans and black leather boots. He walks with that rolling gait that barrel-chested men with short arms often have. Your average residents of The Drive, they are not.

'I'm very pleased to meet you both.' I offer my hand and hope they don't notice me surreptitiously checking afterwards to make sure that none of their spray tan has come off on me.

'Is this it then?' Mr Watkins asks, cocking his head at the substantial, detached, seven-bedroomed house with an expression of slight disdain.

'It is,' I reply. 'It hasn't been on the market long, and properties on this road tend not to hang around.'

'Yeah, yeah. You can spare me the spiel, sweetheart,' Mr Watkins tells me. 'To be honest with you, I'm not sure it's what we're looking for now that we're seeing it in the flesh, so to speak. However, we're here now so we might as well take a look.'

I'm determined not to let him put me off my stride, but something inside me is silently screaming, 'It's seven bedrooms, in one of the most desirable streets in one of the most desirable towns in Kent, and you're not sure it's what you're looking for? What the hell?' I focus on keeping my professional smile in place as I unlock the door and follow them into the hallway. This house is stunning. If I had the money, I'd buy it myself. The current owners have lavished attention on it, keeping the period details where appropriate and modernising elsewhere. The oak floor in the hallway has the kind of sheen that quietly reassures you that it was very, very expensive, and the gorgeous kitchen has every gadget you could ever ask for, including one of those taps that dispenses boiling water. There are bifold doors leading out onto a deck and then the garden. At night (I know this because I've seen the pictures), subtle lighting illuminates the deck. Upstairs is even better, with ensuite bathrooms to five of the bedrooms, and a sumptuous family bathroom with a roll-top bath. I wasn't lying when I said it wouldn't hang around; I'm frankly amazed it hasn't been snapped up already.

Mr and Mrs Watkins, however, seem totally impervious to the house's charms and are wandering around somewhat disconsolately. Things go from bad to worse when they step out onto the deck.

'That driveway at the front,' Mr Watkins asks, 'is that all the parking there is?'

'It can easily fit four cars, according to the vendor, and I have no reason to believe otherwise.'

'Hm. We entertain a lot of visitors, so I'm not sure four-car parking spaces is cutting it, darlin'. It's also a bit overlooked, isn't it?' He points to the windows of the neighbouring houses. 'I was hoping for somewhere a bit more private at this price point. More discreet, for my work. You get me?'

I don't get him at all, but I can practically hear Roxanne's voice hissing in my ear, telling me to ask questions: if this isn't the house for them, we'll never know what is unless we ask.

'What line of work are you in, Mr Watkins?' I ask, hoping that will shed some light on his car parking and privacy needs. Mrs Watkins has wandered back into the kitchen and I'm dimly aware of her prodding at the ovens in my peripheral vision.

'Gail and I are in the adult entertainment game,' he informs me, so matter-of-factly that it takes a moment for his words to sink in. 'Obviously, we're not act-ors any more, we're past all that malarkey, so we've switched over to being content creat-ors.' I can't help noticing his strange inflection of the words 'actors' and 'creators', with heavy emphasis on the second syllable, as if he's trying to make himself sound lah-di-dah. It's very out of keeping with the rest of the way he speaks. I still haven't fully digested the meaning of what he's telling me though, so I fill the silence pretty much on autopilot.

'I see,' I reply. 'So you need discretion for...'

'We're looking for a home primarily. We've both done well out of the industry and things have got even better since we changed tack, but we also need a place we can work in if we want to. That means we need car parking for actors, film crews and so on, plus privacy. We couldn't do a garden scene here, not in a million years.'

Come on, Alex. So they're porn stars; everyone needs a place to live. Be professional and stop judging them. It's really hard though, as my mind is currently wondering whether their orange glows are 'all over' tans, and my stomach is rebelling against the mental images that I'm conjuring up. One thing we can agree on straight away though, The Drive is not for them.

'Have you ever considered a career in the adult entertainment industry?' Mrs Watkins has rejoined us and her voice breaks into my reverie.

'I'm sorry, what?'

'I'm just saying—'

'Gail's right!' Mr Watkins exclaims enthusiastically, cutting his wife off. 'You've got a nice face and a decent rack on you from what I can see. What's it like down below? Most producers still prefer a shaved pussy, because it's easier for the camera to get a decent view of the action, but there's a growing market for hairy, as long as it's trimmed and under control. Nobody likes a growler, right? I mean, there's a niche for everything, but that's not a part of the market I'd get into. Far too many weirdos.'

'Mr Watkins, I—'

'I mean, what are you, mid-twenties? I reckon you'd have ten years of making decent money, especially to begin with. Our industry is obsessed with the new, so you'd probably be looking two to two and a half thou for your first job alone. We could even bring in your current job as a theme. I can see it now, "Naughty estate agent will do anything to earn her commission", or maybe even a virginal vibe, for the first one anyway.'

I'm at a loss for words; nothing in any training manual or anything that's happened to me before could remotely prepare me for this, and I literally have no idea what to say. On the one hand, Mr Watkins's remarks are so impossibly offensive that I'm sure Roxanne would have no issue with me tearing him off a strip, marching back to the office and filing a complaint against him. But the completely dispassionate way he's just summed up my physical appearance and my earning potential makes the whole conversation seem more comical than offensive in a bizarre way.

'My Gary is obsessed with his work,' Mrs Watkins explains. 'It's all he ever thinks about. If it's not for you then no biggie, but he's right when he says you could do well. He's a very driven man where his career is concerned, and he'd take good care of you.'

'If you don't ask, you never get,' Mr Watkins agrees. 'If I only get a one in a hundred hit rate, that's still one. Like I said, our industry is obsessed with new talent. No worries at all if you're not interested, but you really could go far.'

'Thank you, Mr Watkins,' I eventually manage to croak. 'I'm very happy in my current line of work though.'

Completely unperturbed, he reaches into his back pocket and pulls out his wallet. 'Let me give you my card,' he says, extracting a black business card with gold swirly writing on it and handing it to me. 'Just in case you change your mind.'

'They did *what*?' Roxanne explodes when I get back to the office and tell her about my encounter.

'They offered me a job as a porn star. I didn't know what to say or anything.'

'Do you want to make a complaint? We can certainly refuse to do any more business with them.'

'What about? I was thinking about it on the way back in the car. Yes, the way they sized me up and asked about my personal grooming was incredibly offensive, but they weren't perving at me. The way they spoke was oddly sexless, as if they were remarking on my shoes or something equally innocuous. That's what made it so weird, particularly with him. If he'd been a lech, I would happily have slapped him and kicked him in the balls, but in his mind he was making a perfectly normal job offer, almost in the same way as Sarah would offer me a job working for her.'

'She hasn't, has she?'

'What?'

'Sarah. She hasn't tried to poach you?'

'No, of course not!'

'Hm. I wouldn't put anything past that one. So you're not going to make a complaint about the Watkinses?'

'I don't think so. In a way, it was almost funny. Oh, hang on a minute. He gave me his card.'

I retrieve the black card from the wallet with the house paperwork in it and hold it out to her.

'"Dirk Goldenschafft,"' she reads. '"Director, Goldenschafft Productions."' She turns it over and we both stare at the other side, which features a line obviously supposed to represent a female silhouette, with the text 'Goldenschafft: welcome to the new era of adult entertainment.'

We both start giggling, which degenerates rapidly into full-blown eye-watering, snorting uncontrollable laughter. It's nearly ten minutes before we calm down sufficiently to repair the damage to our make-up and present even the vaguest hint of professionalism, and even then it's touch and go. Giggles break out periodically for the rest of the morning.

11

'What a disgusting, creepy old pervert!' Emma declares when I tell her about it. 'Have you looked him up?'

'Umm, no. I'm not much of a porn watcher. Thomas and I watched it a couple of times; I think he thought it might get me in the mood or make me want to try new things, but all I did was point out that a lot of it looked pretty uncomfortable and chafey for the woman involved. He kind of lost interest in us watching porn after that. Do you and Mark watch it?'

'God, no. I'd be crimson with embarrassment. However, we're not looking for titillation here; this is background research on your client so it's completely legitimate.'

'How much research are we talking about exactly? If you're talking about watching him in action, I might have to pass. I need to be able to look him in the eye without getting flashbacks to whatever he's been up to.'

'Don't be so pathetic. What's his website?'

'Goldenschafft.com.' I have to spell it out for her.

'Hmm. It seems he has quite the back catalogue. There's Gold-enschaffted volumes one to five to begin with, followed by some volumes entitled Goldenschaffted Threesomes, Goldenschaffted MILFs, Goldenschaffted Anal, and that's just the first of five pages. Let's try the first one.' She clicks and exclaims crossly. 'Subscribers only. Sod that for a game of soldiers. I'm not paying money to watch one of your clients shagging. Let's see if we can find him on a freebie site.'

She enters a different address and exclaims triumphantly after a brief search. 'Got him. It looks like an older clip, but I've found "Sexy MILF Brunella takes on the Goldenschafft".' She clicks on the icon and the video begins to play.

'Oh no, this is even worse than I imagined,' I moan as the camera pans away from a close up of the action to take in the actors' faces. 'That's his wife!'

'Athletic, isn't she?' Emma observes as he pushes her legs practically behind her ears and the camera zooms back in.

'I can't watch any more. Make it stop.'

'Don't worry, it's a preview. We're skipping ahead to the climax any second now.'

I'm looking away, but I can tell what's going on by the increasing crescendo of the grunts and squeals. Sure enough, there's a massive sigh from the screen, followed by Emma saying, 'Ugh, he's made a bit of a mess there.'

'Is it over?' I ask.

'I think so. Just a few seconds left.'

Just then, a familiar voice comes from her laptop. 'Brunella,' it says huskily, 'you've been Goldenschaffted.'

'Thank you, Dirk,' Gail's voice replies.

'Oh, God, really?' I exclaim. 'Goldenschaffted?'

'That's obviously his catchphrase,' she giggles. 'It was educational though, don't you think?'

'Not in the slightest. I just hope they find their ideal house through another agent. I won't be able to look either of them in the eye now.'

'Dirk Goldenschafft, you are a naughty boy,' she chuckles. 'What's his real name?'

'Gary Watkins, and she's Gail.'

'Yeah, I can see why they changed them. "Gail takes on the Gary" doesn't have quite the same ring to it somehow, does it? Even if they do alliterate rather charmingly.'

'I think I'll need therapy if I ever see them in the flesh again.'

'That could have been you, walking away with two and a half grand in your pocket, and the knowledge that you'd been Goldenschaffted.'

'Just stop, please. Anyway, they aren't act-*ors* any more,' I tell her, mimicking Gary's inflection. 'They're creat-*ors*.'

'So they'd hire someone else to take on your growler? An apprentice maybe, like a Silverschafft? Let's hope it's not the teaboy Bronzeschafft; that would be really demeaning,' she giggles.

'I don't really want to think about it. You're making me feel queasy.'

'Are you going to tell Thomas about your new porn career?'

'I don't have a porn career, and of course I'll tell him. We don't have any secrets, and I very much doubt I'll see Mr and Mrs Watkins again.'

'I'd like to be a fly on the wall for that conversation.'

* * *

Unfortunately, I realise later that week as I'm artistically arranging a cut baguette, a lump of cheese and a glass of wine on a table in the garden of the house in Dunton Green for a 'lifestyle' photo, Fate has decided to play me a curve ball. Roxanne's assessment of this house was completely correct and, for most people, it would be a non-starter. The garden is spacious and beautifully kept, but there is a constant muted roar from the traffic on the nearby M26 that destroys the tranquillity. The driveway is nearly a quarter of a mile long but it's in a poor state of repair, and the indoor swimming pool will need careful looking after to stop it causing condensation problems in the extension that was obviously built to house it. It's going to require a very specific type of buyer to fall in love with it, but the seclusion of the property means there is one person who I think will be extremely interested.

'Do you see what I mean about that house?' Roxanne asks me when I return to the office armed with my photos and a full set of measurements to lay out the floorplans.

'Yes. When are we actually putting it up?'

'As soon as you've processed the photos and the floorplans. I've written the blurb and the vendors have signed everything they need to. I'm not in any blistering hurry though; it's only going to sit there for months, until the vendors get fed up and start reducing the price.'

'So I can conduct viewings on it?'

'Absolutely. We have the keys. Why, do you have someone in mind?'

'I'm not sure yet. Let's talk commission.'

'I'll take that as a yes. Fine.' She smiles. This is a game we're both used to playing, as Roxanne regularly offers enhanced commission for getting successful offers on difficult properties. 'If you get an offer accepted within one month, I'll offer you one per cent on top of your normal commission upon completion.'

'Five per cent.'

'Cheeky. Two and a half, and that's my final offer.'

'Four.'

'You're twisting my arm. Let's make this fun. Four per cent, dropping by one per cent a week.'

'Done.'

I look up the number and dial before she has a chance to change her mind.

'Goldenschafft Productions, Dirk Goldenschafft speaking, how may I service you?' Mr Watkins answers after a couple of rings, and I have to smother a giggle at the lascivious way he pronounces the word 'service'.

'Hi, Mr Watkins. It's Alex, from Forman's estate agency in Sevenoaks. Is now a good time?'

'Couldn't be better, darlin'. Gail's in the car with me. Say hello, Gail.'

'Hi, Alex, how are you?' Gail's voice trills, thankfully cutting off the replay of Gary's voice saying 'You've been Goldenschaffted' from the video clip that has started replaying in my mind.

'I'm good, thanks, Mrs Watkins. I was just ringing to find out how the house hunting was going.'

'Fucking awful,' Mr Watkins cuts in. 'Honestly, I thought we'd be spoilt for choice waving our kind of money about, but it's all been shit so far.'

'I'm sorry to hear that. The reason I'm calling is that my boss has just shown me the details of a house we're going to be listing in the next couple of days. We are expecting a lot of interest, naturally, but I wanted to offer you the opportunity to have a look at it before it goes on the internet. I think it could be just what you're looking for. Very secluded with plenty of parking and even an indoor swimming pool for relaxing in after a hard day on set.' I have to bite my lip to prevent the snigger that has formed as a result of my unintentional double entendre.

'A swimming pool?' Gail's voice cries out delightedly. 'Oh, Gary. I'd *love* a swimming pool.'

'I guess there's no harm in looking at it.' Gary's voice is decidedly less enthusiastic. 'It can't be any worse than the other shit-holes we've seen so far.'

'I've got a good feeling about this one,' I tell him. 'When would you be able to view it, do you think?'

'We're in the area at the moment, as it happens. Where is it?'

I give him the postcode and we agree to meet at the property in half an hour.

*   *   *

'Now this is a bit more fucking like it!' Gary enthuses as he and Gail step out of the SUV onto the gravelled parking area in front of the house. 'Nobody overlooking us for starters, and the driveway is a decent size.'

'Absolutely,' I agree, making a big effort to look them both in the eye and not think about the fact that I've seen them having sex in close-up. 'And the field next to the driveway belongs to the property as well, so if you needed overflow for film crews and so on, you could add more parking there. Would you like to have a look inside?'

'You betcha.' I unlock the front door and step back to allow them to enter the house first. I follow them down the hallway into the open plan sitting room, dining room and kitchen. Personally, I'm not a huge fan of houses being too open plan, but I reckon Gary and Gail will love it. From their expressions, I'm not wrong.

'This is perfect,' Gail is murmuring. 'I can just see myself curled up in front of the telly over there.'

'Yeah, and we could get loads of equipment in easily without cramping the act-ors.'

'It's five bedrooms, this one,' I explain. 'Three doubles and a single upstairs, and a double down here, so it's not quite as large as the house on The Drive. There is a study through that door though.'

'There's only us, so we don't need that many bedrooms,' Gary tells me as he opens the door and sticks his head into the study. 'This would make a good dressing room, don't you think?'

'Gary Watkins,' Gail tells him surprisingly firmly. 'I'm *not* buying a house just because it works as a set. This is going to be our home, understood?'

'Of course it is, doll,' he soothes. 'But you can't blame me for seeing the potential, can you?'

Gail sighs theatrically and rolls her eyes at me. 'You see what I mean? He's a complete workaholic.'

Their enthusiasm hypes up several more notches when they see the pool. Once again, Gail is waxing lyrical about swimming a few lengths each morning and then curling up with her book, while Gary is extolling the filming potential.

'I don't mind nude swimming,' she scolds him at one point. 'But there will be no sex in that pool, do you understand? I'm not swimming through spunk.' I'm very slightly sick in the back of my mouth but somehow manage to keep my professional smile in place. Just the garden to go, I remind myself.

'There is a little bit of road noise in the garden,' I explain as I stand aside to let them out. 'But it's well muted by the hedges.'

As soon as I follow them, I realise the inaccuracy of that statement. I think the wind must have changed direction because the roar is really obtrusive now.

'It's a lovely space, isn't it?' I yell over the din. 'It reminds me of one of those gardens in a Jane Austen novel. I keep expecting to see Elizabeth Bennett and Mr Darcy on that path over there.' Even by my standards, this is stretching reality a bit, but I really want them to love this house.

'I love that scene where he dives into the lake,' Gail tells me.

'What are you talking about?' Gary asks.

'That Regency series on TV. You remember, don't you?'

'Not a clue,' he replies.

'Jane Austen's *Pride and Prejudice*. You definitely watched it with me.'

'Don't remember, sorry. I was probably working, and we aren't making Jane Austen films, are we. Although—'

'Here we go,' Gail says to me as Gary's eyes light up. 'He's got this bee in his bonnet about making a full-length feature film. Everyone says that there's no market for it because twenty minutes is more than enough for most of our viewers, but he won't be told.'

'I remember the show now and I've had an idea. We start with some bird walking through the garden all demure, wearing a long dress and carrying one of them umbrella things—'

'A parasol?' I suggest.

'Exactly. She spots the sexy gardener, she's all heaving bosom and then wham!'

'Wham?'

'Yeah. Into the action. What did you say the series was called?'

'*Pride and Prejudice,*' I remind him.

'We could call ours *Ride and Prejudice* maybe, although that might be a bit subtle. Give me another Jane Austen story.'

'*Emma*?'

'No. Can't do anything with that. Next.'

'*Sense and Sensibilities.*'

'*Sex and Sensibilities.* That has a bit of a ring to it. Next?'

'*Northanger Abbey.*'

His face lights up. 'That's the one. We'll call it *Big Wanger Abbey*. Lots of horny monks with massive cocks. What do you think?'

'I think you're a genius, sweetie,' Gail replies, planting a kiss on his lips. I suspect she's humouring him, but he doesn't spot it.

'I'll leave you to have a bit of a wander and I'll meet you back by the front door,' I tell them. I leave the front door open so I can hear them, and the tone of their voices when they come into earshot gives me cause for hope.

'What do you think?' I ask when they reappear.

'You've played a blinder,' Gary tells me. 'We've had a chat, and it's just what we're looking for. So, here's the deal. We're not going to mess you around; we'll come straight in at the asking price provided it comes off the market right away and nobody else gets to see it. What do you say?'

'I'll have to check with the vendors, of course, but I don't see a problem with that. I'll try to contact them as soon as I get back to the office and I'll give you a call once I've spoken to them.'

'Perfect. Oh, and Alex?'

'Yes?'

'I hope you're going to get a decent commission for this, but if you ever need a little extra, you know where I am.'

'Thank you, Mr Watkins. I'll bear that in mind.'

I can't help chuckling as I drive back to the office. I'm not sure what is amusing me more, my four per cent bonus or Gary's ludicrous Regency porn movie idea.

12

When my phone starts ringing on Saturday afternoon with a video call from Thomas, I nearly drop it in my excitement. I've tried to distract myself in various ways to pass the time; the kitchen is spotless and I've even done a load of Emma's washing for her, but the day has passed agonisingly slowly.

'Hiya,' I beam as his smiling face fills the screen.

'Hiya yourself.'

'So, how is it?'

'It's amazing, really it is,' he enthuses. 'I've learned so much already, and my painting style has been completely transformed.'

'So you're not doing the neo-cubist impression thing any more?' I ask, confused.

'No. Jorge explained that the word "impression" implies restraint and control. If I *im*press something on something, I'm coercing it. He's encouraged me to think about *ex*pression, which is setting myself free and letting the art tell its own story. It's revolutionary. I'm so excited. He really is a genius.'

'I'm so pleased for you. What are the people on your course like?'

'Oh, they're all really lovely and talented. It's like I've found my tribe, you know? It feels like a proper community where we all help each other out. When you first arrive, Jorge assigns a student who has been here for a few weeks already to be your mentor and help you find your way around. I have Catriona, and she's been brilliant. In fact, she wanted to say hi to you. I hope you don't mind.'

He turns the screen slightly and a woman's smiling face appears. I take in her short ash blonde hair, freckles, and the rings in her nose and bottom lip.

'Good to meet you. I'm Cat,' she says in a broad American accent. 'I just wanted to say hi and let you know that I'm taking good care of Tom for you.'

Tom? Thomas has always hated being called Tom.

'Umm, nice to meet you too, Cat,' I reply.

'Oh my Lord!' she exclaims. 'I can*not* get enough of your British accents. I've been getting Tom to read me random stuff just so I can listen to him, haven't I, Tom?'

'You have, and it's the least I can do in return for all the help you've given me,' he replies affectionately. I'm alarmed to detect a tiny prickle of jealousy forming deep within me as I observe their easy familiarity.

'Well, I'll leave you lovebugs to catch up,' Catriona says after a slightly awkward pause. 'Come find me when you're done, Tom. We're going out for breakfast, Alex. Tom has never tried biscuits and gravy, can you believe that? It was good to put a face to your name.'

'You two seem to be getting along very well,' I observe slightly caustically when she's detached herself from my boyfriend and (hopefully) gone out of earshot.

'She's lovely, isn't she?' Thomas replies, completely missing the point. 'Such a brilliant artist too. Her latest concept is aston-

ishing. I'd describe it to you, but you have to see it to truly understand it.'

'Is she exhibiting in the same show as you?'

'Yes, although I feel a bit nervous every time I think about that.
Jorge says I need to chill out and have confidence in my own ability
though, because nerves show on the canvas. We've been doing
regular meditation sessions, and he's encouraged me to take herbs
to help.'

'What, like herbal teas?'

'No. More medicinal than that.'

'You're not smoking weed are you?'

'Don't freak out. It's just a little bit every now and then.
Everyone is doing it, it's fine. It just helps to calm me down so I can
focus.'

'Is that a good idea? Isn't it illegal?'

'Relax. It's totally legal here. There are licensed retailers and
everything, although Jorge has his own specialist supplier.'

'What kind of college encourages its students to take drugs?'

'That's what's so amazing about this place. It doesn't feel like a
stuffy college at all. It's more like a big family with Jorge at the
centre of it. We don't have lectures or any of that stuff. Instead,
Jorge encourages us to find new ways of expressing ourselves and
getting rid of the inhibitions that hold us back. We did an entire
workshop in the nude a few days ago. I was super embarrassed at
the start, but I've never felt so liberated.'

I don't like the sound of this at all. 'Was Cat there?'

'Everyone was there, and we all agreed it was a brilliant move
from Jorge. It's transformed the atmosphere in the dorm as well. I'd
never realised what a barrier clothes were, and how we hide
underneath them. We should totally do a naturist holiday when I
come back; you'll see what I mean.'

I like the idea of that even less.

'Talking of clothes, or rather the lack of them,' I say in an attempt to interject a little bit of me into this one-sided conversation, 'I had an interesting job offer the other day.'

'Really? I didn't know you were looking to move jobs.'

'I'm not. But I did a viewing for this couple and it turned out they work in the porn industry. The guy's stage name is Goldenschafft – have you ever heard of anything so ridiculous?'

'Dirk Goldenschafft?' Thomas replies.

'Yes. How do you know him?'

'I think someone mentioned him to me once,' he says quickly. 'What's he like?'

'You've watched him, haven't you.' I sigh.

'No.' His shifty look betrays him. Great. So far, in this call that I've looked forward to all week, I've learned that my boyfriend is prancing around naked in front of a girl he's way too affectionate with, smoking weed and getting off to porn. An image pops into my head of him and Catriona, stark naked and smoking a joint together while watching one of Dirk's films. Maybe she's more into it than I am. I tell myself firmly that I'm being irrational, but I still feel uncomfortable.

'You said something about a job?' he prompts, unsurprisingly keen to shift the focus of our conversation away from him.

'Yes. Dirk, or Gary as he's called in real life, suggested I might like to make a film with him.'

'Oh, wow. What did you say?' The expected tone of horror and outrage is missing, I note to my dismay.

'I said no! What on earth did you think I would say?'

'I hope you didn't turn him down because of me.'

'Of course you were part of the reason. That and the fact that getting my kit off and having sex with a stranger in front of a camera is both a massive turn-off and literally the most excruciatingly embarrassing thing I can imagine doing. Even if I could get past all of that, what if someone I knew saw it? Can you imagine? I'd be mortified.'

'That's fear talking. If Jorge were here, he'd tell you to take control of that fear, to seize the opportunity to step into the unknown and master it.'

'Are you out of your mind? This isn't trying a new form of painting, Thomas. This is about me being naked, having sex with a complete stranger and being filmed for the gratification of people I have never met and have no relationship with.'

'Or, it's about you harnessing the power of your yoni and using it to celebrate the magic of sex.'

'My what?'

'Your yoni. It's what we call them during our meditation sessions.'

'For fuck's sake, Thomas. It almost sounds like you want me to do it.'

'It's nothing to do with me. I don't own you.'

'I'm not saying you do. But part of being in a relationship is that you only have sex with that one person. That's what monogamy is.'

'Monogamy is a social construct with no underlying biological basis.'

'What?'

'Think about it. Why are we expected to be faithful to just one person?'

'Because that's what being in a relationship means!'

'But who decided that? Did you? Did I? Or have we just accepted a restriction placed on us by society? The whole "one man for one woman" basically comes from organised religion as a way to exert control and stop us from expressing our true natures.'

'Is this another one of Jorge's pearls of wisdom?' I ask sarcastically.

'He's right though. Jorge isn't anti-relationships at all, in fact he's very pro them. But, and this is the key part, he says being in a relationship with someone is about expressing preference rather than exclusivity. It's like soup.'

'I'm sure it bloody isn't,' I mutter to myself.

'Let's say you really like tomato soup,' Thomas continues. 'Would anybody expect you to sign a form saying that you were only going to eat tomato soup for the rest of your life, without so much as looking at another flavour? Of course they wouldn't. You might eat tomato soup more often than any other flavour, because it's your preference, but you wouldn't be chastised and dragged through the divorce courts because you had a bowl of pea and ham to liven things up, would you?'

'Are you having sex with Catriona?' I ask suddenly. 'Is that what all this bullshit is about?'

'No! But what I'm trying to tell you is that it wouldn't make any difference to the way I feel about you if I did. You're my tomato, Alex. Look, I'd better go. The others are waiting for me and Cat keeps pointing at her watch. We'll catch up next week, yeah?'

After the call disconnects, I sit there staring at the dark screen of my phone for a while. I don't recognise the person I've just been talking to. He looked like Thomas, the gentle boy I fell in love with, but he sounded like someone else completely. I start to wonder whether this art school is more of a cult, and he's being brainwashed by this Jorge person. Tears start to fall silently down my cheeks, and I make no effort to stop them.

* * *

'Can I ask you something?' I say to Callum the next morning after he's finished both his crossword and mine.

'Is this part of the "teach Callum small talk" class?' he asks.

'No. I'm wrestling with something and I'd value a male opinion.'

'I'm not sure I'm going to be able to help, but go on.'

'If I were offered a job in the porn industry, would you advise me to take it?'

He looks completely baffled.

'It's hypothetical.'

'OK. I'd say no,' he replies after a long pause.

'Go on.'

'For starters, there is lots of malware hidden on porn sites. So you think you're just clicking around, but all sorts of nasty stuff is being downloaded onto your hard drive in the background and, before you know it, someone has emptied your bank account or is blackmailing you.'

'Yeah. I think I was talking more about me being on camera rather than as a viewer.'

'Ah. I'd still say no.'

'Because?'

'Because it's something that has implications way into the future. Once you're on the internet, you're there forever. I saw a documentary about it once. There was this woman who had made one scene to get her out of a financial hole when she was a student. She pocketed the money, got on with her life and never thought about it until she applied for, and got, a job as a primary school teacher some years later. She was happy, married, doing something she loved and looking forward to becoming a mother herself at the right time.'

'What happened?'

'One of the parents saw the scene, recognised her and contacted the head teacher anonymously. Within days, she'd lost her job, her husband had left her and everything in her life fell apart. She's now living in a static caravan and flipping burgers. All because she made one scene as a student.'

'Wow.'

'Yes. To me, that's not the worst bit of the story. I mean, it's terrible for her and a waste of her teaching talent, obviously, but there's more to it than that.'

'What's the worst bit?'

'That this woman, who made one slip up, had her life ruined by someone who took the moral high ground but was obviously a consumer of the very same stuff and didn't even have the balls to own up. That's hypocrisy of the first order.'

'Thank you,' I say to him.

'For what?'

'For speaking a lot more sense than Thomas did yesterday.'

13

The check-in queue for our flight to San Francisco is surprisingly long, and I'm very aware of Claire's nervousness increasing as we get closer to the front. She wasn't joking about being an anxious traveller. We agreed it would be easier if I stayed over with her the night before because we had an early start, and I could hear her going back and forth to the bathroom several times.

I haven't had a lot of sleep either, but that's nothing to do with any nervousness about flying. My anxiety is more about what I'm going to discover at the other end. My weekly calls with Thomas haven't improved, and it feels more and more like he's slipping away from me. Claire had made up the bed in his room for me to sleep on last night, but it just emphasised the difference between the Thomas I know and love, and the apparent stranger I've been talking to on the phone. I'm just hoping that seeing me in the flesh will jolt some sense of normality back into him, because I don't think I can contemplate the alternative.

'Oh no,' Claire moans suddenly.

'What's the matter? Do you need to go again? I can keep our place in the queue.'

'No. I should have realised this might happen.'

'What?'

'Over there, in the business class check-in area.'

I glance over but can't work out what she's talking about. A man is checking in, accompanied by a pretty young woman who I assume is probably his daughter.

'What am I looking for?' I ask her.

'At the desk. That's Thomas's father, Jack, and he's got New with him. Thomas must have invited them. Typical that they'd be on the same flight.'

Now that I know who they are, I'm fascinated to see them. 'Why are they coming though?' I ask her. 'Thomas is really rude about them to me.'

'Yes, but don't forget that Jack financed this course, so he's probably keen to see what return he's getting on his investment. At least they're in business, so we won't have to sit near them.'

At this point, Michelle obviously spots Claire, because her face erupts in a huge smile and she starts waving at us and pulling on Jack's sleeve to alert him to our presence.

'She certainly seems pleased to see you,' I remark.

'That's the worst bit about all this. She's impossible to hate because she's so bubbly and friendly. She used to be my hair-dresser until, well...'

Jack and Michelle are now engaged in what looks like a fairly animated conversation but, after a quick word with the check-in assistant, Michelle starts fighting her way through the crowd to get to us. Claire looks like she wants the floor to open up and swallow her.

'Claire!' Michelle shouts when she reckons she's close enough to be heard. Several heads in the queue turn to look at her, but she's oblivious. She really is beautiful: she's curvaceous with long dark hair and large dark brown eyes framed by a flawless face. I nearly fancy her myself.

'Claire!' she shouts again as she barrels into the queue towards us. A few people look surprised, but Michelle is obviously the sort of person that can get away with inconveniencing people, as nobody actually grumbles.

'Hello, Michelle, this is a surprise,' Claire says less than enthusiastically when she finally reaches us.

'Are you going to Thomas's exhibition as well?' Michelle asks. 'I'm so excited. I've never been to a proper art exhibition before.'

'Of course you haven't, you're only nine years old,' Claire mutters quietly. Thankfully Michelle either doesn't hear or chooses to ignore her.

'This is Thomas's girlfriend, Alex,' Claire tells her in a more normal voice, and Michelle turns her megawatt smile on me.

'Of course you are!' she exclaims. 'You must be so proud of him, yeah? Anyway, I've come to rescue you both. As soon as I saw you, I said to Jack that it just wasn't right that you should have to languish in economy while we're living it up in the posh seats, so he's fixing you an upgrade. Come and join us. Excuse me, coming through!'

If the other passengers were good-natured about Michelle barrelling through the queue to reach us, they're nowhere near as happy to move out of the way so Claire and I, plus our baggage, can get past them. By the time we're out of the queue and heading for the business class check-in, we've earned ourselves several scowls and a few grumpy mutters.

'Hello, Jack,' Claire says tightly when we reach the desk.

'Claire.' He nods. 'We're all done here. Karen will look after you and we'll see you in the lounge, OK?' He grabs Michelle's hand and stalks off.

'Mr Walsh has upgraded you on both the outbound and homeward legs,' Karen explains with a smile. 'He must think a lot of you.'

'I'm his ex-wife. I suspect it's a guilt offering. We're quite happy to fly economy,' Claire replies curtly.

'Oh no. Trust me, after this you'll never want to fly economy again. Now, let's get you checked in, shall we? Then you can head off to the lounge for a glass or two of complimentary fizz before boarding the flight.'

Claire may be determined to be unimpressed by the business class experience, but I've never come across anything like this before. I'm used to fighting my way through self-check-in for whichever budget airline can get me to the sunshine most cheaply, so this is a real eye-opener. Karen explains how to find the business class lounge and, after our bags have disappeared down the conveyor belt, we glide through fast-track security.

'Bloody Jack, flashing his money around,' Claire mutters grumpily as we wander through the duty-free area.

'I think it was Michelle's doing mainly. I can see why she's impossible to hate.' I smile. 'Do you think you'll ever stop calling her New? I mean, she's kind of "Not-so-new" now, isn't she?'

'It's not New as in new and old. There's a silent P at the front. It was Thomas's nickname for her originally.'

'I don't get it.' I look at her, confused.

'Pneu, as in pneumatic, as in blow-up breasts,' she explains. 'Thomas is convinced she's had work done. Anyway, it made me laugh at a time when there wasn't much to laugh about, and it stuck.'

'Oh.' I'm not sure what to say to that. I didn't look closely, obviously, but I didn't notice Michelle's chest so it can't have been massively out of proportion to the rest of her.

'There you are!' Michelle envelops us both in massive hugs when we arrive at the business class lounge, as if it's been years since she saw us last, rather than about half an hour. As she presses against me, I find myself surreptitiously trying to gauge whether her chest is unnaturally firm, but I can't detect anything. I suspect Thomas was just being catty about her to try to cheer Claire up, but I'm not sure how I feel about them persisting with the joke. I know it was Jack's affair with Michelle that broke up their marriage, but I'll take a dim view if they're pinning all the blame on her, as if he had nothing to do with it.

'How long have you and Thomas been together?' Michelle asks me once we're settled around a table with glasses of champagne and Michelle has introduced me properly to Thomas's father, Jack.

'Three years coming up,' I reply.

'Wedding bells in the offing? I love a wedding. I'll do your hair and make-up if you like.'

'We haven't talked about it.' This isn't a complete lie; although we've talked a lot about moving in together, Thomas isn't wildly keen on the idea of marriage at the moment, given how his parents ended up.

'Of course you haven't,' Jack cuts in. 'Probably waiting for him to stop messing about with nursery schools and paint brushes and get a proper job.'

'Why did you pay for his course if you feel like that about it?' Claire demands sharply. I notice she's nearly drained her glass already and resolve to keep an eye on her. I doubt the airline would take kindly to her being drunk on the plane, even in business class.

'Because the sooner he realises that he can't make a living from painting, the better. If that means I have to pay for him to hang out in San Francisco with a load of loser hippies for a month, then that's what it takes. What do you do, Alex?'

'I'm an estate agent,' I tell him.

'Halle-bloody-lujah. A young person with a proper job. And do you still live at home, or have you moved out?'

'I share a flat in Sevenoaks with my friend, Emma.'

'Which is exactly what he should be doing, rather than skulking around, poncing off his mother.'

'He does not ponce!' Claire practically shouts. 'He pays rent and does all the man-jobs around the house. You know, the ones my husband would do if he hadn't buggered off with someone half his age. No offence, Michelle.'

'Oh, none taken. You do you, honey,' Michelle replies without a hint of malice. I'm fast coming to the conclusion that I really like her.

'Move on, Claire. Bitterness doesn't suit you,' Jack tells Claire.

'Fuck you, Jack. I'm going to get a refill.'

'Well, it's always good to be honest with each other, I guess,' Michelle observes carefully as Claire storms off in the direction of the drinks table.

By the time we come to board the plane, the hostilities have died down a little, but Michelle and I both agree that the flight will be much easier for everyone if we sit between Jack and Claire to keep them as far away from each other as possible. It turns out that Jack and Michelle have decided to make a holiday out of the trip and will be staying for two weeks, so at least we won't have to put up with this on the return leg.

'I've never been upstairs on a plane before,' I say to Claire as we board. 'In fact, I've never even been on a plane that has an upstairs before.'

'Hmph,' she grumbles. 'It's overrated in my opinion.'

When we get into the cabin, I have to disagree with her. No sooner am I settled into my enormous seat than a flight attendant offers me a complimentary glass of champagne, orange juice or water. I watch carefully, but am relieved to see that Claire opts for orange juice this time. I'm not sure this flight will end well if she gets any more alcohol in her system, and I've got enough to deal with worrying about what I'm going to find at the other end, without worrying about what might happen on the way over as well.

'Have you had a look at the lunch menu?' Michelle leans across the aisle to ask me. 'I'm going to have the lamb for my main, and the chocolate pudding, but I can't decide between smoked salmon with all the trimmings or the caprese salad for my starter.'

'I don't know. How much are they?' Although this holiday hasn't cost me a penny so far, airline food is notoriously expensive so my plan is to eat as little as possible on the plane.

'You are funny!' Michelle laughs. 'It's all included.'

'Oh.' I feel a bit embarrassed, like I've been caught using the wrong knife and fork at a banquet. Michelle obviously picks up on my discomfort because she leans across and gives my arm a squeeze.

'The first time I flew business class with Jack,' she whispers confidentially, 'I asked who I had to talk to about hiring headphones so I could watch a film. Turns out they were in this little cupboard that I hadn't even noticed. Noise cancelling and everything. It really is a different world up here.'

Before long, everyone seems to be on board and the captain is telling us about the flight, which is going to be just over eleven hours long. As we taxi out, my heart fills with a sudden violent longing for Thomas. I don't mind flying, but I never enjoy the take-off, with the engines screaming and the acceleration as the plane thunders down the runway. Thomas knows this and instinctively reaches for my hand when we fly together. As the whine from the engines increases in pitch, I feel terribly alone, even though Claire is next to me. I close my eyes tight and try to focus on the fact that I'll be in the same city as Thomas in less than half a day. San Francisco, here I come.

14

To everyone's relief, we aren't staying in the same hotel. Jack and Michelle have booked themselves into some fancy five-star place at the top of the amusingly named Nob Hill, and Claire and I are a few blocks away in a three-star lower down in the Tenderloin. I don't know what they're getting that we aren't, because this is still one of the most comfortable hotels I've stayed in. I don't have much of a view, admittedly, but that doesn't matter as I literally only plan to use this room for sleeping.

The jetlag means I'm wide awake by five o'clock in the morning and, despite my best efforts, there is no way I'm going to get back to sleep, so after a while I decide to get up and have a bit of an explore. As I stand under the shower, I wonder whether it would be polite to use the internal phone to call Claire's room and see if she wants to join me, but in the end I decide not to. I like her, but I selfishly fancy wandering alone without having to conform to anyone else's agenda. If she asks, I'll just tell her I didn't know whether she was awake and didn't want to disturb her. We've agreed to meet for breakfast at nine and head out on a bus tour of the city afterwards. That should get us back with plenty of time to get changed before Jack and Michelle pick us up to go to the exhibition this evening. Claire was a bit frosty about the idea of us all turning up together, but Michelle argued that it would look even stranger if we all turned up separately and, as usual, got her way by being so charming that it would have been churlish to refuse her.

The street outside the hotel is pretty much deserted as I step through the door, and I'm surprised by how cold it is. A couple of street sweepers are making their way along the pavement, carefully skirting the bags of rubbish that are obviously waiting for the refuse collectors outside each shop and restaurant. I consulted the map in my guidebook before leaving my room, so I turn left towards Union Square with the intention of picking up the Powell-Hyde cable car at the turnaround on Market Street. My plan is to ride it all the way to the terminus at Fisherman's Wharf and back again.

I'm no more than half a block from the hotel when I spot what I assume to be a homeless man sitting on the pavement with his back against the wall of a building. Our eyes meet as he hears me approaching, and he stands up and blocks my path.

'Tourist, right?' he asks.

'Umm, yes,' I reply, trying to work out how I can step around him without appearing rude.

'Wanna tour of the city? Hundred bucks. I can show you the real San Fran, not that shit the tour guides sell.'

'No thank you,' I say firmly but politely.

'How about ten dollars for a cup of coffee then?'

'I'm not carrying any change, I'm afraid.'

'Oh, I get it,' he replies, his voice suddenly bitter. 'You think I'm a worthless piece of shit cuz I live on the streets, is that it? You think you're better than me, little Miss English tourist bitch, huh? You don't know fuck all about me, understand? Fuck you, bitch. Go on, fuck off!'

I'm completely gobsmacked. I've come across homeless people begging in London and, although I don't like being approached, at least they get the message and move on when I don't have any spare change and have to politely turn them down. I've never had someone be so aggressive before, and I can feel panic rising inside me. What if he decides to get violent? He could drag me away and literally nobody would know where I was. Suddenly, my early morning excursion seems like a really bad idea.

'I'm sorry,' I say as I turn back. 'I think I've forgotten something.' I break into a run and don't stop until I reach the safety of the hotel.

'Are you OK, ma'am?' the receptionist asks as I burst through the door, panting from the exertion.

'I just came across the rudest homeless person I think I've ever met,' I explain. 'He was really aggressive and I didn't feel safe.'

'Let me guess, you turned left, and he was about half a block that way? Offered you a tour of the city?'

'That's right.'

'That'll be Jerry. He's got a mouth on him, I agree, but he's harmless underneath. His mind is completely fried, poor guy. I must have talked to him over a hundred times and he still doesn't know who I am. But I found out he absolutely loves peanut butter cups, so I slip him one of those from time to time.'

'Oh.' I'm not sure what to do with this information.

'We have a lot of homeless in San Francisco,' the receptionist continues, 'and the highest density of them are in this area. They might be a little eccentric, especially the ones with mental health issues like Jerry, but they're generally harmless. Just walk on by and try not to make eye contact. Whatever you do, don't give them any money. Or, in Jerry's case, you can pay the peanut butter cup tax if you like.'

'Hello, Alex, what are you doing up so early?' The receptionist's explanation is cut short by the arrival of Claire, looking fresh as a daisy.

'Jetlag,' I explain. 'I couldn't sleep, so I thought I'd see whether I could beat the queues for the cable car. Unfortunately I had a run-in with a very aggressive homeless person on the way.' I peer at the receptionist's name badge. 'Brad here was just explaining that they aren't anything to worry about.'

'The cable car sounds like a brilliant idea. I'll come with you,' Claire declares in a tone of voice that makes it quite clear the matter is not up for debate.

'Here,' Brad says, reaching under the counter and slipping a small confectionary package towards me. 'For Jerry.'

The homeless guy is still there, and I can feel my heart rate quicken as we approach, but I follow Brad's advice and keep my eyes on the pavement. It doesn't make any difference, as Jerry is on his feet as soon as he spots us.

'Tourists, right?' he asks as we approach.

'We're not giving you any money,' Claire tells him firmly as she moves to sidestep him.

'You fucking bitch,' he replies. 'Who do you think you are?'

'Excuse me? What did you say?' Claire stops dead in her tracks and I notice her cheeks are flushing pink.

'Leave this to me,' I tell her firmly. Jerry fixes his eyes on me beadily. 'Wanna tour of the city?' he asks. 'Hundred bucks. I can show you the real San Fran, not that shit the tour guides sell.'

'I don't, but I've got something for you.' I pull the packet of peanut butter cups out of my pocket and offer it to him. Jerry's eyes light up as he takes the packet from me and settles himself back on the pavement, suddenly completely oblivious to our presence.

When we arrive at the terminus on Market Street, it's a little after seven thirty and the queue is non-existent. After a few minutes, a cable car rattles in and I watch, entranced, as it's manoeuvred onto the turntable and pushed round to face the other way. It's ridiculously anachronistic in many ways, but it somehow manages to look completely at home.

'I was reading about these on the plane,' I tell Claire. 'They're pretty much unchanged from when the system was first put in to stop horses dropping dead lugging heavy loads up the steep hills. The cable car itself has no power at all. It grips a moving cable underneath the street that pulls it along, and the brakes are made of wood. Apparently, you can sometimes smell the wood burning when they slow down.'

We clamber aboard, along with a few other early birds, and we're soon on our way. I try to imagine Thomas riding the cable car but, when I do, I see Cat with him rather than me, so I decide to concentrate on the views instead. At one point, we get a superb view down to Alcatraz Island and the bay, and I'm delighted to catch my first glimpse of the Golden Gate Bridge. I am definitely underdressed for this excursion though, as the cold wind whipping past is making me shiver, so we decide to sit indoors for the return journey.

'I expect we'll see it all again on the bus tour later,' Claire tells me. 'This is just about the cable car, so you can say you've been on it.'

'I guess so. Maybe Thomas and I can ride it again tomorrow. I'd love to have a picture of the two of us with it.'

'He's going to be so pleased to see you. I know he's enjoying the course and everything, but I bet he's secretly a little bit homesick.'

'Do you think? I hope so. I mean, I'm really glad he's having a good time, but I worry that it's changing him, and it feels like we're drifting apart sometimes. He seems particularly taken with this girl, Cat, who was assigned to be his mentor.'

'I met her on one of our early calls,' Claire replies. 'I don't think you have anything to worry about. I reckon she's just very friendly. Thomas loves you.'

'You're probably right. I know it sounds awful, but sometimes I wish he hadn't sold that painting. Do you ever wonder who bought it? I think we can probably assume it wasn't that man who was so horrible to him. What was his name?'

'I can't remember,' Claire says, but there's an edge to her voice.

'What is it? Have I said something wrong?'

'No, of course not. It's just... Look, if I tell you, you have to promise not to breathe a word to Thomas, OK? He would never forgive me.'

'Why, what have you done?'

'It was me that bought the painting.'

Whatever I was expecting her to say, it wasn't this.

'I don't understand.'

'I didn't want him to think he'd failed. It was such a big deal for him, and those other people were being nasty because he wasn't part of a group. So I went to the hall and bought one of his paintings on the Saturday morning, when I knew he was with you. Then I texted him, saying that I'd just popped in to pick up something I'd forgotten and noticed the red sticker.'

I remember the way his face lit up when her text arrived. Of course it was her; I should have realised straight away that nobody other than a parent would have bought one of his frankly unintelligible artworks.

'But Claire, that means he wasn't technically qualified to enrol on the course,' I whisper as the implications of her actions start to sink in.

'Of course he was. He'd sold a painting, hadn't he?'

'I don't think it counts if the buyer is the artist's mum.'

'Where did it stipulate that on the entry requirements?

Anyway, the point is you mustn't tell him it was me, because it will destroy his confidence.'

'There's no way I'm telling him,' I agree. 'What happened to the painting though?'

She blushes slightly. 'It, ah, had a bit of an accident in the back of the car when I picked it up. I should have wrapped it more carefully. Unfortunately, it was ruined and I had to dispose of it. Thomas would have been heartbroken to see it that way.'

She must think I was born yesterday.

'So let me get this straight. You bought one of his paintings to make him feel good, then deliberately ruined it and threw it away. Where did you take it? You can't have risked putting it in your own rubbish.'

Her blush deepens. 'I may have detoured via the tip on the way home.'

I'm both appalled and filled with grudging admiration for the way she pulled off her subterfuge.

'Don't worry,' I tell her. 'Your secret is safe with me.'

The jetlag is back in force and I'm struggling to keep myself from yawning as I change into the mini cocktail dress I've bought for the exhibition. I'm both excited and anxious about seeing Thomas, and I take extra care with my make-up and brush my hair until it falls over my shoulders in soft golden waves, the way I know he likes it. My stomach is filled with butterflies as I make my way down to the lobby, but I'm also worried that I'll fall fast asleep before we even get there. I've sent Emma a picture of me on the cable car, along with a description of my encounters with Jerry, but she's obviously busy because she hasn't replied.

Claire is waiting for me in the lobby, but it takes me a moment to recognise her. I think I've only ever seen her in practical clothes, so the sparkling floor-length gown takes me by surprise.

'Look at us, all dressed up.' She smiles as I take a selfie of us together. 'I'd suggest a quick drink in the bar before we go, but Jack and Pneu will be here any minute, so I guess we ought to loiter by the doors so as not to keep the taxi waiting.'

As we approach the doors, a long black limousine glides to a halt on the street outside.

'Typical,' Claire mutters. 'I bet that's them.'

Sure enough, the doorman opens the rear door and Jack appears, looking very smart in a dinner jacket.

'Your transport awaits,' he tells us, indicating the limousine with a flourish.

'You just can't help showing off, can you?' Claire tuts.

'Hey, if you'd rather get a taxi then be my guest. Everyone else will be turning up in limos, but don't worry, I'm sure Thomas won't be embarrassed at all.'

'Fine. When in Rome, I guess.'

'Exactly.'

Once I've navigated my way through the surprisingly small door into the limo without (I hope) giving the doorman an eyeful of my knickers, I settle on the plush leather seat and look around. Michelle, unsurprisingly, is looking absolutely gorgeous in a low cut, wraparound evening dress that shows just enough cleavage to be sexy without being immodest. Looking at her shape, I think it's very unlikely that she's had any cosmetic surgery but, if she has, the surgeon has done a superb job because she looks completely natural. As we pull smoothly away from the kerb, I spot Jerry, who doesn't appear to have moved since this morning. He shouts something as we pass, but thankfully the soundproofing means that we can't hear him.

'Do you think there will be any megastars there tonight?' I ask.

'I don't know, but if Orlando Bloom is there, I won't be held responsible for my actions,' Michelle giggles, earning a sharp look from Jack. 'What about you, Claire? Who's your Hollywood heart-throb?' she continues, ignoring him completely.

'I don't know if I have one. I suppose George Clooney is fairly easy on the eye.'

'Yeah, but he's married now, isn't he?'

'Orlando Bloom isn't exactly single,' I remark. 'Isn't he with Katy Perry?'

'Not married though.' She grins.

'I don't seem to remember you being so concerned about marital status when you started seeing my husband, Michelle,' Claire interjects blandly.

'Enough, both of you!' Jack roars suddenly, making us all jump. 'Tonight is about Thomas, and Thomas only, do you understand? We are going to go to this exhibition and we're all going to behave like adults. Do I make myself clear?'

'Crystal,' Michelle replies soothingly. I decide to distract myself by looking out of the window, which proves to be difficult as the glass is very dark and there doesn't appear to be much street lighting in this part of the city. In fact, the closer we get to our destination, the more run down the view outside gets.

I'm starting to get a very bad feeling about this.

15

'Are you sure this is the place?' Jack asks the driver when the car pulls up outside what appears to be a boarded-up shop in a very sleazy looking neighbourhood.

'Completely, sir.'

'Stay in the car,' Jack commands us as he steps out and heads for the doorway. He knocks sharply and, after a second or two, the door swings open to reveal none other than Cat. She's even prettier in the flesh, her elfin features emphasised by the baggy T-shirt she's wearing, which is emblazoned with the name of the college.

'I think we might be slightly overdressed, if Cat's outfit is anything to go by,' I observe to Claire and Michelle.

After a brief conversation, Jack opens the car door again and leans in.

'We're in the right place. Apparently, the location suits the high-profile clients because it's discreet and they're unlikely to be recognised out here.'

'I think I'd be more worried about being stabbed than recognised,' Claire remarks as she shuffles along the seat towards the door.

'You have my number, sir,' the driver tells Jack. 'Just call when you're ready and I'll be here in five minutes.'

'Thank you. Come on then, let's go and see this art.'

Cat is beaming as she opens the door to let us in. 'Hi, welcome. Oh my, don't you all look gorgeous! So who do we have here? I recognise some faces I think.' She turns to Claire. 'You're Tom's mom, aren't you?'

'That's right,' Claire replies.

'That's right,' Cat parrots. 'Sorry, I'm not being disrespectful, I just love your accent and I'm trying to learn it. You're Alex, right?'

'That's me.'

'Cool. Does Tom know you guys are coming? He didn't say anything.'

'It's a surprise,' I tell her, just managing to stop myself from adding 'Not that it's any of your business.'

'Oh, wow! Tom's gonna be so happy to see you.' She turns to Jack and Michelle and a small frown appears on her forehead. 'I'm sorry,' she says. 'I don't think we've met.'

'I'm Jack, Thomas's father, and this is my partner, Michelle,' Jack explains curtly.

'Oh.' She pauses just long enough for me to pick up that she obviously knows about the thorny relationship Thomas has with his father, before switching back into full-on welcome mode. 'That's so great how you're all coming together for Tom. Okay, so we have a mixture of artwork on display this evening. There are two works by our founder, Jorge Henriksen, along with a few pieces from some of our alumni. Pieces that have a red sticker are already sold, but if you see anything that interests you, just talk to one of the stewards and they'll help you guys out.'

'How do we recognise the stewards?' Michelle asks.

'They're wearing T-shirts with San Francisco College of Artistic Expression on them like mine. You can't miss those guys. Feel free to help yourselves to drinks and snacks as well. The cookies were made in college and there are two types. Ordinary chocolate chip and some special ones. Now, if I could just grab your invitations?'

Claire and Jack hand over their email printouts, which Cat places on the top of a small pile on the table weighted down by a small Buddha statue.

'OK,' she declares. 'Go and have fun.'

'Do we get a catalogue or something?' Jack asks.

'Jorge isn't a fan of catalogues,' Cat replies. 'He says they get in the way of the art speaking to you. Also, unlike most exhibitions, the artists are with us tonight, so if you want to know more about a piece, just ask a steward and they'll get the artist for you. Each piece has a title and brief description next to it, along with the name of the artist.'

'I see. Thank you.'

As we enter what I assume to be the main room of the gallery, it quickly becomes obvious that we are massively overdressed. Most of the other people in the room are wearing jeans and T-shirts. I'm furiously scanning the room for Thomas, but I can't see him. My initial pang of disappointment is tempered by the fact that Cat made it clear that he'd be made up to see us, so he must be here somewhere.

'Hi guys.' A steward with a tray of glasses appears next to us. 'We've got white wine, apple juice or water.'

'Wine,' we all reply in unison.

'No problem,' he replies, smiling and turning the tray. 'I just need to remind you that the legal age for drinking alcohol is twenty-one, so please drain your glasses quickly if the feds turn up.'

'Cheeky bastard! How old does he think I am, twelve?' Michelle hisses as he moves away.

'If the cap fits,' Claire murmurs.

'I reckon he says that to everyone,' I interject swiftly before things start to escalate again. 'He's trying to flatter us.'

'Hi and welcome!' Another steward has appeared from nowhere. 'Would you guys care for a cookie? We've got the normal ones on the left here, and the special ones on the right.'

'What's special about the ones on the right?' Claire asks.

'It's a secret recipe, unique to the college,' he stage-whispers conspiratorially. 'They've got a special ingredient that helps make the artwork really pop.'

'I'll have one of those then,' Claire tells him, helping herself to one of the special biscuits.

'Are you sure that's a good idea?' Jack murmurs to her as he waves the steward away. 'I don't like the sound of this "special ingredient" and, if the kitchens here are anything like the rest of the place, the chips in your biscuit are probably mouse droppings.'

'Nonsense, Jack. When in Rome, remember?' As if to emphasise her point, she takes a large bite.

'What's it like?' Michelle asks as Claire chews.

'Interesting. It's like a normal chocolate chip cookie, but there's a slightly bitter undercurrent. It's odd, but not unpleasant.'

Just then, my gaze falls upon a very familiar figure wearing a bobble hat, and my heartbeat quickens.

'There's Thomas,' I announce, and we all set off towards him. He's facing away from us, talking to another man, so he doesn't see us approach.

'Hello, stranger,' I say when we get within earshot of him.

He spins around and his mouth literally drops open. I'm feverishly trying to find the expression of delight in his face, but I can't see anything. It's just surprise.

'Bloody hell!' he exclaims. 'What are you all doing here?'

'Language, Thomas,' Claire intones automatically after she has swallowed the last of her biscuit.

'Sorry, but this is such a surprise. Why didn't you say you were coming?'

'Duh!' I reply. 'Surprise was the whole point. Are you pleased to see us?'

'Of course I am. Why are you dressed like that?'

'Stupidly, we thought we were coming to an upmarket event,' Jack replies caustically. 'If I'd known we were going to be in an empty shop unit in some godforsaken neighbourhood, I might have dressed differently. Where are all the A-list celebrities your principal boasted about?'

'There was a special showing for them earlier. So private even we weren't allowed to come. They bought a few pieces though, including one of mine.'

'That's brilliant. I'm so proud of you!' Claire tells him.

'Do I get a kiss?' I ask, slightly miffed that he hasn't even hugged me hello.

'Of course. Sorry.' He leans forward and places the briefest peck on my lips.

'You must be boiling in that hat,' Claire observes, pulling it off his head and gasping with horror as she does so.

'What have you done to your hair?' she asks.

'I needed it for an artwork, so I cut it,' Thomas tells her as he runs his hand over his buzz cut. 'Cat says this look suits me.'

'If you want to look like a prison inmate, maybe!' Claire retorts. 'What do you mean, you needed it for an artwork?'

'All in good time. Have you had a look around?'

'No, we've only just arrived.'

'OK. So the big pictures on the far wall there, they're Jorge's. That one on the left had a price tag of fifty thousand dollars, and it was already sold when I got down here. He's a legend, that man.'

'Is he here?' Jack asks, scanning the room again.

'He'll be along in a bit, I expect,' Thomas tells him. 'Then the ones surrounding Jorge's are SFCoAE alumni. They're a lot cheaper, a couple of thousand up to around five thousand. Everything else is by current students.'

'And your hair?' Claire asks again.

'We've just finished a project where Jorge encouraged us to step outside the usual boundaries and really put something of ourselves into our art. It's in the next-door room. I'd recommend you start in here though.'

'Are any of these yours, Thomas?' Michelle asks, looking around dubiously. I don't blame her; the kindest way to describe most of the artwork on display is 'experimental'. I certainly wouldn't want any of the stuff I've seen so far in my flat. As well as the paintings on the walls, there are plinths with what I assume are sculptures, but it's very difficult to tell what most of them are supposed to be. One looks like it might be a baby from some angles, but just a load of nails welded together from others. I read the plaque on the plinth, which tells me it's called *Children Hurt* by someone called DD Majors.

'I'll be back in a minute, OK?' Thomas says and disappears in the direction of the door we came in through.

We have no alternative but to make our way aimlessly around the room, trying to look appreciatively at the artwork on display. It's a real hodge-podge, and I still can't say I've seen anything I like when Claire suddenly exclaims, 'This is one of Thomas's, and it's sold. Look!' We gather in front of the painting. Even I can see that this is very different in style to the stuff he was doing before. This looks like someone has just thrown paint at the canvas. There are random splodges of different colours not only on the canvas, but over the frame as well. I look at the caption, which tells me this is called *Unconstrained,* by Thomas Walsh. The price is five hundred dollars and, as Claire has already observed, it appears to have been sold.

'I don't get it,' Michelle observes sadly after a couple of minutes.

'I think he's trying to...' Claire begins, but that's as far as she gets before her words dry up.

'It looks more like an industrial accident than a work of art,' Jack observes crossly.

'Oh, you've found one of Tom's! Isn't it brilliant?' Cat enthuses from next to me. I turn to see she has Thomas in tow. 'I love the way he's refused to be confined by the frame. It speaks of wild freedom, don't you think? It's like "Nobody puts Tom in a box".'

'But what is it supposed to be a picture *of*?' Michelle asks, still looking confused.

'It's not a picture *of* anything, that's what's so great about it,' Cat tells her. 'It's an *expression*. Emotion on a canvas. Tom's innermost feelings represented in paint.'

'Ah, good evening. You must be the family of Tom, yes?' As soon as my eyes move to the latest person to join us, I know that this is Jorge. He looks just as he did in the publicity photos on the website.

'He is such an emerging talent, *ja*? He is really starting to find himself here. Have you seen his work from the project we just did? Extraordinary. He and Catriona seem to inspire each other to greater and greater things. I'm so pleased that he has decided to extend his stay with us.'

What? This is the first I've heard about Thomas extending his stay and, from the expressions on Jack and Claire's faces, I'm guessing it's the first they've heard of it too.

'I've signed up for another month,' Thomas says, a little sheepishly. 'I was going to tell you.'

My heart falls to the floor. Jorge is obviously completely unaware of the bomb he's just dropped and, after clapping Jack on the shoulder jovially and telling him how proud he must be, he wanders off to talk to someone else.

'When was this decided?' I ask softly.

'A few days ago. Cat and I talked about it, and we both agreed that another month would help us reach the next level.'

'Tom's my muse.' Cat smiles at me. 'I hope you don't mind me borrowing him for another month.'

Of course I bloody mind! However, I'm not going to make a scene in the middle of this exhibition, so I just smile back at her. There will be time to get to the bottom of this tomorrow.

'I knew you'd understand,' Thomas says, completely misreading the situation. 'Do you want to see the project pictures now? Cat's is incredible.'

'I might need to sit down for a minute,' Claire says feebly. 'I'm not sure I'm feeling very well all of a sudden.'

'Let me get you some water,' Cat offers and rushes off.

'This is your doing,' Jack snarls at Thomas. 'You've given her such a shock you've made her ill.'

'Leave him alone,' Claire tells him. 'It's not him. I wonder whether there was something in that biscuit that didn't agree with me.'

Thomas pales. 'Mum, which biscuit are you talking about?'

'The one I was offered, the special one.'

'What were you thinking?' he exclaims. 'Don't you know what those are?'

'Don't get bolshy with me. The guy said they were a college recipe, and I thought I ought to try them.'

'They've got magic mushrooms in them, Mum. They're hallucinogenic, for God's sake!'

The shock of what Claire has done seems to paralyse us in some sort of weird tableau, which is accentuated by the fact that we look so different from everyone else here, and nobody else has noticed so they're all still moving about and chatting while we stand still and silent, feverishly trying to work out what to do next.

16

As we start to unfreeze, I worry that Jack is either going to have a coronary or beat the living daylights out of the nearest person, but Michelle swings into action, soothing him and begging him not to make a scene, for Thomas's sake. Cat reappears with a glass of water and we guide Claire to a chair. Thomas manages to find an empty bucket to act as a receptacle if she vomits.

'How could you be so fucking irresponsible?' Jack hisses at his son once we've done all we can for her.

'This is San Francisco, Dad, not Croydon. Jeez, you people need to be more streetwise. Didn't they tell you about the cookies when you arrived?'

'They just said they were special biscuits,' Claire says miserably. 'How was I supposed to know they had magic mushrooms in them?'

'Look. What's done is done,' Michelle interrupts. 'Why don't I stay with Claire while you guys go and look at Thomas's other artwork. Then, when you're done, we can call the limo and get her back to her hotel, OK?'

'I'll be fine. Don't worry about me.' Claire tries to flap her away.

'Nonsense. I'm taking care of you and that's that,' Michelle declares, crouching down next to her. 'Go on, the rest of you. The sooner you're finished, the sooner we can get Claire safely tucked up in bed.'

That seems to be the end of the argument, so we allow Thomas and Cat to lead us into the next room, which is filled with yet more weird art.

'So the project we were asked to do,' Cat explains enthusiastically, seemingly fully recovered from the drama already, 'is to create a work of art that was more than just an expression. It had to have something raw, something of us in it. Jorge is so clever, the way he comes up with these ideas.'

I stop at the first artwork, which appears to be a triptych. The first frame has nothing in it except a brown piece of cloth roughly cut into a letter B. Next to it, and slightly lower down, is a similar frame except the cloth in this one is a very pale yellow and cut into an S. The cloth in the final one is completely white and cut into a T. The plaque tells me the work is entitled *All of Me* by Simon Tan and is on sale for a thousand dollars.

'Can you see it?' Cat asks me.

'I'm not sure what I'm looking for,' I reply.

'All of me. He's taken that concept literally and turned it into art. What you're looking at are Simon's blood, sweat and tears. He's soaked each cloth with one of those things and then placed it in the frame. See?'

'That's disgusting,' Jack observes, but thankfully Cat doesn't hear.

'This is Thomas's,' Cat tells us, indicating a frame a metre or so away. It contains a crudely painted picture of a small boy standing on a lawn, crying and holding a football. It looks like this one is just painted in watercolours, but after the blood, sweat and tears triptych, I'm wary. The scene is observed through a window, and the lead framework across it is very obviously made from Thomas's hair. The picture is entitled *Lost Boy*.

'Go on then. Tell us what's happening here,' Jack demands.

'It's adult Tom looking through the window of himself to the child he feels was never understood,' Cat explains.

'What a load of self-indulgent horseshit,' Jack states matter-of-factly.

'Come and have a look at Cat's,' Thomas suggests stiffly, evidently keen to move us away from any further analysis of his emotions as he leads us over to another frame. This one has a watercolour picture of a woman in it. She's naked, standing up and facing forwards. It could be quite pretty; the body is painted accurately in soft brown hues, but it's ruined by a series of brightly coloured jagged lines radiating out from between her legs, like a three-year-old vandal has grabbed their poster paints and tried to draw pubic hair on it. There's also a bright red vertical line in the middle of the other lines; I don't think you need to be Einstein to work out what that is supposed to be, although it's very crudely painted again. I look at the plaque. *Sugar, Spice and All Things Nice: The Power of a Woman* by Catriona Davis. The price is also a thousand dollars. Who would pay a thousand dollars to have some horrific primary-coloured vagina on their wall, I wonder?

'Every time I look at this picture, I'm blown away again,' Thomas says in awed tones.

'Aww, thanks honey.' Cat looks at him with pure adoration in her eyes and a nasty feeling settles in the pit of my stomach.

'I'm sorry, you're going to have to explain it to me,' I say.

'It's genius,' Thomas says. 'The majority of the body is representing sugar and spice and all things nice, which is what little girls are supposed to be made of, according to the nursery rhyme. So the paler colours are created with a pigment made mainly from sugar and spices dissolved in water. With me so far?'

'I think so. What about the hoo-hah though?'

'So that's where the power of the woman is, and this is the really clever bit. You see how the lines are jagged?'

'Yes?'

'Cat painted them during a series of climaxes. It's like one of those heartbeat monitor things, but each wiggle represents a wave of her orgasm instead. It's visceral, don't you think?'

'Bloody hell. How many climaxes did you have to have to do this?' I ask Cat.

'There are seventy-two lines, one for each year between the beginning of the women's suffrage movement in the US in 1848 and women finally getting the vote in 1920.'

'You had seventy-two orgasms while painting this? You must be exhausted!'

'No,' she laughs. 'I'd never have been able to do anything else. I painted as many lines as I could during each one.'

'Even so. I'm amazed you haven't given yourself repetitive strain injury.'

'I didn't have them all on my own. Everyone helped.'

'I'm sorry?' I can't let that remark go unchallenged.

'I mean, I did some by myself using a toy, but I'm lucky in that I'm hypersensitive to touch. So the other guys on the course would touch me until I came, and then I could paint on the lines.'

'When she says guys, that's a generic term that includes girls too,' Thomas adds by way of explanation. I'm just about to ask him whether he was one of these 'guys' helping her out when Michelle appears, looking flustered.

'Sorry to interrupt, but I need a little help,' she says.

'What is it?' Jack asks.

'Well, the good news is that Claire isn't feeling sick any more. The bad news is that the mushrooms have kicked in properly.'

'There you are!' Claire exclaims, tottering over to us. 'Jack, did you know that Michelle was made of candy? I was sitting there, feeling really grotty, and suddenly I caught a whiff of her. She smells delicious and I want to lick her, but she keeps running away.'

'I explained this, Claire,' Michelle says, forcibly holding her at arm's length. 'You're not yourself right now. I'm not made of candy, it's just my perfume.'

'I'm more myself than I've ever been,' Claire declares, before turning to Jack. 'Hello, fucker. What are you doing here?'

Jack's jaw drops open, but before he can say anything, Claire switches her attention back to Michelle.

'You want to stay away from him. He's not who he says he is. He tempts young people to fall in love with him using his house made of sweeties and keeps them there as his slaves until they get old and wrinkly. Then he just throws them out on the street and replaces them with new young people. He'd love you because you're made of sweeties. I want to eat you up.'

'Mum,' Thomas begins.

'Don't Mum me,' she retorts. 'I don't know who you are. You look like my son, but he went to America and got his head cut off. You're an impostor.'

'We really need to get her out of here,' I say to Jack. 'Can you call the limo?'

'Yes. I'll do that now.' He pulls out his mobile phone.

'Who are you calling, the child catcher?' Claire demands, before turning to Michelle. 'He's hungry. He needs a child to eat. Make sure he doesn't spot you, because you're his favourite flavour. Can I lick you?'

'Why don't we step outside and get some fresh air?' Michelle suggests. 'I've heard there's a magical chariot on its way to take us to a beautiful palace.'

'My beautiful palace is gone,' Claire wails suddenly, looking on the verge of tears. 'It was stolen from me by a wicked witch. You'll protect me from her, won't you?'

'Of course I will,' Michelle soothes. I'm in awe of the way she's managing to stay calm despite the fact that Claire is obviously talking about her. 'Come on. Let's get you outside.'

It takes nearly ten minutes to guide her to the door, as she insists on grabbing nearly everyone we pass and sharing some totally random conspiracy theory with them, but eventually we're outside and sighing with relief as we manoeuvre her into the limo.

'Did you guys have a good time?' the driver asks. 'I expected you to be there a little longer.'

'It turns out there wasn't much to see,' Jack tells him flatly as we pull away.

* * *

'Are you going to be OK with her?' Michelle asks me as we extricate a still rambling Claire from the limo. 'I can stay if you like, I'm sure Jack won't mind.'

'Thanks, Michelle. I'll stay in her room tonight to make sure nothing happens to her, and hopefully she'll be back to normal by the morning.'

'Let me give you my number, just in case. If you give me yours, I'll send you a text and then you can get in touch if it all starts to get a bit much. I'll call you tomorrow anyway, just to see how you are.'

We exchange numbers and then the limo disappears into the night. I just hear a faint call of 'Bitch' that tells me the homeless guy is still down the road, before I start trying to cajole Claire through the doors.

'Is everything all right?' There is a different receptionist on duty this evening, but the fact that I'm pretty much propping Claire up is obviously causing him some concern.

'It's fine. She just had a bit too much,' I explain. 'I'll look after her.'

'If you need anything, just call down, OK?'

'Thanks. I will.'

It takes a few attempts to get Claire to remember what she's done with her room card and, at one point, she becomes completely fascinated by a biro in her bag, but eventually I get her into her room, at which point she tries to crawl, fully clothed, into the bed.

'Umm, Claire?'

'What?'

'I think you should probably take your dress off before you go to bed. You'll ruin it otherwise.'

'Too tired.'

'Please? I'll help you.'

'Who are you? Find Alex. She's a nice girl. She'll help me. She's going to marry my Thomas, you know. Big wedding cake. Are you made of cake?'

'No.'

'Are you sure?'

'Very. Let me help you with your dress.'

'OK.'

After a bit of pushing and shoving, we manage to get the dress off her. There's no way I'm risking trying to get her to brush her teeth or anything, so I tuck her up in bed and sink into a chair. I can't remember the last time I felt so tired, but my mind is still whirling around the events of the evening. There's definitely something going on between Thomas and Cat. I have no doubt about that. My eyes are just starting to droop when my phone pings with a message. It's from Thomas.

Sorry about tonight. I need to talk to you. Where are you staying? I'll
come round tomorrow.

I type out the name of the hotel and send it to him. Normally, a
phrase like 'I need to talk to you' would keep me awake churning
all night, but I'm so tired that I just can't keep my eyes open. I may
have got Claire into bed, but that's a step too far for me. I fall asleep
in the chair, still in my cocktail dress.

17

'You look terrible. Are you OK?' Thomas asks when I meet him in the hotel reception at eight the next morning.

'I've been better,' I tell him. 'The jetlag is still awful, not helped by the fact that I can't have got more than two hours' sleep last night. Your mum was up and down like a yo-yo. At one point she was convinced there were thousands of spiders walking around on the ceiling and started to get a bit hysterical.'

'Where is she now?'

'Sleeping it off, lucky her.'

'Would you rather go back to bed for a few hours? I can always come back later.'

'No. I'm only here for three more days, I want to make the most of it.'

'Let's go and get something to eat then. There's a really good diner not far from here. They do pancakes, waffles, all the good stuff.'

'Sounds perfect.'

He takes my hand and leads me out onto the pavement. The

sensation is familiar and reassuring, until I realise that he hasn't kissed me again.

'It was a hell of a surprise seeing you all yesterday evening. Mum and Pneu in the same room too,' he says after we've navigated our way past Jerry and explained that we don't want a tour of the city right now, but we'll definitely look him up later.

'We wanted to come and show our support for you.' I tell him all about Claire's invitation and us meeting up at the airport, but I leave out the part about Jack paying for the flight upgrade. I'm not sure why.

'Hm. I'm not sure Dad is on board with the whole support gig. He was really snappy with everyone.'

'I think he was just a bit surprised by the venue. Michelle is nice though. She was brilliant with your mum, wasn't she?'

'Hmph.'

Sensing that this conversation has gone as far as it's going to, I attempt to change the subject.

'One good thing about the jetlag is your mum and I were up early yesterday to ride the cable car. I'd love to do it again with you while I'm here.'

'Only tourists ride the cable car, and the queues are immense, especially at weekends.'

'Oh. What about the Golden Gate Bridge? I always fancied watching the sun set over the bridge with a glass of wine.'

'Why have you really come here?' he asks sharply.

'To see you and support you at your exhibition. I told you.'

'Sounds like you're more interested in seeing the sights,' he huffs.

'I kind of hoped to do both. You know, see the sights with you.'

'Yeah, well, I don't know how much time I'm going to be able to get away from the college. Jorge is very demanding and we're on a strict schedule. You should have told me you were coming.'

I stop and, because I'm still holding his hand, Thomas is forced to stop too.

'Aren't you glad I'm here?' I ask.

He doesn't answer immediately, which frankly tells me everything I need to know.

'Fine. Go and have breakfast on your own then,' I snap, feeling the tears springing to my eyes. 'I tell you what, go and have breakfast with Cat. She's probably in need of another orgasm by now.' I wrench my hand out of his and start powering along the kerb in the direction of the hotel. Jerry spots me coming and starts to get to his feet.

'No, Jerry,' I snarl at him before he has a chance to say anything. 'I don't want a tour of the fucking city, OK?' I'm just about to reach the door when Thomas catches up with me and grabs my arm.

'Don't be like that, Alex. I'm sorry. Of course I'm glad you're here, it's just a big surprise, that's all. Come and have breakfast.'

I stand there for a moment, trying to work out what to do while I catch my breath. Part of me really wants to tell him to get lost, but I worry I might not see him again before I leave if I do that. One way or another, we have to straighten this out.

'Fine,' I sigh. This time, he doesn't even hold my hand as we make our way along the pavement. Jerry studies us curiously as we pass, but wisely keeps his counsel. After ten minutes or so, Thomas leads me into the diner.

'Let's order, and then we can talk,' he suggests. 'I'm going to have the pancakes with bacon and maple syrup. It sounds weird but it's delicious.'

'I'll have that too, with a strong coffee.'

Thomas gives our order to the waitress and then turns back to me. 'What's going on, Alex?'

'What do you mean?'

'Why were you were so upset back there? You kind of went from nothing to really angry in half a second. It's not like you.'

He's trying to deflect this on to me, I realise, and my anger surges up again.

'Oh, I don't know,' I begin sarcastically. 'Let's start with you signing up for another month out here without telling me, and then maybe we can talk about what the hell is going on between you and Cat. If there's time, maybe you can explain why you've been so weird on our phone calls too. In fact, let's start there, because I have a nasty suspicion that the other things stem from that.'

He looks down at the tablecloth and starts tracing his finger over the checked pattern. I'm starting to wonder whether he's actually going to tell me anything at all when he finally starts to speak.

'It's been life changing, coming out here. I know that sounds corny, but it has. It's like my eyes have been opened and there's so much more to the world than I ever thought there was. It's not just the course, although that is amazing. It's this place, the people I've met. I feel like a completely different person out here.'

'Tom.'

'What?'

'Cat calls you Tom. Jorge did too. You always hated being called Tom at home.'

'Yeah, but it suits the person I am here in a way it didn't at home. It's hard to explain.'

'I'm not sure it is,' I tell him as the penny starts to drop. Our conversation is interrupted by the arrival of our drinks.

'What do you mean?' Thomas asks once we're alone again.

'What you're telling me is that you've come out here and been on this incredible journey of self-discovery and re-invention, and your life back home with your mum and me suddenly seems incredibly boring and pedestrian.'

'No, that's not what I mean. I—'

'Tell me about you and Cat.'

'What about me and Cat?'

'She's in love with you.'

'No she isn't.'

'Thomas, Tom, whoever the hell you are now. I may be many things, but blind isn't one of them. You're having a thing with her, aren't you?'

'No. Well, not exactly.'

'What does that mean?'

'Look, Jorge is very hot on confronting what he sees as societal norms.'

'I know that. You told me that on the phone.'

'He believes that anything where we have to fit into a mould or expectation stifles us and cuts off our creative flow. He's all about experimentation and doing what feels right in the moment.'

'What does that actually mean, though?'

'What it means is that our relationship as it was is conforming to exactly the kind of societal norms that Jorge is talking about, can't you see? I'd like to re-imagine us as something less restrictive. I still have feelings for you, and I want to be with you when I get back home, but I need to be totally free to make the most of every experience while I'm here. If something, or someone, happens, then I need to be able to pursue that and see where it goes. Same for you, obviously.'

What?

'OK, look,' I tell him, trying to keep my rising temper under control. 'I'm really tired and my mind is a bit foggy, but it sounds like you're suggesting that we have some kind of relationship sabbatical while you're out here, so you can do whatever you like with Cat and anyone else that catches your eye, and then we're just supposed to pick up as if nothing has happened when you get home. Is that what you're saying?'

'That's a great way of looking at it!' His eyes light up enthusiastically. 'A sabbatical. I knew you'd understand.'

He's unbelievable. I stare into his eyes trying to work out if he has any idea what he's suggesting, but all I see is an excited puppy look. Suddenly, everything is totally clear and I know exactly what I'm going to say.

'No,' I tell him.

'What?'

'I said no. Let me explain how this looks from my perspective, shall I? What is happening here is that you're trying to come up with a load of frankly bollocks reasoning to try to convince me to give you the green light so you can do whatever you like with Cat and not feel guilty about it. It's called having your cake and eating it. Unfortunately for you, Cat and Jorge, I'm incredibly dull and conventional where relationships are concerned, and this proposed arrangement basically sounds like you get to shit all over me from a great height and I'm just supposed to lap it up. If you love someone, like I love you and I thought you loved me, you don't ask for "sabbaticals" to chase other people. You're obviously incapable of doing the right thing and making a choice, so I'm going to make it for you.'

'Here you go.' The waitress smiles as she places in front of us two plates of thick pancakes surrounded by crispy rashers of bacon and liberally drizzled with maple syrup.

'I'm sorry. I've suddenly realised I'm not hungry,' I tell her. 'Can I have this to go?'

'Of course you can, honey,' she says, picking my plate back up. 'I'll be right back.'

'What do you mean? What choice?' Thomas asks.

'I mean it's over. You and me. Finito. Done.' I feel weirdly unemotional as I say the words, and I realise that, despite hoping I was wrong, I've been mentally preparing for this moment for the last couple of weeks.

'You're throwing three years of history down the pan, just like that?' he asks.

'I'm not throwing anything anywhere. You've already done that. Be honest with me, Thomas. You're already sleeping with Cat, aren't you?'

He sighs deeply, but nods his head.

'I knew it. And that's why we're over. I'm worth more than that, even if you evidently can't see it. Goodbye, Thomas.'

I get up from the table and walk over to the counter where the waitress has just finished boxing up my breakfast.

'You have a nice day now,' she says.

'I doubt it, but thank you,' I reply.

A thought occurs to me, and I turn back to a miserable-looking Thomas, still seated at the table.

'One more thing. Why are you so horrible about Michelle?'

'You know why. She broke up my parents' marriage.'

'Did she? Or did your father take a fancy to her and decide to re-imagine his relationship with your mother, setting himself free from the mould that was stifling him? It would appear you're a lot more like him than you want to admit. I'd reflect on that if I were you.'

He makes no attempt to follow me this time, and the tears fall freely as I make my way back to the hotel. When I reach Jerry, I stop and hand him the box containing my breakfast.

'I still don't want a tour of the city, Jerry, but hopefully this is still warm. Enjoy.'

'You're a goddamned crazy English fucking bitch,' he tells me as he opens the box and sniffs the contents, but he's smiling so I think he means it as a compliment.

* * *

I'm woken up by my phone ringing. For a moment, my heart leaps into my mouth, hoping it's Thomas calling to say that I've got it all wrong, he's not sleeping with Cat at all and the whole sabbatical idea was a stupid joke.

It's not Thomas. It's Michelle.

'How's Claire this morning?' she asks.

'I don't know,' I tell her groggily. 'It was a difficult night, but I left her fast asleep earlier. I think she's over the worst.'

'You sound dreadful. Are you OK?'

'Not really.'

'What's up?'

'Oh, just stuff. Don't worry about me.'

'What stuff?'

'I found out Thomas is sleeping with Cat. We just broke up.'

'I did think they seemed very close. How did you find out?'

I fill her in on the events of the night and my disastrous breakfast.

'The worst bit,' I tell her at the end, 'is that I'd really like to go home now, but I'm stuck here for three more days. I have no intention of seeing Thomas again, obviously, but Claire is going to want to spend as much time as she can with him, so I'm basically stuck moping around the hotel until it's time to leave.'

'That, at least, I can do something about. Why don't you try to get a couple of hours' kip and I'll pick you up at noon. Jack's got a work issue he needs to sort out, so he's not going to miss me.'

'Thanks, but you don't need to take pity on me, Michelle. I'm a big girl, I can look after myself.'

'I know, and this isn't pity. You're doing me a favour, because at the moment I'm also stuck here with nowhere to go. Be in the lobby of your hotel at noon, OK?'

'OK.'

I'm just crawling back under the covers when there's a tentative knock at the door. Sighing, I slip on a dressing gown and pad across to open it.

'I'm so sorry about last night,' Claire tells me. 'It never occurred to me that the biscuits were spiked. Did I make a terrible fool of myself?'

'You were... interesting,' I tell her.

'Oh, God. Was Thomas embarrassed? There's nothing worse than embarrassing your children in front of their peers. There was one time when he was little, and—'

'I'm really sorry, Claire,' I interrupt. 'The truth is that I hardly got any sleep last night and I've had a difficult morning so far. I don't want to be rude but I really need to go back to bed. Do you mind?'

'Of course. I'm so sorry. What would you like me to tell Thomas? He'll be disappointed not to see you.'

'I'm sure he'll be just fine. Go and have fun with your son.'

I gently close the door before she has a chance to say anything else.

18

I am so looking forward to getting home, I think as I stare out of the tiny aeroplane window at the receding lights of San Francisco. Claire, next to me, is pretending to be absorbed by the in-flight magazine, but I'm pretty sure she's only doing that to avoid conversation. As soon as the seatbelt sign goes off, I will spare her blushes by raising the partition between the seats. Unsurprisingly, things have been a little awkward between us since she found out about the break-up. I don't blame her; she's been kind enough, but Thomas is still her son, however shittily he treated me.

Jack and Michelle, thankfully, have been absolutely brilliant, so the trip hasn't been a complete disaster. Michelle showed up at noon on Saturday armed with a credit card that she told me badly needed a dent putting in it, so I ended up having much more fun than I ought to have done after dumping my useless boyfriend. She practically dragged me into Neiman Marcus and insisted on buying me a series of designer outfits.

'Michelle, I can't let you spend your money on me,' I'd protested initially.

'It's Jack's money, and he's told me I'll be in serious trouble if we don't go full *Pretty Woman*.'

'Is he inferring we're prostitutes?'

'No, he means spending some serious cash in exchange for lots of sucking up.'

'I'm already at my baggage allowance. I won't be able to take any more home.'

'Nonsense. You're in business class, aren't you? You're allowed extra baggage. In fact, I've heard it's now compulsory.'

When we'd worn ourselves out and spent way more than my monthly salary between us, she'd taken me back to their hotel so we could show off our purchases to Jack. I was a bit uneasy about this, as I couldn't see how he'd be pleased about Michelle spending so much on a woman he'd only met once and probably wouldn't see again. It turned out I was wrong.

'I'm sorry my son is such an arsehole,' he'd told me when we first arrived. 'But apparently retail therapy works wonders in these situations, so I hope you're feeling a little better.'

For the rest of my stay, they took me under their wing, so I haven't really seen Claire apart from at breakfast a couple of times. As well as the shopping trip, I got my wish to watch the sun set over the Golden Gate Bridge and we did a day trip to the vineyards in Napa Valley, which loosened all of our tongues rather more than perhaps was wise. The most interesting thing I learned was that the account I'd always been given about Jack and Claire splitting up wasn't completely true. Yes, Jack was still legally married to Claire when Michelle came on the scene, but he'd already moved out of the family home.

It took a couple of bottles of wine over dinner to relax him sufficiently to get the whole story, which was that he and Claire had struggled to conceive, and Thomas was the miracle result of several rounds of IVF. Because of this, Claire had absolutely doted on him from the day he was born, which Jack didn't mind too much to begin with as he was focused on the businesses, but it eventually led to serious rows about her approach to parenting as Thomas grew up.

'She does absolutely everything for that boy,' he'd told me bitterly. 'How is he ever supposed to learn how to cope with reality when she cocoons him like that? He seriously thinks he's going to have a career as a painter, and she actively encourages his fantasies. I mean, what the hell even was that exhibition? Pure bloody self-indulgence if you ask me, and that Jorge bloke is just filling their heads with nonsense. Who's going to want a picture of that stupid climax girl's fanny on their wall, hm? And as for that complete mess with all the paint splodges, fuck me. I'd need a whole plateful of those magic biscuits before I'd be high enough to buy that. Thomas needs to wake up, smell the coffee and get a proper job. I'm not saying he has to follow in my footsteps, but he's obviously good with children, so he could train as a teacher or something. Claire and I used to argue all the time about this, but she just couldn't see that she was spoiling him. I was always the bad person, not being supportive enough of her precious boy.'

'If you feel so strongly about him standing on his own two feet, doesn't paying for him to do this course seem an odd way of going about it?' I'd asked, emboldened by my own wine consumption.

'You're right, but he'd have done it anyway. I thought I was helping to protect his savings, stupidly, and I hoped it would open his eyes. If I'd known he'd end up handing over another chunk of money to stay an extra month with that Jorge fraud, I wouldn't have bothered.'

The conversation is replaying in my head as the cabin crew start to come round with our pre-dinner drinks. I think about how Claire laid on the cheese and wine for the exhibition in the village hall because she was worried that people would be nasty to

Thomas, and how she bought the painting so he wouldn't be disappointed. I've always got on well with her, but I can see that Jack has a point. I almost messaged Emma a couple of times to fill her in and ask her opinion, but in the end I decided to stick to sending pictures of my new outfits. There will be plenty of time to pick over the bones when I'm back. I sigh deeply; Thomas isn't my problem any more, I guess, and maybe that'll turn out to be a good thing. If he and Claire are as enmeshed as I now suspect they are, we'd never have gone the distance.

'I'm sorry this trip didn't work out as you'd hoped,' Claire tells me, lowering the partition. 'Thomas is on a journey at the moment, and I think maybe Cat is best placed to support him during this phase, being an artist herself. Who knows what will happen when he comes back to the UK though, eh?'

'I'm sure they will be very happy together,' I tell her, just about managing to sound sincere.

'She seems like a nice girl. She's very different to you.'

'Thanks a lot!' I'm unable to keep the hurt from my voice this time.

'I didn't mean that you aren't a nice girl. You are, and you'll always be special to me, you know that. It's just that he has a connection with Cat through their shared love of art that he doesn't have with you. Does that make sense?'

'Perfect,' I tell her. 'I think I'm going to watch a movie now, is that OK?'

'Of course. I knew you'd understand.'

I smile and raise the barrier again before I say something I might regret.

* * *

Despite having a lie-flat bed, I haven't slept well on the flight, so my mind is firmly on sleep as I drag my cases up the stairs to our flat. Relief at being home is washing through me as I turn the key in the door and pull the suitcases through into the living room, but it turns out to be very short-lived.

My first thought as I survey the carnage is that we've been burgled. It literally looks like there has been a minor explosion in here. There are dirty clothes on the floor, unwashed crockery and glassware on all the surfaces, along with a fair number of empty bottles. The surfaces in the kitchen are covered in ring marks and the sink is piled high with unwashed pots and pans. In disbelief, I take a picture and send it to Emma with a comment.

WTF??

I wait for a couple of minutes, but there's no answer. She must be in a meeting or something. There's no way I'm going to be able to sleep knowing the state of the flat, so I start gathering up some of the clothes from the floor. I retrieve a pair of men's underpants from beneath the sofa; no prizes for guessing who they belong to, although my stomach heaves slightly when I allow myself to consider how they might have ended up there. There's something else under the sofa as well, but it's further back and it takes me a bit of contortion to retrieve it. When I do, my irritation with Emma turns murderous.

It's a pair of knickers. I guess that's not a surprise in some ways, given what I've already found, but the fact that I recognise them is. They're mine. I know damned well that I haven't lost any knickers under the sofa since we've lived here, so that leaves only one possibility. Being very careful not to touch the gusset or any part of them that might have come into contact with her skin, I lay them out on the floor and take a picture to send to Emma.

You stole my knickers??? For fuck's sake, Emma!

Even if I wash them, there's no way I'm going to be able to bring myself to wear these knickers again. Some things are just too personal to share, so I walk over to the bin to throw them away, only to discover that it's rammed full to the point of overflowing. With a growl, I start to tug at the bag, but it refuses to budge. It's obviously caught on something inside. I summon all my strength and give a mighty pull, and whatever is stopping it gives up the struggle as it suddenly comes loose. My victory is short-lived, however, as whatever it was snagged on has made an enormous tear in it, and all the rubbish spills out onto the floor.

That is the final straw. All the events of the last few days combine with my tiredness and frustration and I sink to the floor, sobbing uncontrollably. I vaguely hear the sound of my phone pinging with a message, but I can't be bothered to get up and look. I'm completely overwhelmed and it takes me a moment to realise that the wails of despair filling the room are coming from me.

My orgy of self-pity is interrupted by a knock on the door. I wipe my face on my sleeve, leaving dark smudges of lipstick and mascara on the white cotton, before getting to my feet and peering through the spyhole.

'Are you OK? I thought I heard crying,' Callum's voice says as I start to open the door.

'Ah,' is all he says when he takes in the terrifying mess that my face must be in. 'Is there anything I can do?'

'Not unless you're Mary Poppins,' I mumble, indicating the shambles behind me. 'Sorry, I'm just really tired from the flight and I'm probably overreacting. Don't worry, I'll be fine.'

'You have something attached to you, did you know?' he observes. 'It looks like the lid from a yoghurt pot. It's, umm, there.' He points to my hip and, to my horror, I realise he's right. For a moment, we both just stare at the film stuck to my jeans and then, unexpectedly, I start to giggle at the thought of how utterly absurd I must look, with make-up smeared all over my face and bits of rubbish stuck to me.

'Are you sure you don't need a hand?' Callum asks as my laughter builds into full-on snorts that make my nose run. I've now got snot running down my face in addition to everything else, but that just makes me laugh all the harder.

'Sorry,' I tell him as I fight to get myself under control. 'I think the jetlag is making me a little bit crazy.'

'How did the yoghurt lid get there?' he asks, still evidently transfixed by it.

'I had an argument with the bin.' I turn and carefully remove the lid, leaving a smear of yoghurt on my trousers.

'I think the bin won,' he replies. 'I've just noticed there's something else, on your backside. I'm not sure, but it looks a bit like a bit of filling from one of those steak pies.'

I look where he's pointing and he's right.

'Oh, God. That's disgusting!' I exclaim.

'Why don't I sort out the bin for you while you get changed?' Callum offers.

'It's OK. Thank you, but I can do it.'

'The evidence would suggest otherwise.' He smiles. 'I don't mind, honestly.'

My resolve crumples as a new wave of tiredness washes over me. 'That would be very kind, if you're sure.'

'Of course. Just show me where the bin bags are.'

My plan to change my trousers and go straight back out to carry on tidying up the mess is derailed as soon as I sit down on the bed for a moment to catch my breath. When I open my eyes again, I'm horrified to see that my bedside clock is telling me it's past midday. I hurriedly pull on a clean pair of jeans and dash out into the living room.

For a moment, I wonder whether everything that happened earlier was a bad dream. The flat is beautifully tidy, the dirty plates and cups are evidently in the dishwasher, which is humming quietly, and the rubbish and ring marks in the kitchen are all gone. The dirty laundry is in a neat pile in the corner with a note on top.

I wasn't sure which clothes belonged to whom, or what settings you use for your wash, so I hope you don't mind me leaving these. Callum.

I'm both mortified and ridiculously grateful. I'm wondering what I can get him as a gift to say thank you when my phone beeps to remind me there is a message waiting. It's from Emma.

Shit, I got my days muddled up and thought you were coming home tomorrow. I was going to clean it up tonight. Really sorry about the knickers – it was an emergency, I promise! I will buy you new ones if you like. Glad you're home though, I have exciting news!! Exx.

19

'It's so lovely to have you back. Here you are.' Emma shoves a bag at me as she comes through the door. I pull out the contents to discover that she must be feeling properly guilty, because she's bought me two pairs of considerably more expensive knickers than the ones she stole. I had to throw those ones away again; Callum must have found them next to the bin, as he added them neatly to the laundry pile along with all the other clothes. At least he would have thought they were Emma's rather than mine. The idea of Callum handling my knickers is nearly as unpleasant as Emma wearing them. I know I'm probably over-sensitive about it, but in my view the only people who should be having anything to do with my underwear are me or a person that I'm intimately involved with. It's strictly off-limits to anyone else.

'Thank you,' I reply. 'I would prefer it if you never went anywhere near my underwear drawer again though. I mean, what kind of emergency was it? Actually, don't tell me. It's probably better that I don't know, given where I found them.'

'Where were they?' she asks, completely unfazed.

'Under the sofa. There was a pair of man's pants under there too. Mark's, I presume?'

She does have the decency to blush a little now. 'Ah yes,' she murmurs. 'That would explain it.'

'I hope you cleaned the sofa.'

'It's fine. We put a towel down.'

'Not the green one?'

'Yes, why?'

'Oh, God. I touched it this afternoon. It was in the pile that Callum left. I feel sick.'

'What was Callum doing here?'

'It's a long story and it's not relevant. What the hell has been going on while I've been away?'

'That's what I meant when I said I had good news. Mark and I decided to do an experiment.'

'If it's got anything to do with your sex life, I don't want to hear it. I've had more than enough of that for one day.'

'We thought we'd see what it would be like to live together,' she explains, ignoring me. 'Although Callum keeps himself pretty much to himself when I'm round there, I'm still aware of him, you know? And obviously you're normally here, so we've never been just the two of us together. And it was lovely. In fact, that's what I was going to talk to you about. Mark and I have decided to move in together.'

'What? But you've only been going out for about five minutes.'

'I know! But we fit together perfectly. Not just sexually, but in every other way too. I love him and he loves me, so why hang around?'

'I see.'

'You don't seem very happy about it. I thought you'd be pleased for me.'

I sigh. 'I am pleased for you, honestly. You'll need a live-in housekeeper if the state of the flat when I got back was anything to go by, but I'm glad you and Mark are so happy together. It does leave me in an awkward situation, though.'

'Why?'

'Because the whole of the rent falls to me if you move out, and I can't afford that.'

'But that's the other genius part, don't you see?'

'No. Enlighten me.'

'Thomas can move in when he gets back from America! It's high time you two took the next step.'

'There's a small wrinkle in that plan,' I tell her ruefully.

'What?'

'Thomas and I have split up.'

Her face falls. 'You're kidding.'

'Nope.' She listens in appalled silence as I fill her in on my trip to San Francisco, the disastrous exhibition and Thomas's request for a relationship sabbatical.

'What a bastard,' she breathes when I've finished. 'Are you sure he isn't under the spell of this Cat person though? He does seem to be acting way out of character. Maybe, when he gets back—'

'No. We're not getting back together.'

'Hold on before you go all Taylor Swift on me. Imagine he comes back and tells you it's all been a terrible mistake and he loves you. Maybe he goes one step further and proposes. Then what?'

'I would tell him where to stick it.'

'Isn't that cutting off your nose to spite your face? You've been very happy with him for ages.'

'That's before he basically asked me to step aside while he got it on with someone else and assumed I'd be fine and just wait until he was done. Plus, if he can do this once, he'll do it again. Also, and this is probably the biggest thing, I've realised that he'd expect me to do everything for him that his mother does now if we moved in together, and I'm definitely not up for that. I need to be with someone I can respect, and who respects me in return. Mollycoddled mummy's boys need not apply. Anyway, I don't want to talk about him any more. The point is that he won't be moving in, so I guess I'd better start looking for somewhere to live.'

'I'm sorry. I'll stay until the end of the contract, you know I will. But this was never going to be forever, was it?'

'It's fine.' I smile at her as brightly as I can. 'I'm happy for you, really. Now, tell me what kind of emergency justifies you going into my room and rifling through my knicker drawer.'

'I thought you didn't want to know.'

'I probably don't, but I need to make sure it never happens again. So, what was it?'

'It was lovely having Mark here and all to myself,' she begins, 'but we, ah, weren't particularly focused on the mundane stuff like doing laundry and washing up.'

'Really? You could have fooled me,' I reply sarcastically.

'Yeah, I know. I was fully intending to clear it up before you got back. Anyway, I kind of ran out of clean underwear.'

'I was gone for, like, five days!'

'Yeah, but I had a bit of a laundry backlog before you went, and I didn't get around to clearing it.'

'So let me get this straight. You run out of underwear because you're completely disorganised and wrapped up in Mark but, rather than taking that as a sign to do some washing, you decided to help yourself to mine instead? What else have you taken?'

'Nothing. It was just the one pair. I didn't think you'd mind.'

'I don't mind you borrowing the occasional outfit if you ask me first. Any form of underwear and I really, really mind, Emma. OK?'

'Yeah. I'm sorry.'

'You'd better get Callum a gift too. The reason this flat is so clean is down to him.'

'How so?'

'Let's just say that breaking up with Thomas, excruciating jetlag and the state of the flat was all a bit much when I got home. He happened to be passing and offered to help clean it up.'

'So he helped you. He didn't do it all himself.'

Now it's my turn to blush. 'I was going to help, but I had something on my trousers, so I went to get changed and kind of fell asleep. By the time I woke up, he was gone and everything was done.'

'Wow. Perhaps I should have a chat with Mark about keeping him when we move.'

'I'm sure he'd love that,' I laugh. 'Where do you think you'll go?'

'I don't know. I'd like to stay around here if I can. It's so convenient for work. Too early to start thinking about that just yet though. We've still got a few months on the contract, but I have this amazing estate agent friend, so I'll probably call her nearer the time.'

'I'm not sure she's going to help you. She's heard that you're a slovenly tramp with a penchant for stealing other people's underwear.'

'I've got a few months to bribe her.' Emma smiles. 'Talking of which, do you fancy takeaway tonight? My treat.'

* * *

I'm feeling conflicted as I get dressed for work the next morning. There's no doubt that Emma has proved much more challenging to live with than I'd anticipated, but I have enjoyed it for the most part. I really love our flat, and it will be a wrench to move out. I did do some sums when I was waiting for sleep to come last night, but there was no way I could find to afford to take the flat on myself and eat as well. If I'm honest, it would also be too big for me and, even though the boys I shared with in Tonbridge were pretty disgusting, it was still better than living on my own. Maybe I'll have a look and see what's out there during a quiet moment at work.

My mood isn't improved when I get to work and find a complete stranger sitting at my desk.

'Hi. I'm Ashleigh, can I help you?' she enquires as I walk through the door.

'Yes, Ashleigh, you can. That's my desk,' I tell her.

'Oh! Sorry, I didn't know you worked here. Roxanne told me it was free.'

Before I have a chance to interrogate her any further, Roxanne comes out of one of the meeting rooms at the back.

'Hello, Alex. I see you've met Ashleigh. Can I borrow you for a few minutes?'

'Umm, yes. Of course.'

'Great. We're in the office.'

My mood falls through the floor as I follow her. They say bad luck comes in threes, and it looks like that might be coming true for me. I've lost my boyfriend, I'm losing my flat and, if the fact that my desk has been given away is anything to go by, I'm about to lose my job.

When I get into the office, there's another surprise waiting for me in the form of Roxanne's frenemy, Sarah.

'Take a seat,' Roxanne instructs. 'I think you know Sarah.'

'Umm, yes. Hi.'

'Hello, Alex.'

'I expect you're wondering why Sarah is here, Alex,' Roxanne continues. 'I won't keep you in suspense. The fact is that the housing market in this area is not really growing. Yes, there are new houses going up here and there, but nothing like you'll see if you go to Ashford, for example. What Sarah and I have realised, therefore, is that our two companies are basically fighting over the same limited housing stock. If I do well, Sarah suffers and vice versa.'

'I thought that was how you liked it?' I can't help asking.

'It's fun in some ways, but not practical. So, we've decided to join forces and bring the two companies together as Forman and Hungerford. That means that we no longer need two offices, which in turn means that we don't need the same staffing levels. We've tried to be as even handed as we can be about it, and we're also offering what we hope are generous severance packages.'

So I was right. This is all I bloody need.

'Why me?' I stammer. 'I thought I was one of your top performers. I even sold that unsellable house in Dunton Green.' As I say the words, a feeling of dread settles over me. Maybe Gary and Gail have pulled out.

'You are one of our top performers,' Roxanne says soothingly. 'That's one of the reasons I'm so reluctant to lose you from the sales team.'

'But I love what I do, and I'm good at it. At least, I thought I was good at it.'

'You are. But nothing stays the same forever, does it? We have to move with the times.'

'So that's it?' I ask bitterly. 'Just like that, I'm out of a job.'

'What?' Roxanne looks puzzled.

'That's what you're telling me, isn't it? You're trying to dress it up with all your talk about staffing levels and severance packages, but basically I'm out on my ear.'

'Whatever gave you that impression? Did I say that?'

'No, but you were building up to it. Let's just cut to the chase, shall we? What's the severance package?'

'There isn't one. Not for you, anyway.'

'What do you mean?' This is even worse.

'I was getting to that when you interrupted. I was saying that we have to move with the times, and obviously Sarah and I can't work in the same office together because there would be blood on the carpet, so we're branching out. As well as the existing business, we're going to start an online agency. You know the type; lower fees but the customers have to take their own photos, conduct their own viewings and so on.'

'Right.'

'So I'm going to be heading up the office downstairs while Sarah develops this new aspect of our business, and that's where you come in.'

'I'd like you to come and work with me,' Sarah explains.

There's a pause while I digest this information.

'So you're not making me redundant?'

'No. The opposite. This is effectively a promotion, if you want it.'

'So the reason that there's someone else sitting at my desk—'

'Is because you will have a new, bigger desk. You and I will be working from my home initially, just until we get the upstairs space here reconfigured. What do you think?'

'What made you choose me rather than someone from your existing team?' I ask her.

'Because Roxanne here was always banging on about what a hotshot you were, and how you could outsell any of my agents. How long do you think she waited to ring me up and crow about you getting an offer on that house in Dunton Green before it had even gone properly on the market? I'll tell you. It was less than five minutes. If we're going to make a success of this, I need someone with your kind of acumen.'

I take a moment to think about it. I do love my job, but I can see that this is an opportunity to do something potentially much bigger, and it would look good on my CV even if it didn't work out. Plus, being told I'm a hotshot is quite a nice stroke to my ego after the knocks of the last few days.

'It does sound interesting,' I tell them.

'Is that a yes?' Sarah asks.

'Yes.'

'I can't tell you how happy I am,' she beams. Roxanne doesn't look quite so delighted, I can't help noticing.

'Just out of interest, what would have happened if I'd said no?' I ask.

'It would have put us in a difficult position,' Roxanne replies. 'We couldn't have kept both you and Ashleigh.'

'Where did she come from? I don't know her, and I thought I knew all the other agents in the area.'

'She's one of mine, but she's new. Still a little bit green but she shows lots of promise.'

'Who would you have kept?'

'Thankfully,' Roxanne says with a tight smile, 'that's a question we won't have to answer.'

20

Any disquiet I may have felt about possibly losing my job to a trainee is quickly swallowed up by the whirlwind of my new role. Sarah practically frogmarched me to the door as soon as the meeting finished, and all my working hours since have been spent holed up at her house. The new, bigger desk won't materialise until the conversion of the upper floor of Roxanne's office building is complete, so we're currently working in Sarah's sitting room, which is festooned with whiteboards and flipcharts that we have to pack away religiously at the end of each day so her family aren't inconvenienced.

I was a little unsure on the first day, because I'm used to seeing Sarah as the enemy, but she's actually a really nice person and, dare I say it, considerably less prickly than Roxanne. So far, most of our work has been conducting research into our competitors and working out ways to differentiate ourselves. It's stimulating work and I'm really enjoying having a more creative role. It's almost, but not quite, making up for the shitshow that is the rest of my life. Even with my substantially larger salary, there's still no way I could afford to take the flat on by myself, and my dreams at night are haunted by Thomas. There was one particularly nasty one where I went round to Claire's house, only to find her breast-feeding him. She'd turned and looked at me with pure loathing in her eyes and said, 'You'll never be able to look after him like I do. You'll always be second best.' Then Cat had sauntered in and started drawing pictures on the wall of her and Thomas having sex in different positions, like some kind of comic book Kama Sutra. It was so vivid that it woke me up with a start, and it took me a moment or two to realise it wasn't real.

I haven't seen Callum since I fell asleep on him, but Emma promises me faithfully that she thanked him profusely on our behalf. She had better have done, because it's Sunday morning and I'm heading up the hill with the paper tucked under my arm. I'm hoping that nothing will have happened to disrupt our crossword club breakfasts but, given how this week has been so far, it wouldn't surprise me to find Callum has a wife and family now. It seems incredible that it was only just over a week ago that I was having that appalling breakfast with Thomas. For some inexplicable reason, the homeless guy pops into my mind, which makes me smile and mutter 'goddamned crazy bitch' under my breath.

'I'm sorry, what did you call me?' I turn to see an indignant-looking woman staring at me. I obviously wasn't as quiet as I thought.

'I said I had a terrible stitch,' I tell her quickly. 'This hill is always steeper than I think it's going to be.'

'Oh, sorry. I thought you said something else.'

I can't help giggling as I continue my journey. I hope Callum hasn't got married and started a family in a week, because I'd quite like to tell him the story.

'Your usuals?' Leah asks once I've settled myself opposite Callum and fed him the cryptic crossword.

'Please.'

I'm just about to start filling mine in when Callum stops me.

'If we're going to do this properly,' he tells me, 'we need the right tools.' I watch in amazement as he pulls two short pencils out of his pocket and hands one to me.

'You can rub it out if you make a mistake,' he explains.

'I need to say a massive thank you for clearing up the flat the other day,' I tell him as I take one of the pencils.

'It was nothing, honestly. I hope you didn't mind me knocking on your door, it's just you sounded so distressed when I came up the stairs.'

'I'm glad you did, although I feel a bit guilty that I didn't help you at all. I literally sat on the bed for a moment and the jetlag got me.'

'Don't worry about it. Emma gushed all over me the other night and gave me the most enormous box of chocolates. Did she tell you about her and Mark?'

'About them moving in together?'

'Yes.'

'Yeah. I'm happy for her, obviously, but a bit gutted for me. I really love that flat, but there's no way I can afford to keep it on my own.'

'You could advertise for a new flatmate.'

'I guess so. What are you going to do?'

'I haven't decided. I could afford to rent the flat myself, but I'm not sure that's a good idea.'

'Why not? Don't you like it?'

'I do, but...' He tails off.

'But what?'

'This is going to sound ridiculous, given how antisocial I am, but having other people around is good for me. I work alone for the most part so, if I didn't share a flat or house, I could literally go for months without social interaction. That's not good for anyone's mental health, even mine.'

Silence descends as we turn our attention to the crosswords. As always, Callum starts filling his in methodically, while I struggle with mine more than usual. To be fair, I'm a little distracted as a thought is bouncing around elusively in the back of my head, and I can't quite pin it down.

'How was your trip?' Callum asks when Leah has deposited our breakfasts. 'This is me asking questions, by the way.'

'Impressive. Well done. The trip was pretty awful, if I'm honest. I think the highlights were being called a bitch by a homeless guy and spending time with Thomas's father and his girlfriend, neither of whom I'm likely to see again.'

'I did overhear Emma telling Mark that you had split up with him. I'm sorry.'

'I'll live, I guess. I got a promotion at work, so that's taking my mind off it a bit, but the evenings are hard because there's nothing else to think about, you know?'

'Not really. I've never been in love.'

Somehow that doesn't surprise me, but I'm not sure what the proper reaction is. I don't want to sound patronising, so in the end I opt for what I hope is safe ground.

'Not even a schoolboy crush?' I ask.

'Ah, well, if you're including those, then I've been in love thousands of times.'

'Really?'

'No, of course not. There was a girl I quite liked when I was in year ten, but I couldn't pluck up the courage to speak to her, so nothing ever came of it. There were a couple of girls I was friends with at university, but nothing more. I'm sure that probably sounds tragic to someone like you, but I'm OK with it.'

'So if, for example, Leah came over and professed her undying love for you...'

'I think we both know that isn't going to happen.'

'But if it did? Humour me.'

'It wouldn't. I'm not her type.'

'How do you know?'

'Because, unlike most of my sex, I'm aware of my limitations. I'm not especially attractive and I'm not particularly interesting.'

'You have a very low opinion of yourself, you know that?'

'I prefer to think of it as being realistic.'

'Shall I tell you what I know about you?'

'Will I be able to stop you?'

'No.'

He nods. 'Go on then.'

'OK. I'll acknowledge that you didn't exactly give a great first impression. The slippers—'

'Which I explained, and which you said you weren't judging.'

'I lied. Also, you were difficult to talk to, but I know why now.'

'Before you go any further, is this going to be a character assassination? Because I can manage those quite nicely on my own.'

'No! I'm just getting the less favourable parts out of the way so we can get onto the good stuff.'

'There is some good stuff then?'

'Oh yes. You're a good friend, I can see that. You're also kind, empathic and, given the right topic, interesting to talk to.'

'Where did you get all that from?'

'The good friend part I got from Mark, via Emma. The rest is personal observation. If you weren't empathic, you wouldn't have knocked on my door when I was bawling my eyes out and you would never have done what you did next if you weren't kind. These are all attractive qualities. You just need to have a bit more faith in yourself.'

'If you say so.'

'So, Leah comes over and professes undying love.'

'Still not going to happen. She likes bad boys, you can tell.'

'How?'

'Oh, I don't know. It's probably something to do with the piercings and the tattoo.'

'What tattoo?'

'Haven't you noticed? To be fair, it isn't visible most of the time, but her T-shirt rode up once when she was bent over wiping a table, and it revealed a small tattoo at the base of her spine. I was too far away to see it clearly, but I think it was a butterfly.'

'So you've decided you're of no interest to her purely because she has a couple of extra ear piercings and a tramp stamp.'

'A what?'

'That's what those lower back tattoos are called. I'm not sure why.'

He sighs. 'Look. I know you mean to be kind, and thank you for the nice things you said, but I'm fine as I am, really.'

'Apart from imminently becoming homeless, you mean.'

'Yes. Apart from that.'

The elusive thought I've been trying to pin down chooses this moment to slam into my consciousness in perfect clarity. It's so absurd that my first instinct is to dismiss it. But as I start to turn it over and examine it, it begins to crystallise and grow roots.

'Can I ask you another question?'

'You just did.'

'Ha ha. How would you describe yourself as someone to live with?'

'I think we're done with my love life, aren't we?'

'I'm not talking romantically. How would Mark describe you, do you think?'

'I'd like to think he'd say I was no trouble. I keep myself largely to myself, I'm not aware of having any unpleasant habits and I'm relatively tidy. Why?'

'Do you watch sport on the TV?'

'That's an incredibly specific question.'

'It's also a very telling one. Do you?'

'No. Where is this leading?'

'I was just wondering something.'

'Are you going to share?'

'I don't know. It's either brilliant or leaping out of the frying pan and into the fire.'

'OK. I'll leave you to it. Are you going to finish that?' He indicates my half-completed crossword.

'No. Help yourself.' As he starts to fill in the clues, I wrestle with the idea in my head some more but, frustratingly, I find I'm getting nowhere. 'Callum?' I ask after a few minutes.

'Yes?' He looks up and I notice he's pretty much completed the puzzle.

'Here's the thing. You need somewhere to live, right, and so do I. You can afford to live on your own but don't want to, and I can't afford to live on my own, and probably don't want to either.'

'Yes.'

'So what I'm wondering is...'

'Yes?'

'Whether you would like to move in with me. As my flatmate, obviously.' I gabble the words out quickly before I can change my mind.

He stares at me for a long time without moving.

'You're right,' I say when I can bear the silence no longer. 'It's a stupid idea. Forget I said anything.'

'Do you think it's a stupid idea?'

'Yes... No... I don't know. What do you think?'

He smiles. 'How would Emma describe you, as a flatmate?'

I ponder for a minute. 'I think she probably finds me a bit uptight.'

'Why?'

'Emma is, how can I say this kindly, more of a free spirit than me, and this is the first time she's lived away from her parents, so it's been a bit of a steep learning curve for her.'

'So you are...'

'Responsible, organised, tidy and probably a bit dull in her eyes. I can't help it. I'm not good at chaos.'

'I learned that the other day. If it's any consolation, Mark is nearly as bad. I dread to think what their place will look like after a few weeks without anyone tidying up after them. That's if they haven't starved to death first. He's a terrible cook and I don't think he's ever used the washing machine in the entire time I've lived with him.'

'Really?'

'Everything goes to the dry cleaner, even his pants.'

'Bloody hell, that must cost a fortune.'

'Yup. But that's how he operates. Pretty much any problem can be made to go away if you throw enough money at it. He can afford it, to be fair. But we're getting off the subject.'

'You're right. OK. Callum, would you like to flat share with me?'

'Are you sure? I'm very different from Emma.'

'That would be a huge relief!' I laugh. 'I love her to bits, but she's not the easiest person to live with.'

'I have a small confession to make before I answer.'

'Which is?'

'I came up with the same idea when Emma and Mark told me they were moving in together. I dismissed it because I was certain you wouldn't want to do it.'

'Is that a yes then?'

'Yes.'

As he turns his attention to the final crossword clue, the reality of what I've just done starts to sink in and I desperately hope I haven't just made the most idiotic mistake of my life.

21

'You're doing *what*?' Emma's face is a picture of horror.

'I'm going to flat share with Callum,' I repeat.

'But you *can't*!'

'Why not?'

'You hardly know him, for starters, apart from that weird little Sunday crossword thing you've got going on. And he's Mark's friend. You can't just kidnap him from under his nose like that.'

'Listen to yourself. He's a grown man, not a pet cat. And as for not knowing him very well, that's true, but I know a lot more than I would if I moved in with a complete stranger. I'm flat sharing with him, Emma, not marrying him. All I need to know is that he knows how to tidy up after himself and he's not a bloodthirsty psychopath, a drug addict or anything else undesirable. What did you expect him to do when you and Mark move in together?'

She fidgets uncomfortably for a minute or two, and a nasty realisation dawns on me.

'Oh my God! You were planning to take him with you, weren't you? I thought the whole point of this was for you and Mark to be on your own, just the two of you.'

'No, of course we weren't! Well, not really. It was just an idea, OK?'

'So he could clean up your mess for you?'

'Look. It sounds bad, the way you say it, but I was thinking about him too, actually. He doesn't exactly have a lot of friends, so I felt guilty about taking Mark away from him.'

'Bullshit. You just wanted him as some kind of house elf. Admit it.'

'I told you, I was only thinking of Callum. Besides, you know you'll hardly see him if he moves in with you, don't you? It won't be like living with me, where you've got someone to unwind with at the end of the day. He pretty much never comes out of his room except to cook, and then he always takes the plate straight back in to eat. You'll feel like you're living alone. Is that what you want?'

'Maybe he only does that because he doesn't want to play gooseberry to the two of you. If you get up to half the stuff over there that you evidently did when I was in San Francisco, that would be enough to drive anyone into their bedroom.'

'That's a cheap shot. I'm just looking out for you.'

'Don't worry about me, I'll be fine. Anyway, I had another thought. You said you'd quite like to stay in the area, didn't you?'

'Yes.'

'So why don't you? You could move across the corridor and Callum could move in here. I doubt the landlords will mind if we swap before the lease officially comes to an end. We've all passed credit checks and stuff, so it should be a fairly simple thing.'

'That's a brilliant idea,' she says after pondering for a moment. 'We'd still be neighbours too, which would be nice.'

'Exactly. You'd be just over the other side of the landing.'

'Or...'

'Or what?'

'Or *you* could move across the corridor and Mark could move in here.'

'Uh-uh. Not going to happen.'

'Why not? It's our flat. I've got just as much right to it as you.'

'I don't think so. You lost all your rights when you gaily announced you were moving out to live with lover boy.'

'So that's what this is about. You're jealous because I'm happy and you're not.'

'I'm not jealous. I'm sticking to my guns. Come on, you even said you were going to start looking for places. That's a clear indication that you didn't expect to live here.'

'Yes, but everything has changed now, hasn't it. I think we should toss a coin for who gets which flat.'

'I'm not going to toss a coin. You are moving out. I've found a new flatmate. End of story.'

'I don't—'

'No, Emma. This is how it's going to be. You can move across the corridor or you can move somewhere else. Whatever suits the two of you. But you are not throwing me out of my home just because I've found someone other than you to move in when you go. Am I making myself clear?'

'Crystal,' she suddenly spits. 'Fine. Have the fucking flat if you feel so strongly about it. Have Callum too. I hope you're blissfully happy together. Just don't come crying to me when you're lonely because you haven't had anyone to talk to for weeks, OK?'

I watch, open mouthed, as she literally flounces into her bedroom and slams the door behind her.

* * *

'I'm sorry,' she tells me when she reappears a little while later.

'You did catch me by surprise. What was that all about?'

'I don't know. I guess I never really thought about the reality of what moving in with Mark would mean. Talking about who is going to live where, I don't know, I found it upsetting. It's like we're getting divorced.'

'We're not getting divorced. As you said yourself, this was never going to be forever. Are you having second thoughts about living with Mark?'

'No, not really. It's just that I feel like I'm being selfish, especially after you called me out on the Callum thing.'

The words 'What's new?' form in my mind, but I manage to suppress them and smile.

'It's not selfish to fall in love, or to want to move your relationship to the next stage,' I tell her instead.

'I know, but it's shitty timing for you, isn't it? There I am, all loved up while you've just split up with Thomas. I haven't been here for you when you needed me.'

'I'm fine. He and I weren't meant to be; I can see that now.'

'What will you do?'

'Lick my wounds and move on. There isn't really any choice, is there?'

'You'll meet someone else.'

'Maybe, or maybe I'll die alone surrounded by angry cats. None of that should stop you pursuing your happiness though. And it's not as if you're moving to Timbuktu. We'll still see each other, won't we?'

She brightens. 'Of course we will. I'll make sure we do. Are you going to move into my room when I go?'

'I guess I'll have to negotiate that with Callum.'

'Are you sure this is the right thing? I can't imagine the two of you living together.'

'As I said before, this is a flat share. I'm not marrying him.'

'So when shall we, you know...'

'Swap over?'

'Yes.'

'I need to talk to Roxanne to make sure there isn't a problem with the lease. It might be that we have to do this informally to begin with, and then firm it up when the lease runs out. It also depends on Mark and Callum.'

Our conversation is interrupted by my phone ringing. When I see the caller ID, I'm surprised to find that it's Michelle.

'Hi, how's California?' I ask, retreating into my bedroom and shutting the door behind me.

'It *was* lovely,' she tells me with a sigh. 'Unfortunately, the police raided one of Jack's nail bars and made a bit of a mess, so we had to come back early for him to sort it out. Anyway, that's not why I'm calling. How are you doing?'

'I'm OK. I've got a new job and my flatmate is moving in with her boyfriend, so lots of change.'

'Wow, you haven't even been back a week. Talk about living life at a hundred miles an hour.'

'Yeah, it does feel like that. I'm sorry you had to cut your holiday short though.'

'Life happens.' I can practically hear her shrug. 'It's a shame, because I think Jack could have done with a bit longer in the sunshine to bring him down after the whole Thomas debacle.'

'He wasn't that upset about the exhibition, was he? I mean, I know it was pretty embarrassing, but—'

'Of course, you'd already gone,' she interrupts. 'You missed the proper fireworks when Jack met up with Thomas for a coffee. Actually, that's not quite right. Jack decided Thomas needed to hear a few home truths and summoned him to the hotel.'

'Uh-oh.'

'Exactly. I did warn him that it might backfire, but he was determined. He kept going on about how Thomas needed to come out from under Claire's apron strings and see the world as it really is, and if she wasn't going to tell him what he needed to know then someone else was going to have to.'

'I'm sure Thomas would have absolutely loved that.'

'Mm. Things got off to a bad start when he brought that girl along with him. The vagina one, what's her name?'

'Cat,' I tell her, feeling a lump form in my throat when I say the name.

'That's the one,' Michelle continues, oblivious to the effect she's having on me. 'So Jack told him that he was hoping to have a chat man to man, and he'd prefer it if it was just the two of them.'

'Wait, weren't you there?'

'God, no. I know Thomas doesn't like me, and I had a kind of uneasy truce with Claire at the time, which I wasn't going to risk by getting involved in any activity that could be even remotely perceived as parenting her precious boy.'

'So how do you know all this?'

'Jack told me, when he'd calmed down enough. Anyway, Thomas did the whole "anything you want to say to me you can say in front of Cat" routine, which got right up Jack's nose, but he decided not to die on that particular hill. So, as Jack tells it, he started to try to explain to Thomas that art is fine as a hobby, but even people who are really good can't make a living from it, and that he needs to have a career plan alongside his passion so he can support himself and any family he might have in future.'

'Sensible advice, but not easy to hear, I suspect.'

'So it would seem. Jack said Thomas went ballistic, started ranting about how Jack had never supported him in anything, that he was only interested in "shagging people young enough to be his daughter", that he wouldn't have left Claire if he'd had any interest in being a father, and so on. Jack said it was like being hit by an avalanche.'

'Bloody hell.'

'Exactly. And then he started yelling that Jack knew nothing about art, and how Jorge was convinced that he was an undiscovered talent that just needed the right market. Jack then told him there wasn't a market for random paint splodges on a canvas and, if there was, you wouldn't need to serve hallucinogenic snacks to the viewers to sell it. He did admit he laid it on a bit thick about how badly Claire was affected in the hope that Thomas would see sense.'

'And did he?'

'Of course not. He just shouted that he'd prove Jack wrong, grabbed Cat by the hand and stormed out. The really weird thing, apparently, was that this Cat girl just sat there with an amused smile on her face through the whole thing, as if it was a show put on for her entertainment. What's that about?'

'No idea. Perhaps she likes a bit of drama.'

'Maybe. So poor Jack came back up, obviously upset by the encounter, but barely ten minutes later Claire called him and tore him off a strip as well. Thomas apparently rang her in floods of tears moments after storming out, and now nobody's talking to anybody. In the meantime, Jack's convinced himself that Jorge is running some sort of cult, and he's spending a small fortune on private investigators and the like to dig up any dirt they can on him. Honestly, I may be young enough to be Jack's daughter, as Thomas so kindly put it, but sometimes I feel like I'm the only grown-up in the room. I hope you don't mind me sharing all of this with you, it's just that it's been a bit intense and I needed another grown-up to talk to.'

I smile. In a funny way, this is all quite comforting, and I almost feel glad that I'm not stuck in the middle of it any more. Obviously, nothing like this ever happened when Thomas and I were together, but there was always an underlying tension in that family, and it's only now that I've realised how much of it I must have absorbed over the years.

'It's fine. It's nice to hear from you, actually,' I tell her, and I mean it.

'So, tell me about the job and the flat.'

I fill her in on everything that's happened since I got back, leaving out the bizarre row with Emma. The more I talk to her, the more I remember how much I like Michelle. She's an attentive listener, and she speaks her mind clearly but kindly. By the time we disconnect, we've arranged to meet for coffee and I've somehow agreed to let her do something different with my hair, which I'm already regretting. What I can see, increasingly clearly now that I'm observing from a distance and I know more of their story, is why Jack fell for her.

22

Who knew that two people moving across a landing could be such a logistical nightmare? I woke early this morning, excited for the day ahead but also nervous. It's partly Emma's fault, because she's been alternating between wild excitement about moving in with Mark and crushing doubt that this is all happening too quickly, and some of her nerves have rubbed off on me. But I'm also facing the unknown with my own new flatmate, so I'm nervous on my behalf as well. The issue that we can't seem to get our heads around is which order to do things in. I can't move into Emma's room until she's gone, but she needs Callum's room to be free to put all her stuff in initially. Callum, on the other hand, can't move until I have. It's pouring with rain, so putting stuff outside temporarily is a no-no, even if we could summon the energy to lug it up and down the stairs.

'Here's what we're going to do,' Mark announces as we're pondering the issue over breakfast at the café on the ground floor. 'Callum has the least amount of stuff, so we'll move him first. Then we'll move Emma, and then we can retreat into our own flats to sort the rest out. Fish and chips for dinner at ours when we're done.'

'Umm. Where is my stuff going to go?' Callum asks, looking unconvinced.

'We'll move all the furniture in yours and Alex's living room up to one end. That should give us enough space to get your stuff in there to begin with. Then, once Alex has moved into Emma's old room, you can put it away.'

'I don't like that idea,' Callum replies, surprisingly firmly. 'I've got expensive equipment that I don't want you falling over or treading on when we're moving Emma. Let's do Emma first, into your living room, then Alex and finally me.'

'Have you seen the size of her bed? How are we supposed to fit that into our living room? At least you've only got a single bed.'

There's something about Mark's tone that makes me feel a bit protective about Callum all of a sudden. 'I think Callum's right,' I declare. 'Besides, Emma's bed comes apart so you can stack it in a pile.'

By lunchtime, we've made good progress, but Callum has forbidden us from touching any of his furniture until he's moved his computer and other fragile items to safety, so he's currently dismantling them and carrying them gingerly across the landing. I agreed that he could put them in my new room temporarily so they were out of the way, thinking it would just be a computer and a few other bits and pieces. So far, I've seen three enormous widescreen monitors make the journey, and he's just reappeared with a fourth, which is strapped to a bracket that wouldn't look out of place in Frankenstein's laboratory.

'Bloody hell, Callum. How many computers have you got?' I ask.

'Just two. A personal one and a work one, but I sometimes run a lot of programs simultaneously on the work one, so I need lots of screen space.'

'You're fighting a losing battle there, Alex,' Mark quips. 'I've lost count of the number of times I've told him one screen for each eye is more than enough for anyone. If you ask me, he's compensating for something.'

Eventually, after we've eaten the sandwiches Emma fetched from the supermarket and Callum has finished moving a seemingly never-ending series of black boxes with wires hanging out of them, we get around to moving his furniture. His single bed and desk are a doddle to deal with after Emma's enormous divan, but he also has a large squishy sofa, which takes a fair amount of wriggling to get through the doorways.

'Right, that's all of it done,' Mark declares as we finally deposit the sofa next to the bed in Callum's new room. 'We'll leave you to get yourselves shipshape and see you at eight, OK?'

'Do you need any help?' I ask Callum when Mark and Emma have left.

'I'll be fine, thanks. I'll come and get my stuff from your room and then I'll be out of your way.'

He's as good as his word, and I set about arranging my things and making the bed. I sigh with pleasure as I take in the extra space and put my head around the door into the ensuite bathroom. I wasn't unhappy in the other room at all, but this is definitely better, I think to myself as I plug in my radio alarm clock and glance at my watch to get the correct time.

'Callum, it's half-past four. Do you want a cup of tea?' I call across the living room, but there's no reply. His door is closed, so I cross the living room and knock. Still no reply. I give a few louder knocks, but nothing. I can hear him moving around, so I know he hasn't met with an accident, but this presents me with a dilemma. If I leave him and make a cup of tea just for me, he might think I'm being selfish. However, his door is closed and he could be naked behind it for all I know. Bursting in on him in the nude on his first day is not how I want this flat share to start. In the end, I decide to leave it and retreat to the kitchen. As I boil the kettle and fish out the teabags, I start to wonder whether moving him in was such a good idea after all. If he's as reclusive as Emma said, it is going to be very odd living with him.

'Is there enough in the kettle for two cups?' Callum asks, startling me out of my reverie.

'Bloody hell, Callum! You made me jump.'

'Sorry.'

'I did bang on your door to see if you wanted some tea, but you didn't answer.'

'Ah, yes. I probably ought to explain about that. I quite often listen to music on my headphones, so I won't hear if you knock on the door. The best thing to do is send me a WhatsApp. Now that we're living together, we probably ought to have each other's numbers anyway, don't you think?'

'Why headphones?'

'It's for your benefit, actually. It means I can listen at a reasonable volume without disturbing other people.' He smiles. 'It also helped sometimes when Emma came to stay. They weren't always terribly discreet.'

'Hm. Maybe I should have bought some. What do you listen to?'

'All sorts. My parents always had music playing when I was growing up, so I listen to a lot of the stuff from their era, but I like classical as well.'

'I'm not really into classical music,' I admit.

'A lot of people say that. My answer is always the same.'

'Which is?'

'You're just not listening to it loud enough.'

* * *

For some reason, I'd assumed that Callum was the kind of man who would wear full-length pyjamas, probably paisley. He isn't.

I found this out first thing this morning, when I stumbled out of my bedroom in my dressing gown to make a cup of coffee and found him in the kitchen, wearing nothing but a tight T-shirt and boxer shorts. My first thought was how much better he looked without his horrible glasses on, but then my eyes took in the rest of him. Either computer hacking requires considerable strength or Callum works out. The sleeves of his T-shirt were wrapped tightly around his biceps and the rest clung to his torso, leaving very little to the imagination. Legs that a rugby player wouldn't be ashamed of completed the look, although it was all undone by the ridiculous slippers on his feet. I'm not that impressed by muscle generally; it sounds like a cliché, but personality generally matters more to me. Thomas is a beanpole with a hollow chest and skinny arms and legs, but his personality made up for it in spades. Until he turned into a Cat-shagging arse, of course.

'I'm sorry about my appearance.' Callum had blushed when he'd spotted me looking at him. 'You always forget something, don't you, and in this case it would seem my dressing gown is still hanging on the back of my door in Mark and Emma's flat. I'll try to get it back today.'

'Don't worry on my account. You're decent enough,' I'd told him. 'Start wandering about in the nude and we might have to have a chat. Oh, and no sitting on the sofa in your boxers scratching your balls either, please.'

'Really?' He'd feigned disappointment. 'I usually like to sit on the sofa scratching my balls for at least half an hour on a Sunday before walking up the hill.'

'Ha ha. So you're still going to the café for breakfast then?'

'Of course. It's my Sunday treat. You?'

'I'd better. There's this bloke I meet and do the crossword with every week. He'll only fret if I don't turn up.'

* * *

'Callum?' I ask after he's finished both crosswords as usual.

'Mm?'

'Have you ever considered wearing contact lenses?'

'No. Why?'

'It's just that you looked so different in the kitchen this morning without your glasses on. If you don't mind me being honest, I'm not sure they do anything for you.'

He considers this for a moment. 'You know your rule about not sitting on the sofa scratching my balls?'

'Yes. What's that got to do with it?'

'I have a rule of my own. I'm not going to become your pet project, OK? This isn't some romcom where we have a montage of you transforming the nerd into a beautiful hunk that no girl can resist. I'm happy as I am.'

'Sorry, I didn't realise it was a touchy subject. I'll back off.'

He sighs. 'It's fine. I know you mean well, but it's one of the things I used to find frustrating about living with Mark. He was always trying to give me fashion advice, but his idea of fashion is chinos, expensive shirts and brogues. That's not me at all. I'm quite happy in a comfy pair of jeans, a T-shirt and a decent pair of trainers.'

'Noted.'

'Can I ask you a question?' he pipes up after a couple of uncomfortable minutes have passed.

'Of course.'

'Why estate agency?'

'You sound like you disapprove.'

'Not at all. I'm just curious and this is part of the whole asking questions thing.'

'I think it's probably because I'm fundamentally nosy,' I tell him after I've pondered for a moment or two. 'I'd also like to think I'm good with people, professionally anyway, and it's tremendously satisfying when you show someone a house and you see their eyes light up as they fall in love with it.'

'But you're not going to be doing that any more in your new job, are you? Do you think you'll miss it?'

'Goodness me, Callum. Not only are you asking questions but it seems that you're actually listening to the answers!'

'Am I not supposed to do that then?'

'Most men don't. It's a good thing, trust me.'

'I can't really see what the point of asking questions is if you're not going to listen to the answers. Anyway, do you think you'll miss your old job?'

'I did, but this is testing me in new ways, and it's exciting to be building something from scratch. I'm currently working on the packs that we're going to send out to people when they list with us. Hints and tips to ensure a successful viewing.'

'I read somewhere that baking bread is a good idea, because it makes the house smell homely. That kind of thing?'

'Yes, that kind of thing. Tell me about you. Why hacking?'

'I was always good with computers, so it was a no brainer to study computer science at university. When I graduated, I had this notion that I'd do something that was in the public interest, so I joined the Metropolitan police in their cyber crime unit. That proved to be a big mistake.'

'Why?'

'I was really enjoying myself and, without blowing my own trumpet, I think I was pretty good at the job. But that proved to be my undoing. They asked me to help out the paedophile unit because they had some particularly heavily encrypted computers that they couldn't crack.'

'Did you crack them?'

'Of course, but part of me wishes I hadn't. When we got in, there were over ten thousand images of children, all neatly organised into categories. I only saw a few of them, but that was enough. I literally ran out of the room to the gents and threw up. It broke me. I resigned from the Met just over a month later, but those pictures still haunt me to this day.'

'But don't you get special training and counselling to deal with stuff like that?'

'Yes, but I was only there to do this one job so I didn't get it. Nobody lasts very long, even with the training. It changes you, because you either become immune to it, which is dangerous, or it builds up until you can't take any more. There is counselling and supervision of course, but you can't unsee what you've seen.'

'I'm sorry.'

'Sometimes it takes a couple of wrong turns to find where you belong. I just wish my wrong turn hadn't been quite so traumatic. I love what I do now, so it's worked out well in the end. What are your plans for the rest of the day?'

'Not much. I might call in to see my parents at some point if they're around. What about you?'

'My parents are in Scotland. We speak regularly and I try to get up there to see them at least twice a year, but we're not especially close. My older sister lives near to them; she's married and has given them two grandchildren to dote on, so I don't think they miss me that much.'

'I bet they do. How come you don't sound Scottish?'

He smiles. 'My father is the Scottish one. He moved south with his work when he was in his twenties, met my mother and stayed down here for her. It was always his dream to move back to Scotland one day, but they didn't actually manage it until he retired. Much to his disappointment, I don't share his love of his home country. I like it down here, where the weather is better.'

'I'm trying to imagine your sister. Is she literally a female version of you?'

'God, no. She's completely the opposite of me. She's loud, gregarious, life and soul of the party. Mum always used to say she wished she could scoop out some of Morag's social skills and inject them into me, as well as injecting some of my calmness into her. I must admit, I do wish I was more like her sometimes.'

'Why are you so down on yourself all the time?'

'Like I said before, I'm just realistic. Morag is funny and interesting, and I'm not.'

'Right, new rule,' I announce. 'You have to stop running yourself down. You are interesting, actually. You have a cool job, you're obviously into your music and you're good to talk to when you relax. Do we have a deal?'

Callum sighs. 'I'll do my best.'

As we walk back down the hill after breakfast, we lapse into silence, but it's companionable rather than uncomfortable. Callum may not want me to make him into a project, but I'm not entirely sure I'm going to be able to resist. As well as the honed body, there's an attractive personality lurking under his protective shield, and I definitely want to see more of it.

23

'I have *so* much to tell you!' Michelle says excitedly as I open the front door to let her in. She's carrying two enormous bags full of hairdressing paraphernalia which she dumps unceremoniously on the floor before looking around the room.

'This is nice,' she observes. 'Where's the flatmate?'

'In his room. You probably won't see him.'

Callum and I have been living together for just over a month now and it's been pretty smooth sailing. In fact, after the chaos of living with Emma, it's a welcome relief. He does still spend a lot of time in his room, but I've managed to cajole him into eating with me in the evenings and I've discovered that, unlike Emma, he's a more than competent cook. He's slowly coming out of his shell as well, and I'm enjoying his company more and more. I was right about his physique; he goes to the gym at least three times a week. When I asked him about it, he simply said that his job was very sedentary and he found that exercise helped to clear his mind. He did invite me to join him, but I politely declined. Prancing about in Lycra really isn't me.

'Shame. I'm curious to meet your mystery man,' Michelle tells me with a wink.

'Behave. He's not my man and he's not that mysterious. He just likes to keep himself to himself. Cup of tea?'

'Lovely. Remind me what happened to the old flatmate? I forget her name.'

'Emma,' I tell her as I pull my phone out of my pocket and WhatsApp Callum to see if he wants tea. 'She lives across the landing with her boyfriend, Mark. I think we're better friends now we're not living together, although I make sure she always comes over here when we meet up. Their flat is a tip.'

My phone pings straight away with his reply, and I grab three mugs from the cupboard after reading it.

'Who are you messaging?' Michelle asks curiously. 'Is there a new boyfriend on the scene?'

'No. It's the flatmate.'

'Bit weird. Why can't you just knock on his door?'

'He listens to music on his headphones, so he doesn't always hear me knock. I'm used to it now. Anyway, you said you had news?'

'I do. Do you remember me telling you that Jack had hired private detectives to dig up any dirt on Jorge?'

'Yes. Did they find any?'

'Did they ever. I believe our friend Jorge is currently residing in a police station, undergoing a series of very uncomfortable conversations.'

'Really?'

'Oh yes. It turns out that the San Francisco College of Artistic Expression was nothing more than a massive con trick. Jorge Henriksen is actually Craig Matthews from Luton with a terrible Scandinavian accent.'

'You're kidding.'

'Nope. It started with one tiny error in Jorge's bio and, when they picked up on that, it was like pulling on a loose thread. The whole thing just started to unravel.'

'What was the error?'

'Apparently, he said he was the number one expert on the subject of ancient Maori ceramics, but there's no such thing as ancient Maori ceramics. The Maoris worked almost exclusively with wood. That was the trigger for the investigators to start digging deeper. It didn't take them long to find out that Jorge Henriksen had appeared, seemingly out of nowhere, around five years ago. There were no immigration records for him, no registered birth certificate or passport. Here's where it starts to get a bit shady. They told Jack that they managed to "gain access" to his apartment, which I suspect is code for they broke in, but they found a British passport in the name of Craig Matthews in his bedroom. The picture was Jorge, only without the beard and long hair. They also found plenty of documents relating to Jorge, which they said were probably forgeries but had to leave behind for the police. A bit more searching found that Craig Matthews was on a wanted list, because he'd entered the country on a tourist visa but hadn't left.'

'This all seems a bit elaborate, doesn't it? I'd understand if he was taking people's money and disappearing, but the college was real. He was teaching the students.'

'The college wasn't any more real than him. Yes, he taught them, but it wasn't registered and he was creaming off a fat profit. The dormitory and studio were illegally occupied squats and, every time he got evicted, he'd just find a new place and tell the students some horseshit about artistic differences with the landlord or whatever. And as for the so-called gallery, it was exactly what it looked like – an empty retail unit that he'd broken into.'

'But what about the carefully curated list of celebrity clients?'

She laughs. 'So carefully curated that they didn't exist. Do you remember when Thomas said they weren't allowed to meet the celebrities?'

'I'm not sure I do.'

'Yeah. The students were kept away during the supposed "celebrity showing". They were told it was for security and so on, but that wasn't true either. The reality is that there were no celebrities.'

'But I saw sold stickers on some of the artworks. If there weren't any celebrities, who was buying them?'

'Have you ever heard of a convincer?'

'No.'

'Neither had I, but I have now. I'll give you the example Jack gave me. Let's say you're running an investment scam and you want to persuade someone to hand over a hundred thousand pounds. That's a lot of money, right? People are going to be wary. So what you do is persuade them to give you a thousand as an initial investment. You ring them up a few days later and say "Guess what, we've managed to double your investment. Here's two grand", and they're like "Woah, I like this" and hand over the hundred thousand, thinking they're going to double up like before.'

'I'm guessing that they don't?'

'Of course they don't. They get an apologetic "I'm sorry, it didn't work out this time" call if they're lucky, but basically the money has gone. It all works on greed. If they turn around and say they're out after the first "investment", then the scammer is down by a grand. But they never do.'

'How does this apply to Jorge?'

'He tells his students he's well connected, right? He always puts one of his own artworks into the exhibition and, crucially, it always sells. What makes him even cleverer is that he puts in some alumni artworks as well, and they sell too. Then, he makes sure each student sells an artwork, but for a much lower price. That's the convincer.'

'Go on.'

'Think about it. Jorge sells a painting for maybe thirty thousand dollars. The students see alumni works going for a few thousand, and they also pocket a couple of hundred. The message is clear. "You're on the road to success. It might be three hundred dollars this time, but it will soon be thousands and tens of thousands. You know this because you see it happening in front of your very eyes." Except it isn't. Jorge isn't selling anything to anyone. All he's doing is putting a ridiculous price on his work and then adding a red sticker. The alumni paintings are also fake. To be fair, he does pay out on the fake sales of the student paintings, but what's a couple of hundred dollars when you can sell them another month in the squat at six thousand dollars on the back of it?'

'Bloody hell. Does Thomas know?'

'No. He and Cat did their extra month and are now travelling in the Far East.'

'I bet Jack loves that.'

'Actually, he's kind of OK with it. In his eyes, seeing the world is a good thing, because it gives you insight into other cultures and broadens your horizons. Claire, on the other hand, is pulling her hair out. She hates the fact that she doesn't know where he is, and Jack really loves that.'

'I bet he does. Can I ask you something personal?'

'Of course. If I don't like it, I'll just tell you to piss off.'

'Do you ever find the age gap between you and Jack problematic?'

Michelle smiles. 'You think it's odd that I should be in love with a man so much older than me, particularly when we don't seem to have much in common, don't you.'

'I can't say I've given it much thought. It just occurred to me,' I lie.

'Bullshit!' she laughs. 'Thanks for trying to be tactful though. What most people see is a hard-nosed businessman who may or may not be exploiting his employees. But those people haven't worked for him. Yes, he's successful, but that's not through exploitation. Do you know how modern slavery works?'

'I think so. People come over expecting a better life, only to find themselves being paid a pittance by their bosses, who then take all the pay back for putting them up in disgusting accommodation. They're trapped because they owe the slavers a huge debt for bringing them here.'

'Exactly. And what happens to these people when the slave traders are found and shut down?'

'I hadn't thought about that bit.'

'If you're illegal, you might get deported, but hardly anybody is. If you're unlucky, you get transferred to a new slaver and it goes around again. If you're lucky, you meet someone like Jack, who pays you the going rate and helps you to find accommodation you can afford. He's actually a good man, and his employees love him.'

I'm not sure I believe her, but I smile anyway. I'm far too busy digesting her earlier bombshell and marrying it up to my experiences when I was in San Francisco.

'Anyway, enough of my prattling,' Michelle tells me with a smile as I hand her a cup of tea. 'Let's see what we can do with your hair, shall we?'

* * *

I have to confess that I've been very nervous about letting Michelle loose on my hair, but a couple of hours later I'm looking delightedly in the mirror. She's applied gentle highlights and, although she's cut it a little shorter than I'm used to, I love the way it frames my face.

'This is fantastic!' I enthuse. 'What do I owe you?'

'Call it thirty quid for the chemicals. I did the cut for fun.'

'Are you sure?'

'Of course. I love being a lady of leisure, but I do miss my job sometimes. Oh, hello. You must be Callum.'

'Hi,' Callum replies as he heads for the kitchen.

'He's a bit shy. Be gentle with him,' I murmur to Michelle.

'Gentle, my arse,' she replies with a broad grin. 'He's gorgeous, or at least he could be with a decent haircut and glasses that didn't make him look like a fifty-year-old.'

'Don't. He's made it very clear he doesn't want to be anyone's pet project.'

'Hm. We'll see. Callum?' she calls.

'Yes?' He reappears from the kitchen looking wary.

'Do you mind me asking who does your hair?'

'I go to the barber when it gets annoying. Why?'

'I was just thinking. I'm all set up and I'm finished with Alex. I could give you a little trim while I'm here if you like.'

'Thanks, but I'm fine.'

'I won't do anything radical, but I couldn't help noticing it's well below the collar line at the back. And, like I said, I'm here and set up. Why don't you take a seat and I'll give it a quick once over. Save you a trip to the barber.'

Callum looks at me, obviously hoping that I'm going to save him, but this is too good an opportunity to miss, so I just shrug my shoulders and say, 'What have you got to lose?'

I'm reminded of one of those cute online videos where people rescue stray dogs and cats. They fight viciously against any human interaction until they realise they're not getting anywhere, at which point they suddenly give up and become completely docile. Callum looks exactly the same.

'That would be very kind of you, if it's not too much trouble,' he says to Michelle.

'No trouble at all.' She grins. 'Alex. How about another cup of tea all round?'

24

'I thought she said she wasn't going to do anything radical,' Callum moans as soon as Michelle has left. I'm sitting on the sofa in the living room and he's examining his head in the bathroom.

'I think it suits you,' I offer. His trademark floppy mop is gone, and he now has it cut short at the back and sides, with a longer top that she's styled into the beginnings of a quiff.

'It's weird, and I've never used products in my hair before.'

'It's modern,' I counter.

'Well, I suppose I'm stuck with it now, so I'd better make the most of it.' He reappears, looking morose.

'You just wait. You'll be fighting them off next time you're at the gym.'

The corners of his mouth finally turn up a little. 'You think?'

'Oh yes. All the girls will be whispering to each other, wanting to know who the handsome hunk with the huge biceps is.'

'You're embarrassing me now.'

'Sorry,' I laugh. I'm not sorry really. Despite my ban on him running himself down, Callum still seems unable to see what I see in him. It's frustrating, because I'm sure he'd like to meet someone, but it's never going to happen until he starts to build some self-confidence. I study him as he wanders into the kitchen to retrieve the tablet computer that we use for our online grocery shopping. Within a week of moving in, he'd set us up a joint email account, imaginatively called CalandAlFlat12, and used it to create the login for our online shopping. The way it works is that we can both add items to the list, he pays and I reimburse him for half of the general bill, plus any extra things I order just for me. It would never have worked with Emma – goodness only knows what she would have considered were general items – but it works very well with him.

'What did she say that stuff was called?' he asks as he navigates to the haircare products.

'I think she used a salon-only brand, but any hair wax will do. They're all much of a muchness, I reckon.'

'Hm.' He selects a product and adds it to the basket before closing the browser and turning to me.

'Do you really think it's an improvement, or are you just saying that to try to cheer me up?' he asks.

'It really is an improvement. Turns out there's quite a good-looking guy under all the camouflage, you just have to let him out.'

That seems to be all the encouragement he needs as, having deposited the tablet back in the kitchen, he retires back into his room.

'Don't forget Emma and Mark are coming round tonight,' I call as he closes the door. The muffled grunt from the other side lets me know that he's heard.

* * *

'What have you done to Callum?' Emma demands. We're sitting on the sofa making steady progress through a bottle of wine while the boys are out collecting the takeaway.

'Hey, don't point the finger at me. Michelle persuaded him to have a little trim after she'd finished with me, and that was the result.'

'He looks completely different. I did a double take when I first clapped eyes on him. It was only the glasses that gave him away. If he lost those and maybe grew a bit of stubble, he'd be kind of hot, don't you think?'

'You should tell him that. I'm trying to get him to work on his self-esteem, so any remarks about his increasing hotness would definitely help. I'd love him to get confident enough to sign up for online dating. He's much more interesting than he gives himself credit for and, unlike most of the men you come across online, he's not a dick.'

'And what makes you such an expert on online dating all of a sudden?' she asks.

'Don't get excited, I'm not talking from personal experience. I'm just going on what I've heard from Ashleigh at work. Anyway, this is about Callum, not me. I reckon he'd get snapped up pretty quickly, don't you?'

'Why haven't you snapped him up then?'

'I'm not in the market, but I admit I might be tempted if I were.'

'Still getting over Thomas?'

'It's not that so much. It's just that I'm kind of happy with the way things are right now. I'm enjoying my job, living with Callum is surprisingly easy, and I've got my best friend across the corridor. I don't feel the need for anything else at the moment.'

'What about sex? Don't you miss that?'

'A bit, but not enough to make me want a man in my life.'

'Fair enough. It's still kind of weird though.'

'What?'

'Well, you were always the one with the boyfriend while I was single. Now you're single and I'm the one with a boyfriend.'

'And how are things with Mark?'

'Oh, lovely as always. I'm currently trying to teach him to use the washing machine instead of taking everything to the dry cleaner.'

I can't help laughing.

'What?' she demands. 'What's so funny?'

'The blind leading the blind, don't you think?' I reply.

'Ha ha. I'll have you know that I'm transforming into a domestic goddess, actually. I even boil-washed some towels the other day. What do you say to that?'

'Umm, why?'

'This video came up on TikTok. What it said was that all this washing at low temperatures that we're encouraged to do now is turning our washing machines into breeding grounds for bacteria and all sorts of other nasties.'

'Doesn't the detergent get rid of them?'

'Not according to the video. Anyway, it said you should do a boil wash every so often to kill off all the nasties, so I put the towels in. I swear they've come out softer and fluffier than they used to be. You should try it.'

'You're giving me advice on how to operate the washing machine now? Kind of ironic, don't you think?'

'It's up to you.' She shrugs. 'I was just trying to be helpful. In the spirit of which...'

'Yes?'

She lowers her head bashfully. 'I'm sure you know this, but you *really* don't want to mix the colours when you're boil washing.'

'Oh dear,' I laugh.

'Mm. Mark's being very good about it, but I don't think he was exactly delighted to find that his white towels had turned a fetching shade of grey.'

'I'd tell him to sod off and wash his own towels.'

'It's a journey we're on together. We reached peak shithole a couple of weeks ago, and we realised we were going to have to do something about it, so we've divided up the chores. He's doing most of the cooking, and some of it is surprisingly edible. We did have to throw away a casserole dish after his first attempt at a stew, because he misread the recipe and stuck it in the oven at two hundred degrees for six hours, but he's had some successes too. He likes to experiment. We had chicken cooked in tomato soup the other day.'

'Sounds disgusting.'

'It was nice, actually. The soup made a kind of sauce for the chicken. You should try it.'

Thankfully, Mark and Callum reappear before Emma can give me any more bizarre recipe tips.

'Callum totally pulled in the chippy,' Mark tells us excitedly as they come through the door.

'He's exaggerating, as usual,' Callum replies as he sets the bag down on the table. An enticing vinegary aroma is coming out of it, and my mouth begins to water. Emma can keep her chicken in tomato soup; this is what delicious smells like.

'What happened?' Emma asks.

'Mr Swanky New Hairstyle rocks up to the counter, flashes the poor helpless girl on the till a megawatt smile and says "Four cod and chips please" in a tone so sexy I swear her underwear melted. She was putty in his hands.'

'You know you're talking complete bollocks, don't you?' Callum sighs.

'Not completely. Yes, I might be exaggerating just a tiny bit, but you should have seen the smile she gave him, and the way she kept tucking her hair behind her ear. That's a thing, isn't it? I'm sure I read somewhere that girls playing with their hair is a sign they're attracted to you.'

'That or nits,' I offer.

'Shouldn't she have been wearing a hairnet?' Emma asks.

'You're getting off the subject. The point is that Callum pulled and, even if you don't buy the hair flicking, I'm certain she gave us extra chips.'

'That I can get on board with,' Emma laughs. 'Perhaps we should send him over in his underwear next time; who knows what extras we'd get?'

'I am here, you know,' Callum calls from the kitchen where he's getting out plates and cutlery. 'Besides, I have no idea what you thought you were watching, because I didn't see any of the things that you've just talked about. We went to the chippy, we got fish and chips, the girl smiled politely when I paid and we came home. That's what happened. The way you're describing it makes it sound like there was a soaring soundtrack by a string orchestra as our eyes met over the fryer.'

'You just weren't reading the signals, that's all,' Mark tells him.

Although the conversation flows easily for the rest of the evening, my conversation with Emma and Mark's remark stick in my mind and I find myself distracted, turning over various scenarios. How would I feel if Callum had a girlfriend? What sort of person would he go for? Would he want someone quiet like him, or a foil to bring him out of himself? Despite living with him for a while, I realise I still know precious little about this side of him apart from his dislike of tattoos, and I'm curious.

'Callum?' I ask when the others have gone and we're clearing up.

'Yes?'

'How would you have felt if what Mark was saying earlier was true?'

'About the girl in the chip shop?'

'Yes.'

'It wasn't, though.'

'I know, but what if it had been? What if she'd properly come on to you? How would you have felt?'

'Terrified, I expect.'

'What would you have said?'

'I don't know.'

'OK, let's role play. Hello, handsome, what can I get you?'

'Stop. You're making me cringe.'

'Fine. What sort of woman do you go for?'

'I don't really go for any particular type.'

'Nonsense. All boys have a type. If you picture your ideal woman in your head, what does she look like? What personality does she have? We know you're not a great fan of tattoos, but what are the other red lines?'

'You're right. I'm not wild about tattoos, but I can honestly say that's about as far as I've got. I either like someone or I don't and, let's face it, beggars can't be choosers.'

'I'm going to get a bloody jar and make you put a tenner in it every time you run yourself down. I reckon I'll be a millionaire in a month.'

'Sorry. Old habits. Do you want a cup of tea before I go to bed?'

'No thanks.'

I reflect on our conversation as I watch him moving about in the kitchen. I think he'd do really well with someone who was quiet like him. A librarian, perhaps, although the only person I know from school who became a librarian was one of the wildest girls in our year. I don't know who was more shocked when she announced her intention to join the library staff, her English teacher or her friends. Anyway, she's married with children now, so totally not suitable for Callum.

'Whatever you're thinking, don't.' Callum's voice startles me out of my reverie.

'I have no idea what you mean.'

'Of course you don't. Let me help you. First, Mark dropped a load of bullshit about the girl in the chippy fancying me, and then you started asking me all sorts of questions about what kind of person I would go for. Finally, while I'm minding my own business making a cup of tea, I notice you watching me with an intense expression on your face. I may not know very much about women, but I like to think I know a bit about you, and if that wasn't a matchmaking face then I don't know what is. I might get a jar and make you put a tenner in it every time you try to project manage me.'

I sigh. 'You've got me.'

'What were you imagining? If it was a librarian, you'll have to put an extra twenty quid in the jar just for being such a cliché.'

'It definitely wasn't a librarian.'

'Hm. Goodnight then.'

I've still got half a glass of wine, so I switch on the TV to give me something to look at while I finish it. It's the late-night news, which is full of the usual depressing stories, so I turn it back off. I'm unsettled, and I can't quite put my finger on the cause. Emma asking why I haven't snapped Callum up is part of it, for sure. The truth is that the more time I spend with him, the more he grows on me and, if I'm brutally honest, part of the reason I've been fishing to find out what sort of girl he might go for is because I want to see how many of those boxes I tick. Underneath the image he projects to the world is a man who I've come to see is quietly comfortable in his own skin, and that's surprisingly attractive. Yes, it's massively frustrating that he doesn't show his qualities more easily, but getting to know him is a bit like digging for hidden treasure. Look in the right place and there's gold aplenty. You just have to be patient until he knows you well enough to hand you the map. I reflect on all this as I finish my wine, but it's not the full reason for my jitters.

It's only as I'm brushing my teeth that the answer comes to me. Callum wears his lack of social ability almost like a medal, yet he literally just read me like a book. What is that about? Is he secretly paying as much attention to me as I am to him and, if he is, what does that mean?

25

'Are you feeling all right?' Sarah asks, concern on her face. Our new office was declared ready two weeks ago and we moved in last weekend. Although it's generally a much better working environment than her living room, the lights are very bright, particularly in contrast to the darkness outside. Or maybe they just seem that way on this winter afternoon.

'Sorry.' I smile weakly at her. 'I've got a pounding headache for some reason. I don't know whether it's the lighting in here or something else.'

'I know what you mean,' she replies. 'I might see if we can get it toned down. Look, it's nearly time to close up anyway, and you've worked your socks off all week. Why don't you get away and start your weekend a bit early?'

'Are you sure?'

'Of course. You're white as a sheet. Have you got any painkillers?'

'No, but there's a pharmacy in the block of shops under my flat, so I'll call in there on the way home.'

'Will you be all right to drive?'

'Yes, I think so. It's not a migraine, just a really bad headache.'

'Good. Off you go then, and hopefully it'll clear soon. See you on Monday.'

'Thanks, Sarah.'

It's definitely the lights in the office, as the pounding in my head decreases slightly once I get outside. The cold fresh air is probably helping too, but I'm still going to need some painkillers to see it off completely. I drive home with the window open and slot my car into its usual space behind the flats, before walking quickly through the passageway that leads from the car parking area to the front of the building where the shops are.

'Hey,' a voice calls out from behind me as I reach the front of the building and turn towards the pharmacy. I turn around to see a man leaning against the wall. He's wearing a hoodie, tracksuit bottoms and trainers and smoking a cigarette.

'Sorry, were you talking to me?' I ask.

'Yeah. Here's the thing. I've lost my wallet with my bank card and everything, and I need to get back to Orpington, 'cos my missus is about to have a baby. You couldn't spare us a tenner, could you?'

'Sure,' I tell him, fishing in my purse and handing him a ten-pound note. For a moment, I'm reminded of homeless Jerry in San Francisco, but this guy doesn't look homeless. His clothes are clean and his trainers look expensive.

'Thanks. You're a lifesaver,' he replies. He takes another long draw on his cigarette as I turn to leave. I'm just about to head into the pharmacy when I spot a very familiar figure carrying a gym bag coming round the corner.

'Hiya, you're back early,' Callum says when he reaches me.

'I've got a headache so Sarah let me go early. I'm just going to grab some painkillers. Good workout?'

'Yeah, not bad. I thought I'd reward myself with some chocolate from the newsagent. Do you want any?'

I smile in spite of my throbbing head. 'I could murder a Double Decker.'

'No problem. See you at home.'

I decide to bypass the pain relief on the shelf and go straight for the stronger stuff you can only get over the counter. After assuring the assistant that I'm not on any other medication or pregnant, I leave with a box of ibuprofen-based pills that she assures me will kill most headaches stone dead. I'm relieved to see that the guy with the cigarette has obviously moved on and head into the passageway, quickening my pace.

'Oof!' I exclaim as someone bumps into me. Suddenly, I can feel my bag being pulled off my shoulder and, on instinct, I try to grab it.

'Just give it over,' hoodie man grunts as I grip the handle as hard as I can. He's yanking at it, trying to get me to let go, and it feels like my arms are being wrenched out of their sockets. Still, I stubbornly hang on, pulling back in return. The problem is that he's much stronger than me and it's all I can do to keep my balance.

In the end, the bag decides its own fate, as the stitching holding the handles on gives way and hoodie man flees with his prize. I'm stunned, unable to take in what has just happened, staring stupidly down at the straps still in my hand as if the bag will magically reattach itself somehow.

'What the—' I hear hoodie man's voice at the end of the passage, followed by a thump. I raise my eyes to see that Callum has blocked his path, and they're engaged in a much more serious tussle for the bag. I'm just about to yell at Callum to leave it when hoodie man suddenly escapes from Callum's grip and runs out into the darkness.

'He's gone,' Callum mutters, pinching his nose to try to stem the flow of blood. Hoodie man obviously landed at least one punch. 'Sorry. I did get your bag back though.' He hands over my now extremely sorry-looking bag.

'Are you OK?' I ask.

'Yeah, it looks worse than it is. What about you? He didn't hurt you, did he?'

'I don't think so. It all happened so fast.'

'Good. Let's get inside. We're running on adrenaline now, but it won't be long before the shock kicks in. Can you see my glasses anywhere?'

I glance around and I'm quickly rewarded by a distinctive gold glint. However, as soon as I pick them up, it becomes obvious that they're broken beyond repair. The lens has popped out on one side, and the frame is bent completely out of shape.

'I'm sorry,' I tell him as I hand them to him. 'Will you be able to manage without?'

'I've got a spare pair indoors. Come on.' He slings his gym bag over his shoulder and holds out his hand, which I take without thinking. He's right about the shock. We're barely through the door before I start shaking uncontrollably.

'It's fine, you're safe,' he soothes as he leads me carefully to the sofa and helps me to sit. 'Have a bite of this.'

He reaches into his bag and pulls out the Double Decker. 'Sugar helps,' he says, handing the bar to me. My hands are shaking so hard that I can't even open the wrapper so, after a moment or two, he gently takes it out of my grasp, opens it for me and then hands it back.

'Will you be all right if I leave you here for a moment? I'll be as quick as I can,' he asks, and I nod. He disappears into the bathroom and I listen to the sound of running water as I take a tentative bite from the chocolate bar. I'm still shaking as he crosses into his bedroom, reappearing a minute or so later wearing a fresh T-shirt and carrying two glasses of amber liquid.

'Whisky,' he tells me as he holds the glass up to my mouth. 'The good stuff, which is why I'm holding it rather than letting you spill it everywhere. Have a sip.'

I follow his instructions and feel the heat spread through my body as I swallow the fiery liquid.

'Th-thanks,' I mutter.

He sits down carefully next to me, taking a large swig from his own glass. There's a brief clatter as he sets it down on the table, and I realise that he's shaking too.

'A-are you OK?' I manage to ask.

'Yeah. Don't worry about me. I reckon I'll have a couple of cracking black eyes in the morning, but otherwise I think I'm fine. Here.' He holds the glass up to my mouth again and I take a bigger sip. I can feel its soothing effect, and I'm relieved to find that the trembling is starting to ease off.

'You ought to call the police,' he continues after a few moments. 'What he did to you was assault and we should report it.'

'I'm not sure,' I tell him. 'What will they do? He'll be long gone by now, won't he? They might decide to arrest you for assaulting him.'

'It will probably come to nothing, I agree. But what if he tries to mug someone else, and nobody is there to stop him? I don't know about you, but I don't think I'd sleep easily if I hadn't at least reported it.'

'You're right,' I sigh. We decide that it's not a 999 emergency so, after a bit of research, we find the Kent police website and navigate our way through the online forms to report the incident. At the end, I receive a crime reference number and a promise that someone will be in touch if they need more information. It's a surprisingly banal process, and I've pretty much stopped shaking by the end.

'I think you're going to need a new handbag,' Callum observes after trying to see if there's any way to reattach the straps.

'Why me? I'd already given him a tenner.'

'Yeah, but that was probably a ruse to see what was in your bag, and your bank card is in your purse, isn't it? He'd get quite a few contactless payments out of that before you managed to get it stopped, and I guess your phone is in the bag too.'

'It is.'

'So he'd probably be able to sell that.'

'Fucking bastard,' I mutter angrily.

'If it's any consolation, you were putting up a hell of a fight from the tiny bit I saw. I don't think he was expecting that.'

'It wasn't enough though, was it. Thank you. You didn't have to do that, you know.'

'What did you expect me to do? Stand back and say "Well done mate, off you go"?'

'No, but—'

'I just did what any decent person would have done. How's your headache, by the way?'

'Oddly enough, it's gone. I might go and have a shower though. I feel dirty.'

'Umm, I'm not sure that's a good idea. If the shock comes back, the last thing you need is to be standing upright on a slippery surface with lots of hard edges around you. I'll run you a bath in my bathroom and you can soak in that. At least you'll be lying down already if you get the wobbles.'

I'm so grateful to him that I follow his instructions without a murmur of complaint, getting up and heading for my room carrying my tattered bag. As I close the door behind me, the shock hits me again and I have to sit on the bed for a little while to let the worst of the shaking pass. Callum is right about the bag; it's way beyond saving so I methodically empty the contents onto my dressing table before placing the bag and handles in the bin. By the time I come back out wrapped in my dressing gown, Callum is nowhere to be seen but he's filled the tub and added a decent slug of bubble bath from what I can see. He's also placed my glass with the remains of the whisky on the side. I close and lock the bathroom door behind me before slipping out of my dressing gown and stepping into the hot water. As I allow my body to sink beneath the surface, I inhale deeply. The smell of the bubble bath is familiar, but I can't place it at the moment. This is the first time I've been in here since Callum moved in and I can't help looking around. It's very Callum. Everything is in its place; the toothbrush and toothpaste neatly stacked in a glass next to the basin, the traditional razor in a little stand with a brush and shaving soap, and a small collection of aftershave bottles on the shelf under the mirror. Seeing the bottles brings my mind back to the bubble bath. Why does it smell so familiar, I wonder, and why do I find the scent so soothing? I reach for the glass and take a small sip. I've never liked whisky, but tonight I'm really enjoying its numbing warmth.

All of a sudden, my mind joins the dots. The smell of the bubble bath is the smell of Callum. I've caught hints of it countless times before, but it's never really connected with me.

Tonight, it has a whole new meaning. It's the smell of home, the smell of safety.

I stay in the bath until the heat starts to go out of the water, before wrapping myself back into my dressing gown and stepping out into the living room. Callum is sitting on the sofa and glances up.

'How are you doing?' he asks.

'Better, thank you.'

'I hope you don't mind, but I emptied your bin while you were in there.'

My immediate feeling of irritation about him invading my privacy is swiftly replaced by gratitude. He must have realised that the bag would continually remind me of the attack and he's quietly done the right thing.

26

It's no good. I can't sleep. Every time I close my eyes, the incident replays in my head like it's on a never-ending loop. I roll over and glance at the clock. Half past two in the morning. With a growl of frustration I throw off the covers, swing my legs out of the bed and flick on the bedside light. It takes a moment for my eyes to adjust to the sudden brightness but, when they do, they fall immediately on the small pile of items from my handbag on the dressing table. Seeing the confirmation of what happened earlier flips a switch inside me and, before I know it, my vision blurs as the tears start pouring down my cheeks. Even though the man in the hoodie didn't physically assault me, I still feel violated and unsafe. I've heard of muggings, obviously, but I never thought it would actually happen to me and the worst part is that it could have been something so much worse. What if he'd been a sexual predator? Would I have been able to fight him off if Callum hadn't come to my rescue? A picture forms in my mind of me pinned against the wall unable to move while hoodie man yanks up my skirt, and I have to shake my head hard to get rid of it.

'Come on, Alex,' I tell myself firmly. 'This is the shock talking. He just wanted your bag.'

It's not much comfort, however, and the tears continue to fall. When they eventually begin to subside, I realise there's no way I'm going to be able to go back to sleep any time soon, so I pull on my dressing gown and pad out into the living room with the intention of making a cup of tea. To my surprise, there's a beam of light under Callum's door. Suddenly, I feel like an awful person. Yes, I was the primary victim, but I haven't given any thought as to how this might have affected him. Maybe he can't sleep either. I cross the living room and knock softly but, unsurprisingly, there's no response so I retreat to my room and grab my phone to send him a message.

Are you awake? Do you want a cup of tea?

His response is immediate:

Are you OK? Why are you up?

I can't sleep. So, tea?

I'd love one if it's not too much trouble.

I flick the switch on the kettle and pull a couple of mugs out of the cupboard. The mundane tasks are soothing, even though it feels very strange to be up and about at this time of night. Emma and I would often go out clubbing until the small hours when we were younger, but it's a long time since those days. Callum is still in his room so, when the tea is made, I carry the mugs over and knock gently on the door again.

'It's open,' his voice says from the other side. I'm not sure what to expect when I walk in, but it's not Callum sitting at his desk fully clothed. In front of him the four enormous screens are filled with windows containing incomprehensible-looking text. It reminds me a bit of a villain's lair in a James Bond movie.

'What are you doing?' I ask as I place his mug of tea on the coaster on his desk.

'Working,' he replies simply. 'I was going to do this next week, but I couldn't sleep either so I thought I'd do it tonight instead. Are you all right?'

'I'm still a bit shaken up,' I tell him. 'Do you mind if I sit with you for a bit?'

'Not at all. You can help yourself to my thinking couch if you like. It's not very exciting though, I'm warning you.'

'That's fine,' I say as I perch on the arm of his sofa. 'I think I've had more than enough excitement for one day. So, tell me what you're doing.'

'Why?'

'Because I'm interested. I've never seen a hacker at work before, and it will take my mind off things.'

'OK, but don't blame me if it bores you senseless. Basically, there are three main types of penetration test that we do. There's white box testing, where we test a single system for a particular flaw. The customer knows exactly what we're going to do and when, and they give us the necessary access to their systems so we can carry out the test.'

'Got it,' I tell him.

'Black box testing is the opposite. The customer doesn't share any details with us or give us access. We effectively behave like an unprivileged outside attacker.'

'A hacker.'

'Exactly. Then the final one is grey box testing, where we get some information but not all. This is to simulate an insider threat.'

'But what are you actually testing for?'

'All sorts of things, depending on what the client wants. So we could test their internal network hardware, their Wi-Fi access points, their external web application, cloud environments and so on. Where do you think the greatest security risk to an organisation typically lies?'

'I don't know. I've never really thought about it. The website?'

'And why do you think that?'

'It just seems that's the most vulnerable bit because it's public facing.'

'You aren't wrong. Any part of the software that is publicly accessible is obviously a risk, but the greatest risk is actually posed by your people.'

'Disgruntled employees?'

'They don't have to be disgruntled. Have you come across phishing?'

'I've heard of it. That's the one where they try to get you to click on a link in an email, isn't it?'

'Yes. Typical examples are emails that look like they've come from your bank, advising you that someone's tried to access your online account and you need to click a link to change your password. The link takes you to a site that looks legitimate. It asks you to enter your username, your old password and your new one, and then the hackers have everything they need to empty your account. But there are also corporate versions, so you might get something from the HR department or the CEO, telling you to do something. Even though most companies give regular training on this stuff, people still fall for it.'

'And you do that?'

'Yes, if we're asked to. Obviously, nothing bad happens when the users click the links in our emails. We just send them an automated response reiterating the things to look out for and explaining that it was a training exercise. One of my colleagues did get a bit carried away once and sent out an email that purported to be from the CEO inviting everyone to a corporate party to thank them for their hard work and giving a link for them to click on to indicate their acceptance. When people found out it was a fake, there was a lot of bad feeling.'

'What happened?'

'The CEO was massively unimpressed and that colleague doesn't work for us any more.'

'But a fake party doesn't sound very threatening.'

'On the surface, no. But the danger is in the link. You could unwittingly be downloading a virus, key tracking software or anything. Once something like that is on your corporate network, you're putting the company at risk.'

'So what are you doing at the moment?'

'I'm trying to gain access to the server that has our customer's sales data on it. It's very valuable information, so unsurprisingly the server that stores it has several layers of security.'

'And you're doing it in the middle of the night because?'

'Partly because I couldn't sleep, but also because hackers aren't polite and don't work from nine to five Monday to Friday, so we have to replicate that. Plus companies quite often carry out maintenance activities overnight, and sometimes this means they have to temporarily disable a firewall or back up a system, so it can be slightly easier to get in.'

At that moment, one of the windows on a screen bursts into life and countless lines of text begin to appear.

'Aha!' he exclaims triumphantly and begins typing furiously. I don't think I've ever seen anyone type so fast; his fingers are practically a blur on the keyboard as he focuses intently on the screen. He's clicking between various windows, entering commands on each, and soon several of them are churning out lines of unfathomable text. It's difficult to see from the sofa, so I move closer and perch on the end of his bed so I can watch over his shoulder.

'What does all that mean?' I ask, looking at the scrolling lines of text.

'It means I'm through the final layer and the internal API is talking to me.'

'What?'

'Sorry.' He types another flurry of commands before continuing. 'APIs are like little windows into a system. So, imagine you're booking a flight on the internet. You enter where you want to go and the dates, and the web page will post that into an API. The server at the other end of the API will work out what options are available to you, and then send it back through the API to your browser. Does that make sense?'

'I think so.'

'Great. So this one gives out sales data based on what I request. I have a choice now. I could either start asking it for confidential sales data or I could cripple it, thus bringing any part of the business that needs to use that data to a standstill. Which do you prefer?'

'They both sound pretty awful.'

'Don't worry. I'm not actually going to do either. All I need to do is prove that I got the API to talk to me by getting a simple piece of data that they can verify as genuine.' He types some more into one of the windows and then takes a snapshot that he copies into a document on one of the other screens.

'What's in this for a real hacker?' I ask.

'Several things. Pride is a big one, but most hacks of the type I'm simulating are for financial gain.'

'How?'

'I could download this company's sales data and sell it to the highest bidder, for example. Information is valuable. Or, if I decided to cripple the API with a denial-of-service attack, I could effectively hold them to ransom.'

'What's a denial-of-service attack?'

'It's when a hacker overloads an API with so many requests that nobody else can communicate with it.'

'Surely you'd get caught though.'

'Not as easily as you'd think. I can route through so many servers that I'm practically impossible to find.'

'Fascinating.'

'You think?'

'Well, the hacking part is interesting, but what I was actually talking about was you.'

'What do you mean?'

'I've never seen you so alive. You are literally radiating joy.'

'I'll let you in to a little secret. I think I'm probably a born hacker. If I didn't have this legal outlet for it, I'd probably be trying to get into the FBI, or the Pentagon or something just for the fun of it.'

'Really?'

'No, not really. At least I hope not. It is a hell of a buzz though, breaking through an organisation's security.'

I sit and watch as he works. There are long periods where nothing happens, and then short bursts of frenzied activity. It doesn't take long before I'm certain he's forgotten I'm even there. After a while, I finally find my eyelids getting heavy.

* * *

When I wake up after a surprisingly deep and dreamless sleep, I am totally disorientated. I'm in my room, but it's also not my room. It's familiar but very different, and it takes me a long time to work out why. It's only when I catch a glimpse of the four enormous monitors, now completely dark, that the events of last night start to come back to me. I gently move my limbs to test out the limits of the mattress and it confirms my mounting fears; I'm in Callum's single bed.

I sit up and look around to try to locate Callum. I'm definitely alone in the bed and, although the room is fairly dark and the curtains are drawn, I can clearly see that his thinking couch, as he called it, is also empty. On the bedside table next to me is a glass of water that I'm fairly sure wasn't there when I came in last night, and my mug of tea has vanished as well. I flush with embarrassment as I realise I must have fallen asleep watching him work and, rather than wake me up, he appears to have tucked me up in his bed and left me to sleep. *But where is he?*

I swing my legs out from under the duvet and cross to his door, opening it quietly. The living room is also in darkness, so it takes me a minute to spot the prone figure stretched out on the sofa with a blanket wrapped around him. When I do, I'm flooded with a whole range of emotions. I'm embarrassed for driving him out of his room but also incredibly grateful that, yet again, he went out of his way for me in the kindest, gentlest way. There's another emotion bubbling inside me as well, but I can't deal with that one at the moment; it's just too complicated and confusing. Pushing it to one side as best I can, I pad across to the kitchen and put the kettle on for a cup of tea. The kettle sounds unbelievably loud in our silent apartment, but Callum doesn't stir. When I've filled two mugs, I carry them carefully over to the sofa where Callum is still sleeping. His face is completely peaceful, despite the angry bruising round his eyes, and I just stand and watch him for a while before I gently bend over him and touch his shoulder to wake him up.

'Here you are, I've brought you a cup of tea,' I tell him as he starts to come round. His arm reaches out to find his glasses and he opens them up and puts them on his nose, wincing slightly as he does so.

'Are those your spare glasses?' I ask, looking at the round black plastic frames.

'Yes. I was wearing them last night. Didn't you notice?'

'I was a bit distracted, sorry. Where have you been hiding those?'

'What do you mean?'

'They suit you so much better than the other ones. You look properly handsome in them.'

'Really? They were literally the cheapest frames I could find.'

'They suit you perfectly. Anyway, I'm so sorry for falling asleep. Why didn't you wake me up and kick me out?'

'You'd had a hell of a day and you looked at peace for the first time. I couldn't bear to wake you, so I just covered you up and then came out here. It's not a problem, really. Did you sleep all right?'

'I can't remember the last time I slept so heavily.'

'You needed it then, and I'm glad I could help.'

I look at him as he sips his tea and another raft of surprisingly complex emotions courses through me. As much as I try to rationalise them and see them as nothing more than gratitude, I know deep down what they are, and that's potentially a big problem.

27

'You're not falling for him. You can't be. I mean, I can see he's pretty hot physically and I know we joked about you snapping him up, but come on. This is Callum we're talking about,' Emma declares matter-of-factly after I've explained my predicament to her over a cup of coffee and a piece of cake. We're in Bluewater shopping centre, ostensibly to get me a new bag, although Emma is all for turning it into a full-on spree.

'What difference does that make?'

'All the difference. You've got Stockholm syndrome, that's what it is.'

'Umm, I think Stockholm syndrome is where you end up falling for someone who's kidnapped you,' I tell her.

'Well, whatever the equivalent is. He came to your rescue and now you think you're falling for him. It's just gratitude, that's all.'

I can tell that she's not ready to engage with this quite yet, so I decide to let it go. Emma sometimes needs a few minutes for a concept to sink in, so it wouldn't surprise me if she came back to it.

'You're probably right,' I tell her. 'It was a bit weird. Did you notice his glasses, by the way?'

'I did. *Such* an improvement. He's actually quite good looking now that you've tidied him up.'

'I haven't done anything to him. The hair was Michelle and he had the glasses already. He just didn't realise that his spare pair suited him much better.'

'Who'd have thought it though? Shy Callum, a hero. I don't think Mark would have done something like that.'

'I'm sure he would have done exactly the same if you'd been in my position.'

'I think he would have run away screaming. Violence really isn't his thing, and the idea of anyone messing up his precious face or spoiling his perfect manicure...' She sighs expressively.

'Trouble in paradise?' I ask.

'No, not really. I love him to bits, but the honeymoon phase is definitely over and we're becoming more aware of each other's flaws.'

'Such as?'

'Apart from the fact that his house training is still very much a work in progress, he is quite vain. Honestly, Alex, I think he takes longer in the bathroom than I do. Sometimes I'd like him to be a bit more rough and ready, you know? Like your Callum.'

'I thought we'd just established that he's not *my* Callum.'

'You know what I mean. Anyway, what are you going to do?'

'About what?'

'Callum, of course.'

Here we go. She's engaging now.

'Nothing,' I say. 'You've made it very clear that I'm just confused because he came to my rescue, but...'

'But what?'

'What if I'm not? What if these feelings are genuine?'

'Do you fancy him?'

'He's good looking, yes, but it's about so much more than that. That's what makes this so difficult. He's kind, and—'

'My granddad is kind. Kind isn't sexy.'

'I disagree. Kindness is a very attractive quality in a man. It was one of the big things that drew me to Thomas.'

'Yeah, and that worked out just brilliantly, didn't it. Can I be honest?'

'Please do. If you keep sitting on the fence like this, I'll never be able to work out what you're really thinking.'

It takes her a moment to realise that I'm joking.

'Oh, very good,' she remarks caustically. 'The thing is, well, I liked Thomas, but I never really got what you saw in him. He's not exactly a heartthrob, is he? You've dated hotter.'

'Like Nathan, you mean?'

'Oh yes. He was so hot he practically sizzled. Didn't you lose your virginity to him?'

'Too bloody hot to handle, that's what he was. And yes, he was my first. Most disappointing sex ever.'

'Really? He looked like the type of bad boy who would have all the moves.'

'Nope. At least none that would please a woman. He was pretty good at pleasing himself though. Did I ever tell you about the time he spanked me?'

'He *what*?'

'Yup. He was in his own little world as usual, while I just lay there and stared at the ceiling, occasionally making appreciative noises to try to speed him up. He suddenly started on this bizarre monologue about how I was a naughty girl and he needed to teach me a lesson. I tuned him out because it was frankly weird but seemed to be helping him along, and then he spanked me.'

'What did you do?'

'I pushed him off, sat up and told him that if he ever did

anything like that again, I'd cut off his balls. We broke up pretty soon after that. That's what I mean. Yes, Nathan was hot physically, and he was a "bad boy", which is exciting when you're seventeen. But it turns out that bad boys are also bad boyfriends. As well as being selfish in bed, he was the most unreliable person ever. We'd make plans to go out, and half the time he wouldn't turn up. I can't remember the number of times he let me down.'

'I wonder where he is now?'

'Probably making a living slapping girls in Dirk's dirty movies.' I giggle. I do my best to put on a deep announcer's voice and American accent. 'Coming to a porn site near you, Nathan Spankalot stars in the latest movie from Goldenschafft productions, *Crap in the Sack*.'

'Sounds positively faecal,' Emma replies.

'Maybe that's his vibe.' I join in with her laughter.

'I'm going to stalk him,' she says suddenly, pulling out her phone. 'He can't be hard to find. Nobody is these days. What was his surname?'

'Tennyson.'

'Like the poet?'

'Yup. Probably the only thing they have in common.'

'Let's try Facebook first.' I sip my coffee as she works. I haven't thought about Nathan in years, and I'm not that interested in finding him now, so my mind drifts back to Callum and how I feel about him.

'Found him. Oh, wow.' Emma's voice interrupts my thoughts.

'What?'

'OK, he's married. Two children, but that's not the surprise. The surprise is this.'

She turns the phone and shows me Nathan's profile picture. It's unmistakeably him, older obviously, but the key features are unchanged. He still has the same piercing blue eyes, although they're behind frameless glasses now.

'Oh,' is all I can say when I see what caught Emma's eye.

It would appear that bad boy Nathan has turned to the Lord, if the telltale white stripe in his shirt collar is anything to go by. I press to see his bio, which confirms it. The Revd Nathan Tennyson is rector of St Mary's church somewhere in the suburbs of Birmingham.

I hand Emma back her phone. It was an interesting diversion, but I've got bigger fish to fry.

* * *

Callum is out when I get back to the flat late in the afternoon, and I'm surprised to feel a pang of disappointment. I've had a really fun day out with Emma and I've spent way more than I planned to, but I've been looking forward to getting back home and seeing him. Despite grilling me extensively, she's still convinced that the feelings I'm having are purely a result of his actions last night, but I'm not at all sure I agree with her diagnosis.

'Pull yourself together,' I tell myself sternly. 'He's probably not even into you.'

The universe is obviously enjoying my discomfort, because the door buzzer chooses that moment to ring. My heart sinks when I glance at the screen. It's Thomas.

'Hello, Thomas. What are you doing here?' I say into the microphone.

'Hi, Alex. Can I come in? Is now a good time?'

I consider for a moment. I don't really want to see him, but he's here and I am a tiny bit curious to find out why.

'Fine,' I tell him, and press the button to open the bottom door before going out onto the landing. I watch him as he comes up the stairs. He's changed; if possible, he's even skinnier than before and he's also quite tanned. What's even more interesting, however, is that I have absolutely no physical response to him at all. My stomach doesn't lurch with desire or hatred; I just feel mildly irritated that he's interrupting my day.

'It's so good to see you,' he says enthusiastically when he reaches the top of the stairs. To my astonishment he leans in to kiss me on the lips. Thankfully, I'm too quick for him and turn to one side so it lands on my cheek.

'What are you doing here?' I repeat.

'I've come to tell you that I'm an absolute arse and to beg for your forgiveness.'

My curiosity is definitely piqued now. 'Really? You'd better come in and tell me more,' I reply.

'I behaved appallingly and I can't tell you how sorry I am,' he tells me once I've let him in and we've settled ourselves on the sofa. I haven't offered him tea or anything; I don't want him to feel too welcome.

'Mm-hm? In what exact ways do you think you behaved appallingly?' I encourage him.

'What do you mean? You were there.'

'Yes, I know I was. I just want to see how well you understand it.'

'I was unfaithful to you.'

'I know. How is Cat, by the way? Do send her my love.'

'I have no idea how she is. Coincidentally, she decided things were moving too fast and she needed space right around the time that my savings ran out.'

'Did she now?' The schadenfreude is too much for me to resist and I realise I'm smiling. Unwelcome as it is, this visit is starting to be a lot more interesting than I thought it was going to be. 'I'm so sorry to hear that. Anyway, you were telling me about how badly you behaved. Please don't let me stop you.'

'It was stupid. I was brainwashed by Jorge. That's the only excuse I can offer. He was always pushing Cat and me together. It turns out he's a fraud, did you know?'

'Yes, Michelle told me.'

'Michelle? As in Dad's Michelle?'

'That's the one. We're friends now, but that's not important. Let's get back to your story because, from what you were just saying, it sounds like you don't think it was your fault at all.'

'I'm not saying that. What I'm saying is that I was over-whelmed, I guess. I was all alone in a strange country, Cat was kind to me and Jorge encouraged it. I lost sight of myself.'

At that moment, we're interrupted by the sound of a key in the door as Callum arrives home. He's obviously been at the gym as he has his bag over his shoulder.

'Oh, umm. Hello,' he says when he spots Thomas on the sofa. 'Sorry, I didn't realise you had guests, Alex.' There's no resentment in his tone, merely confusion.

'Callum, this is Thomas,' I tell him, and I see his eyes widen in surprise. 'I would have told you he was coming, but he just called round unexpectedly. Thomas, this is Callum, my flatmate.'

Now it's Thomas's turn to look surprised. 'Where's Emma?' he asks.

'Emma lives across the corridor with her boyfriend, Mark,' I tell him. 'Callum used to live with Mark, but now he's living here, as you can see.'

'I'll leave you guys to it,' Callum says, and beats a hasty retreat.

An uncomfortable silence descends when Callum's bedroom door closes. Something awkward just happened, and I'm not entirely sure I know what it is. What I do know is that Thomas is at the centre of it, and I'm suddenly anxious to get this visit over and done with so he can leave.

'You were saying?' I prompt Thomas.

'Yes. As I said, I just kind of lost sight of myself because San Francisco was so overwhelming, and I guess I gravitated to Cat.'

'You lost sight of yourself?' I repeat. 'I think you'll find the person you lost sight of, Thomas, was me.'

He sighs. 'You're right. I know how much I hurt you, and I'll never be able to tell you how sorry I am. I'm not the person you saw in San Francisco, you know I'm not.'

'But you became that person, Thomas. That person was inside you and San Francisco let him out. He's still in there, and that's a problem because he'll probably come out again at some point.'

'Would it help if I told you I've given up painting?'

'What? Why?'

'Do you remember the bloke at the art show in the village who asked me how I thought my work was art?'

'No.'

'You were very rude to him. It was funny at the time, but he had a point. I've realised that I'm not an artist. Anyone can fling a bit of paint onto a canvas, but only an artist can make it mean something. I wanted to be a painter so badly that I fooled myself into thinking I could do it, particularly because Dad was so against it. So when Jorge told me I had potential, it was like music to my ears. I was going to prove Dad wrong and become a great artist. I was perfect material for someone like Jorge. The sad thing is that I was really happy in San Francisco. But the truth is it was all a lie and I screwed things up royally with you in the process. Do you think you'll ever be able to forgive me?'

'Do you need me to? Why does that matter now?'

'It matters because I'm back in the UK for good.'

I'm not sure what he thinks that has to do with anything. 'I expect your mother is glad to have you home,' I say eventually.

'I'm living with Dad and Michelle, actually.'

This does surprise me. 'Really?'

'Yes. I think Mum felt lonely while I was away, and Arthur, that's the man you were rude to at the exhibition, appears to have stepped in to fill the gap. I'm happy for her, but it's a bit icky to watch them together. Anyway, I ended up having a long conversation with Dad about everything and we managed to clear the air. We talked for a while about what I should do next, and he agreed I could move into the annexe over their garage for now. I've started teacher training college too.'

'I expect your dad is pleased.'

'Yes. He's even agreed to cover my costs while I'm there.'

'It sounds like everything is working out well for you.'

'Yeah. There's just one thing that isn't.'

'Which is?'

'You. I miss you, Alex. I know I've behaved very badly and I have no right to ask you this, but do you think there could be a future for us?'

I'm gobsmacked. Despite all his protestations to the contrary, he hasn't understood his behaviour at all.

'Of course!' I exclaim enthusiastically. 'I've been waiting and hoping that you'd call, so nothing would make me happier.'

'Really?' He looks so delighted, I almost feel guilty about puncturing his balloon. Almost.

'No, Thomas,' I say firmly. 'Let me replay what you said to me last time I saw you. You said you wanted us to have a sabbatical so you could have a relationship with Cat with a clear conscience. Then, when you got bored or, as it turns out, she got bored, you'd come home where I would be waiting for you.'

'It was a stupid thing to say. I'm sorry. I didn't mean it.'

'But it's exactly what you're still expecting to happen, don't you see? She's dumped you and now you're asking me to let bygones be bygones and for us to pick up where we left off. How is that different from what you suggested before?'

'I guess, when you put it like that...'

'I do. Look, I hope the teacher training works out, but you and I are one hundred per cent over.'

'Can we be friends at least?'

'I don't know. I'm moving on.'

'I see,' he says sadly. 'Do you mind me asking if that moving on includes Callum?'

'There is nothing between me and Callum, and even if there was, it would be none of your business. It was nice of you to take the time to come round and apologise, but I think it's probably time for you to go now.' I get up and walk towards the front door, holding it open for him.

'I really am sorry, Alex,' he says as he walks out. 'I'll see you around, yeah?'

'Yeah.'

28

As soon as Thomas has gone, I WhatsApp Callum to ask him if he wants to join me for a cup of tea. I stifle a snigger as he cautiously opens his bedroom door and scans the room, as if checking for danger.

'He's gone,' I tell him with a smile.

'I assume that was the boyfriend?' he asks as he comes out.

'*Ex*-boyfriend,' I correct him.

'What did he want? Sorry, that's none of my business. Forget I said anything.'

'It's fine. He wanted to apologise for being an arse when he was in San Francisco, and then he asked me if we could get back together.'

A look crosses his face, but it passes so fast it's gone before I can work out what it is.

'Oh,' he says neutrally. 'What did you say?'

'I told him where he could stick it.'

This time there's no mistaking the look on his face. It's pure relief.

'What?' I say to him.

'It's nothing,' he blusters. 'It's just, umm, well, I guess I was concerned that I was going to become the third wheel again, like when I was living with Mark and he started going out with Emma.'

I study him for a moment. I don't think Callum has ever been less than truthful with me, but the way he said that doesn't ring true at all.

'Anyway, how was your day?' he asks, obviously keen to move the conversation on.

'What, before Thomas arrived? Good, thanks. I got a new bag and Emma and I indulged in some general retail therapy. How about you? You don't normally go to the gym on a Saturday.'

He smiles, glad to be back on safe ground. 'I was at a loose end and feeling a bit dozy after working last night, so I didn't want to sit around here in case I went to sleep and really mucked up my body clock. Also, I hope you don't mind, but I've brought home a leaflet I thought you might be interested in.' He reaches into his pocket, pulls out a piece of paper and hands it to me.

'Self-defence classes?' I ask. 'I'm not sure about that, Callum. Aren't they just martial arts in disguise?'

'This one is supposed to be different. I asked at reception and, apparently, it's aimed specifically at women. It focuses on psychology, how to avoid danger and appropriate physical responses.'

'Ha. The appropriate physical response to avoid danger is never to go through that bloody passageway again. That's my plan, anyway.'

'I had a thought about that too, actually.'

'Uh-oh.'

'How would you feel about going down and walking through it right now?'

'Why on earth would I want to do that?'

'Not long after my sister passed her driving test, she was involved in an accident. It wasn't her fault, but her car was written off and, although she wasn't hurt, she was really shaken up. Dad was really good with her and calmed her down to start with, but then he upped the ante. Morag's favourite thing in the world is a Chinese takeaway, so he suggested we had one to cheer her up.'

'That doesn't sound too arduous.'

'There was a catch. She had to drive him to pick it up.'

'Ah. What happened?'

'She did it, although Dad said she drove so slowly it might have been quicker to walk. The point is, he got her to confront her fear straight away, before it could really take root.'

'And you think me walking through the passageway will do the same thing?'

'It's got to be better than avoiding it forever. I could stand at one end and wave a Double Decker if you think a reward would help.'

However much I don't want to do what he suggests, there is a certain logic to it.

'I think I need a bigger reward than a bloody Double Decker,' I tell him.

'Name it.'

'You mentioned Chinese takeaway just now. I think wine is called for as well.'

'Fine. I'll stand at the end of the passageway waving the menu and a corkscrew. How about that?'

I sigh. 'Come on then, let's get this over with.'

* * *

Walking through the passageway the first time wasn't actually as bad as I feared. Callum walked alongside me and that helped me to feel safe. The second time was a bit hairier because he stayed at the end while I did it, and the third time the bastard vanished completely and I practically ran through. I know he was trying to

help, but it took my heart rate a good while to settle down afterwards. In all, he made me do it six times and, although I'm not
completely comfortable with it, it did help a bit. I've promised I
will look at the self-defence thing, and I have had a read of the
leaflet while he's been out collecting the takeaway. It does actually
look good and they offer an online course, so I might have a chat
with Emma and see if she wants to do it with me.

'Here you go, one reward as promised,' he announces, placing
the takeaway bag and two bottles of wine on the table. 'I got extra
wine in case one bottle wasn't enough.'

'I can see you've thought of everything.' I grin, opening the
bottle nearest me and pouring two generous glasses.

I study him as he unpacks the takeaway, placing the little boxes
on the table and opening each one up. Emma's question is
bouncing round in my head. Do I fancy him? He's much more
attractive than he realises, particularly with his new hairstyle and
glasses. Yes, fine. I fancy him. Do I love him? That's a much more
difficult question.

'What?' Callum asks.

'Hm?'

'You're staring at me. Have I got something stuck to my face?'

'No. I was just trying to work something out. Can I ask you a
question?'

'As long as we can eat at the same time. I'm starving.' As if to
emphasise the point, he helps himself to a pancake and starts
loading it up with crispy duck, cucumber, spring onion and hoisin
sauce.

'Do you like living with me?' I ask as I start loading my own
pancake.

'Where has that come from?'

'I was just wondering. I expect it's very different from living
with Mark.'

'You can say that again, but you know that. We've talked about it before.'

'You're right. Sorry.' I focus my attention on the food in the hope that the question I'm actually trying to ask will magically pop into my head.

'What about the fact that I'm a girl?' I ask lamely when we've eaten all the duck and dished out the main courses.

'What about it?'

'Does that bother you?'

'No. Should it?'

'I don't know. I just thought you might miss the blokey banter that you and Mark had, I suppose.'

'Yeah, because we both know I am Mr Blokey Banter. What is this really about? Are you not enjoying living with me?'

'No! Quite the opposite,' I say, more forcefully than I intended. 'I love living with you actually. I just wasn't sure whether you found me... annoying sometimes.'

This conversation is not going at all how I want it to, but how do I ask Callum if he fancies me without actually asking?

'Why would I find you annoying?'

'I don't know. I talk a lot and you like the quiet; maybe it gets on your nerves but you're too polite to say anything.'

'Are you sure you didn't hit your head last night? You're making precious little sense right now. Yes, I'm quiet, but that isn't because I don't enjoy talking to you. You're very easy to talk to, and you make me laugh. I feel' – he pauses – 'comfortable around you.'

OK, time to change the subject. That's totally not the answer I was looking for. 'Comfortable' makes me sound more like the hideous dinosaur slippers than the potential love of his life.

'What are your plans for the rest of the evening?' I ask instead.

'I thought I might turn off the lights and listen to some music. I've got a playlist lined up.'

'Sounds a bit depressing.'

'No, it's good. Taking away all the visual stimulation helps me to focus on the music without being distracted. I might take some wine in as well. You can join me if you like. I have a spare pair of headphones.'

My initial thought is to tell him that I'd almost rather go back and run through the passageway a few more times than spend my Saturday night sitting in the dark with headphones on, but that's swiftly pushed aside by my second thought. I'd be sitting in the dark with headphones on, *with Callum*. Worryingly, despite the earlier comparison to his slippers, my heart still does a little flutter.

'Why not?' I say to him with a smile.

'There will be some classical music, I'm warning you.'

'You'd better play it loud then,' I tell him with a grin.

When we've finished eating and have cleared up, I follow Callum into his room, having topped up my glass first. He reaches into a drawer and pulls out two pairs of enormous over-ear headphones, offering one set to me. I settle myself on his thinking couch while he fiddles about pairing everything up to his computer and turning off the main light. The only illumination in the room now comes from the four enormous screens.

'Ready?' he asks. 'We're going to start with a bit of Supertramp.'

'The logical song?'

'No. That's the song that everyone knows, and it's good, but we're going to listen to "Fool's Overture". It's about ten minutes long, and the first five are purely instrumental. Roger Hodgson, who wrote it, always says that it's made up of three snippets of songs that he had in his head and decided to glue together, but people have all sorts of other theories about what it's actually about.'

He puts his headphones on and gestures to me to do the same

before flicking a switch that turns off the monitors and plunges us into complete darkness.

OK. This is weird. I mean, I understand his point about depriving the other senses so you can focus on the music, and I am enjoying the haunting piano melody, but it's merely a background to the thing I'm most aware of, which is Callum. Even though I can't see him and we're not touching, I'm acutely aware of him next to me. Although the thinking couch is a large piece of furniture, the seating area on it is not very wide, so I can feel the warmth of him and it's doing strange things to me. It's taking all my willpower not to reach out and touch him. It's agony.

'What did you think?' he asks as the monitors come back to life at the end of the song.

'Oh, umm, yes,' I babble. 'Very atmospheric, and the bit at the end was unexpected.'

'He's got a very distinctive voice, hasn't he? Right, time for something classical. I'm going to try you on Beethoven's Seventh Symphony, second movement. It's also haunting, but in a different way.'

I take a sip of wine while he sets it up, and then the monitors go off again and we're plunged back into darkness. I wasn't lying when I told him I'd never really 'got' classical music, but this is totally different to the boring stuff they used to play us in music appreciation classes at school. The melody is sad and incredibly moving. In my imagination, I can see it as the soundtrack to one of those black and white films from the Second World War. This one is of a column of refugees, trudging wearily along the road in the snow and I'm surprised to feel that my eyes are wet. As the strings build, it's almost too much for me, and I reach for Callum's hand in the darkness. By the time it finishes, I feel totally wrung out.

'Not into classical then?' Callum asks with a smile as the monitors come back on and he gently withdraws his hand.

'That was incredible,' I sigh. 'So sad, and yet so beautiful.'

'Hmm.'

'What?'

'I was going to move on to some Elton John, but looking at the effect that had on you, I'm going to try something different. This is a longer one, so if you need to top up your wine or go to the loo, now would be a good time.'

'I'm ready,' I tell him after I've topped up my wine.

'OK, this is Mozart's Requiem. He actually didn't write it all, because he died before he finished it, so quite a lot of it was written by a chap called Süssmayr based on scraps of paper that Mozart left. I'm selecting a few movements that I think might appeal to you.'

Once more the screens go dark and the orchestral music starts, but this time it's accompanied by a choir. As the melodies soar and intertwine around each other, I shift closer and curl into him. Callum doesn't stir but, after a minute or so, I become aware of his arm gently reaching around me and his hand resting on my shoulder, before his thumb starts gently stroking the base of my neck. This is bliss. I feel like I belong here, almost like I've come home somehow, and I can feel all the tension of the last twenty-four hours draining out of me. As the choir starts singing 'Confutatis', I place my hand over his and guide it gently to my mouth, kissing each of his fingers in turn before returning it to my shoulder and leaving my hand covering his. I'm tingling all over now and my breathing is shallow. My heart is thumping away so hard in my chest, I'm surprised he can't feel it.

The music turns more melancholy and, almost like a moth drawn to the light, I turn my head and seek his lips with mine. When they touch, it's like fireworks. Our lips are barely brushing, but it's the most erotic sensation I've felt in ages. His breath is as shallow as my own, I note as I reach up and cup his face in my hands so that I can kiss him more deeply. Our lips part, letting our tongues slide ever so gently against each other, and I can't get enough of it. Callum has either been getting lessons from somewhere or he's a natural born kisser. I am literally fizzing with lust.

And then the music stops and everything changes. Callum can't seem to get away from me fast enough and keeps his back turned to me as he switches the monitors and then the overhead light back on.

'It's been a long day. I probably ought to think about getting some sleep. Do you mind?' he asks, leaving me in no doubt that my presence is no longer welcome.

29

What the hell just happened?

For the second night in a row, I can't sleep as I lie in bed trying to make sense of Callum's abrupt change of mood earlier. The elation and excitement has gone, replaced by a leaden feeling of misery and dread. Have I just ruined everything? Are we going to be so stilted that we have to start avoiding each other? I don't think I could bear that. What if he decides the only option is to move out? Oh God, I've made such a mess of everything.

I wonder what he's thinking. Maybe he's lying awake in bed the same as me. We need to talk about this, I realise. We're both adults and we've done nothing wrong. Well, I might have done, but it's nothing we can't sort out by just talking it through rationally. If he's not into me, then I'll have to find a way to live with that.

But you don't kiss people you're not into like he kissed me!

This is hopeless. Once again, I throw back the covers and flick on the light. I'll go out into the living room and see if his light is on. If it is, I'm going to bang on his door until he talks to me. I open my door and look across the living room.

There is no light under Callum's door.

What now? Even though I'm desperate to have it out with him, I don't think waking him up is going to put him in the right frame of mind for the type of conversation we need to have. I'm not sure I can wait until the morning though. What if I do manage to go to sleep, and then he sneaks out before I wake up? He could be out for the whole day, and I don't think I can keep this bottled up for that long. He might be lying in the dark like I was, I suppose. Retreating back into my room, I pick up my phone and type out a message.

Are you awake?

I watch for what feels like hours, but the ticks stay resolutely grey. He's either asleep or ignoring me. With a groan, I turn out the light, climb back into bed and pull the duvet over me, clasping my phone to my chest. How on earth am I going to fix this? What if I can't fix this? I should *never* have kissed him. If only I could go back and do it differently, not ruin everything.

I'm probably on my third nightmare scenario when I feel my phone vibrate. I bring it out from under the duvet and unlock it to find that the ticks are blue and Callum has replied.

Yes.

Now what? Do I go and bang on his door? Perhaps, given his earlier discomfort, me going into his room in my pyjamas isn't going to send the right signal, so I type out another message.

I'm sorry.

This time, the ticks go blue immediately, and I can see that he's typing. I sit up in bed and turn on the bedside light.

No, I'm the one that should say sorry. I shouldn't have taken advantage of you like that.

How on earth has he figured that one out?

If anyone took advantage, it was me. I kissed you, remember?

His reply is instant.

You're emotionally vulnerable after the attack. I should have been a better friend.

I'm annoyed now. He obviously thinks this is all because of the mugging, like Emma did. I angrily bash out my reply.

I think I know my own mind. If you're not attracted to me, have the guts to just say it, rather than trying to play the morality card.

The ticks go blue, but that's it. He's not typing anything. I sit and wait, but nothing. I'm on the verge of getting out of bed again and storming across to his room when he finally replies.

I am attracted to you. That's the problem.

Enough. My reply is terse.

Living room. Now.

I throw off my bedclothes again and wrap my dressing gown around me before marching out into the sitting room and flicking on the light. After a moment, Callum's door opens and he comes out too. He looks the very picture of misery, and suddenly I'm not sure what to say to him.

'Tea?' I offer eventually.

'Please.' He plonks himself down on the sofa. I try out various opening lines in my head while I'm waiting for the kettle to boil but nothing adequate comes, so in the end I carry the mugs out and set them on the table before sitting down on the sofa opposite him. I'm obviously feeling the need to protect myself, as I draw my legs up against my chest and wrap my arms around them. Callum sips his tea but says nothing.

'What's going on, Callum?' I ask eventually.

'Nothing. Everything. Oh, I don't know!' he cries.

'Talk to me.'

'I can't. I feel so stupid.'

'Why?'

'Because this isn't how it works, OK?'

'How what works?'

'Look. I know you tell me not to run myself down and stuff, but let's be realistic. People like me don't get to be with people like you.'

'I'm sorry, you're going to have to explain. You're not making sense.'

'Alex. Do you have even the faintest idea how beautiful you are?'

'Umm. I'm OK, I guess. I think beautiful is stretching it.'

'You would say that, of course you would. The point is that you're way out of my league. There is no way I could ever be enough for someone like you.'

'Who died and gave you the right to make assumptions about what is and what is not enough for me!' I retort. 'Don't I get any say in this?'

'Fine. Have your say.'

'You are enough. You are more than enough. For God's sake, Callum, I wouldn't have kissed you if I thought you weren't enough.'

'You were probably just caught up in the moment. The music, the darkness, a glass or two of wine. But then, in the cold light of day, when you come to your senses and realise that it's just boring old Callum—'

'You're not boring. You're so far from boring it's unbelievable. I've never met anyone like you before. You're kind, thoughtful, and you actually listen to me when I'm prattling on.'

'I'm safe then. Safe might be what you think you want now, particularly after yesterday, but safe wears off really quickly and then what are you left with?'

'This has sod all to do with yesterday. If you understand nothing else, understand that. This is all about your stubborn refusal to believe in yourself. You assume that safe isn't enough, but I don't look at you and see safe. I see a man that I think I'm falling for.'

I don't know who is more shocked by this revelation, him or me. I'm breathing hard, and he's staring at me. Part of me wants more than anything to take back what I've just said, but hearing my voice saying the words has just cemented how I feel about him.

'I'm scared, Alex,' he says eventually.

'That's normal. I'm scared too.'

'Why are you scared?' He seems genuinely confused.

'Let's see. I've just told you I'm falling for you. I've effectively thrown myself at your feet and I'm at your mercy. I'd say that's plenty to be scared about.'

'What do we do?' he asks.

'What do you want to do?'

'We're flatmates. What if it doesn't work out?'

'Then we're in no worse a position than countless people

whose relationships break down when they're living together. We'll never know unless we try though, will we?'

'I'm not... you know... experienced.'

'I'm not expecting bloody Casanova! These are all things we work out on the way. Besides, if your kissing is anything to go by, I reckon you might be a bit of a natural.'

At last, the faintest glimmer of a smile appears on his lips.

'Was it OK?'

'It was more than OK. It was hot as all hell. You did things to me, Callum.'

He blushes. 'I've never kissed anyone like that before.'

'Then aren't I a lucky girl?' I grin at him, and he smiles back.

'Can I kiss you again?'

'I thought you were never going to ask!' I exclaim, getting up and moving to join him on the other sofa.

This time, when our lips meet, there's nothing tentative about it. It's still gentle, but there's an intensity to it as well as we let down our barriers and make ourselves fully vulnerable. It's amazing.

'Callum?' I ask when we come up for air some time later.

'Yes?'

'I'm really glad we've cleared the air, but it's four o'clock in the morning and we probably ought to get some sleep.'

'You're right,' he sighs as I gently start to untangle myself from him. I'm still wearing my pyjamas, but my dressing gown seems to have made a bid for freedom, as it's lying on the floor. I scoop it up and turn towards my room.

'I'll, er, see you in the morning then,' Callum offers as he picks up our mugs of cold tea and carries them towards the kitchen to wash them up. As he stands at the sink, I throw my dressing gown in the general direction of my bedroom door and run up behind him. I press myself up against him, wrapping my arms around his chest. Now that we've cleared the air and I know he feels the same about me as I do about him, I can't bear the idea of being separated from him, even for a few hours.

'Umm, I just had a thought,' I tell him.

'Yes?'

'You could spend the rest of the night in my room, if you like.'

He turns around and I can see the fear has come back into his eyes.

'I don't have any expectations, don't worry,' I reassure him. 'We can just cuddle and go to sleep.'

'I'd like that,' he replies, stacking the clean mugs in the rack to dry and pulling the plug.

'Come on then.' I take his hand and lead him to my room.

When I wake the next morning, I'm briefly convinced that the events of the previous night were nothing more than a wishful dream. It's only when I roll over and see Callum lying next to me that the truth sinks back in. I was as good as my word; we had a fantastic cuddle, with quite a lot more kissing, but it didn't go any further than that. Slowly, I stretch out my arm and stroke his shoulder.

'Mmm-hmmph,' he murmurs, turning over onto his back and slowly opening his eyes. I can see he's just as disorientated as I was yesterday morning for a moment, but then he turns to me and his face lights up.

'Good morning,' he murmurs.

'Good morning yourself. Did you sleep OK?'

'Mm. I had lots of dreams.'

'Was I in any of them?'

He smiles. 'What do you think?'

'I don't know. Now you've discovered what a fantastically

talented kisser you are, I might have been discarded for someone hotter.'

'There is no one hotter than you.'

'You're a smooth talker, you know that? I'm going to have to watch myself around you.'

'I mean it,' he protests.

'I know. And I can't tell you how good it makes me feel to hear you say it. Has anyone ever told you you're pretty hot yourself?'

'I think you may have mentioned it last night. I still don't see it, but I'm happy to take your word for it.'

'You do that. Are we going up the hill for breakfast?'

'Oh, that is a difficult question. We could stay here.'

I smile. 'We could, but I don't think my morning breath is going to do it for you, especially after that takeaway. We've got the whole day ahead of us and, in case you haven't noticed, we're living together so I'm not exactly going anywhere.'

'How is that going to work?' he asks. 'Normally, people don't move in together until they've been dating for a while. This is the wrong way round, isn't it?'

'Think of it as a head start. We've already sorted all the boring things that take the shine off a relationship, like who does the laundry and who takes the bins out, so we can just concentrate on the fun stuff.'

'Hey, don't let me stop you taking the bins out if you get the urge,' he laughs as he slides out from under the duvet and heads for the door. 'Any time, just let me know.'

'That's what I like about you.' I grin as I get out of the bed. 'Always thinking of others.'

I stand in the doorway and watch him as he heads into his bathroom. If I ever wanted to know what winning the lottery feels like, I reckon I have a pretty good idea right now.

30

'Bloody hell, you don't hang around!' Emma exclaims when I call round after lunch to tell her. 'How did you get from "I think I have feelings" to "We're together" in less than twenty-four hours?'

'I didn't say we were together, I just said things had moved on.'

'Tell me what happened. I want to know everything.'

'It kind of started when he invited me to listen to some music with him in the dark.'

'What?'

'I know, I thought it was a bit odd too, but it was really nice, and we ended up having a bit of a kiss.'

'Did you now? And...?'

'And then he suddenly came over all weird and practically threw me out of his room.'

'Hang on. You're jumping ahead and I don't want to miss a single detail. Tell me about the kiss.'

'It was good.'

'Good? That's like saying it was nice. Damning with faint praise.'

'No, Emma, it was *good*.'

'What, as in "fuck me" good?'

I can feel myself blushing as I nod.

'Wow. Who knew he had that in him. But then you say he threw you out? Oh no.' She starts to giggle. 'Wouldn't it be the worst irony if it turned out that you were actually a shit kisser and he couldn't bring himself to break the news to you.'

'Based on what happened later, I don't think that's the case,' I say defensively.

'What do you think it was then? Tell me, blow by blow.'

'We were listening to Mozart's Requiem, possibly my new favourite piece of music by the way, and having a bit of a cuddle, and then we started to kiss. But then, when it ended and he put the lights back on, he wouldn't even face me. He just said he'd had a long day, needed to sleep and asked me to leave.'

'Oh Lord, this is just too good,' she chortles. 'I can almost picture the scene. You and Callum chewing each other's faces off in the dark while listening to moody gothic music, like a couple of lovestruck vampires. Are you going to start dressing in identical black and wearing lots of eyeliner?'

'Fuck off. It was romantic actually. You had to be there.'

'I'm pretty glad I wasn't. So, anyway, why do you think he couldn't face you when the lights came on after this hot session?' She holds her hand out in a fist, slowly extends her index finger, and waggles her eyebrows suggestively.

'An erection? Oh, shit, I didn't think of that. He would have been mortified, knowing him,' I breathe. Emma is practically crying with laughter now. 'I'm glad you think it's so amusing,' I tell her crossly.

'Come on, Alex. Surely you can see the funny side of it? So far, it's literally the most inept love story in the world. What happened next?'

'I'm not sure I want to tell you, if you're going to be like that about it.'

'I'm sorry, I'll try to behave. Please, what happened next?'

'I went to bed, but I couldn't sleep, and we ended up having this conversation about it over WhatsApp, and he told me he thought I was attractive.'

Having tried to compose herself when she realised she was upsetting me, Emma is now laughing again.

'What now?' I ask.

'I'm literally knocked off my feet by the levels of romance here,' she corpses. 'Hey, Vladimir, forget ze chocolates, flowers and champagne. Zey are so last century. Now ve just haff to text ze women and zey come running.'

'It wasn't like that, your Russian accent is appalling and who the hell is Vladimir?'

'All vampires are called Vladimir, it's a well-known fact.'

'Apart from Dracula, you mean.'

'Yeah, apart from him. So, he sends you this amazing text that has you salivating with lust. What then?'

'We went into the sitting room and talked it all through, and then we kissed some more, and then we went to bed. End of story,' I tell her curtly, and she does at least have the grace to stop laughing.

'Same bed or different beds?' she asks after a brief pause.

'Same bed, but nothing happened. We had a cuddle and a kiss. We're taking things slowly.'

'Why? Don't you want to get to the main event? When Mark and I got together, I think we were naked within twenty minutes.'

'I need to go at his pace. It's fine, actually. It means we get to spend time doing things that are normally only cursory waypoints leading to the main event. With Thomas, you could almost set a timer. Two minutes kissing, quick squeeze of the girls, and off we go. This is much better, trust me.'

'Hm. You might be on to something there. I'll give you that one.'

'Thank you. It's about the only positive thing you've had to say so far.'

'I'm sorry. It is funny though. I'm happy for you, really. Are you happy?'

'Honestly?'

'No, I want you to lie,' she says sarcastically. 'Yes, honestly. I'm your best friend. You're supposed to tell me these things.'

'I don't think I've ever been so happy.'

'Wow.'

'I know you don't see it, and he certainly doesn't, but he's got so many amazing qualities. Plus, I already know what he's like to live with, which is a bonus.'

She draws me into a hug and holds me tight for a while. 'I'm delighted for you. You deserve it.'

'There's something else I wanted to talk to you about,' I tell her when we break out of the hug. 'How do you feel about doing a self-defence class with me?'

'No.'

'Why not?'

'Look, I get why you might want to do it, after what happened, and you know I would normally be one hundred per cent behind you. But anything that involves going to the gym and wearing Lycra is totally not me.'

'That's what I said at first, but Callum's found an online course. No gyms, no Lycra.'

'Really? Let's have a look then.'

I show her the leaflet and it's not long before we're logging onto the website to find out more. An hour later, we've completed the first section and fixed a time next weekend for our next session. I check my watch and I'm horrified to see it's nearly six o'clock.

'Shit, I'd better go. Callum will be wondering where I am,' I tell Emma as I leap to my feet.

'Under the boyfriend's thumb already?' she teases.

'It's too early to be referring to him as my boyfriend, and it's nothing to do with anyone being under anyone else's thumb. We normally cook dinner together on a Sunday, that's all.'

* * *

Callum is standing in the kitchen peeling potatoes when I get back.

'I'm sorry I'm late. Emma and I started that self-defence course and lost track of time a bit.'

'It's not a problem. I've put the meat in, and I'll do the vegetables when I've finished these. How was it?'

'Yeah, interesting. What have you been doing?'

'Not a lot. I had a video call with my family.'

'Did you say anything about me?'

'God, no! If I'd told them about you, my sister would be on the first flight down here to check that you're an actual person and not a blow-up doll or an imaginary friend. I have a suspicion my parents think I'm gay, so it will be quite the surprise for them too. These things have to be handled gently and at the right time.'

'Why would your parents think you were gay?'

'The fact that I've never had a girlfriend, I guess. They used to hint every so often that they'd be fine if I was, as if they were trying to tell me it was OK for me to come out of the closet.'

'Based on the extremely scientific evidence that I've accrued over the last twenty-four hours, I don't think you're gay,' I tell him as I wrap my arms around him from behind. 'Of course, I'll have to do a load more tests to be absolutely certain, but I'm looking forward to them.'

'What kind of tests?'

'You'll have to wait and see,' I say, reaching up to give his earlobe a little nibble. 'I think you'll like them though.'

'How am I supposed to concentrate when you're doing that? More importantly, if I accidentally stab myself and have to go to A&E, what on earth will I tell them?'

I sigh and release him. 'Emma said ours was the most inept love story she'd ever heard. Bit rude, don't you think?'

'You told Emma about us?' He doesn't sound pleased.

'Of course I did! She's my best friend. What's the problem? Not embarrassed about me, are you?'

'Of course not. You know how I feel about you. The point is that she'll tell Mark.'

'And that's a bad thing because?'

He doesn't get a chance to answer because we're interrupted by a furious pounding on the door.

'I think you're about to find out,' he sighs.

He crosses to the door and, moments later, Mark breezes in followed by Emma.

'Not *interrupting* anything, are we?' Mark asks before enveloping Callum in a huge bear hug. My eyes flick across to Emma, who mouths 'sorry' at me.

'My, but you're a dark horse aren't you?' Mark continues. 'Congratulations, mate. I can't believe you pulled and I wasn't even there to be your wingman. And all by saucy text message, I hear.'

Callum breaks out of the embrace, absolutely puce with embarrassment. 'It wasn't like that,' he mumbles.

'Of course it was like that. It's so typically you. What was it, a few little nudies to get each other in the mood before moving in for the kill?'

'Leave him alone,' I tell him firmly. 'Apart from the fact you're obviously embarrassing the hell out of him, our sex life is absolutely none of your business.'

'You're right. I'm sorry. I was just excited because this is such a big thing for Callum. I'm over the moon for you, mate, honestly. When's the wedding? I need time to get my best man's speech organised.'

'Mark,' Callum says quietly.

'Yes?'

'Fuck off, will you?'

Mark laughs uproariously. 'Point taken. We'll get out of your hair and leave you two lovebirds to it, whatever *it* is.' He winks lasciviously at this point. 'Come on, Emma, we'd better go and break the news to that girl in the chippy. Of course she'll be heartbroken, poor thing, so no more extra chips for us, I suspect.'

'I am so, so sorry,' she says to Callum as he follows them to the door.

'It's fine. It had to happen sooner or later, and I guess it's better to lance the boil and let him get it out of his system.'

'Do you see why Mark knowing is a bad thing?' Callum says to me once we're alone again and he's back at the sink.

'He was a bit full-on,' I agree.

'Thank you for coming to my defence.'

'I meant what I said. Our sex life is nothing to do with him.'

'We don't have a sex life.'

'Not yet,' I reply with a smile. 'But I'm hopeful.'

31

'How was your weekend?' Sarah asks me when I walk into the office on Monday morning. 'Did your headache clear up?'

It takes me a moment to connect with what she's said. So much has happened that Friday seems like a lifetime ago.

'Yes, thank you,' I reply once I've joined up the dots.

'You still look a little pale.'

'I'm fine, just a bit tired. I think it took it out of me a bit.' This isn't true. The real reason I'm tired and pale is that Callum and I didn't get much sleep for the third night running. He stayed in my room again last night and let's just say things have definitely moved on. My body tingles as I think back to it; although we kept whispering about going slowly, we somehow ended up naked and then there really was no going back from there. The first time was a little brief, but it wasn't long before he got his second wind and the second time was much more satisfying. I might have to banish him to his own room tonight though, as I really have to get some decent sleep soon. The problem is that, while my brain knows I need to sleep, my body definitely has other ideas where Callum is concerned.

'I'm going to get a coffee from down the road, do you want one?' Sarah asks. 'The caffeine might help.'

'Lovely, thank you.'

Although we haven't gone live with our website yet, there is still plenty to do and I quickly get lost in the work. We've had to adapt our model to offer professional valuations, photography and floor-plans as our focus group results proved that people have completely unrealistic expectations of what their house is worth and very little idea about how to make it look appealing, so we've been searching out freelancers in each area that we can pair up with. Our aim is to cover the whole of the south-east of England on launch, with plans to expand into other areas later, and it looks like we're pretty much there. The only place we haven't covered yet is Eastbourne, and I've got a list of people to call today to see if we can fix that. Sarah is working with a company that's going to do various bits of magic to ensure that we are the first listing people see when they search online so, after drinking our coffees, we each bury ourselves in our work, not even pausing to chat with Ashleigh when she brings the post up shortly before midday. In fact, it's not until after lunch that I get around to sifting through it. There are a couple of envelopes for Sarah, but I'm surprised to find a letter addressed to me. I open it and slide out the card inside. Although I haven't seen it for several months, the female silhouette is instantly recognisable. The text, however, catches me by surprise.

Goldenschafft Productions is delighted to invite you to the launch party
for their first feature-length film,
BIG WANGER ABBEY
on Saturday 12th December.
Drinks and Canapés from 6 p.m.
RSVP

My first reaction is that this must be some kind of mistake, but then I turn the card over and read the spidery handwriting on the other side.

Alex,

Hoping you'll be able to join us, as the original idea came from you. Please bring a plus one if you'd like to.

Looking forward to seeing you,

Gary and Gail xx

'What's that?' Sarah asks, indicating the card in my hand.

'It's an invitation to a party in just over a month's time from a couple I sold a house to,' I tell her.

'Bit odd, isn't it? We don't normally get party invitations from clients.'

'This one is especially odd.' I fill her in on the whole story of Gary and Gail, along with Gary's feature film ambitions.

'So he's made a porno in the style of Jane Austen?' Sarah asks at the end, clearly disbelieving.

'I very much doubt it bears any resemblance to anything Jane wrote.'

She picks up the invitation and studies it. 'It says here that the idea came from you. What's that about?'

'Honestly, I don't know. I remember him talking about it when I showed them the house, and he asked me to name some Jane Austen novels, but I didn't contribute any more than that. I don't have a secret second career in adult entertainment, if that's what you're thinking.'

'I'm glad to hear it.' She smiles. 'Although I guess it's not technically a conflict of interest, clients might struggle to take you seriously if they'd seen you, how can I put it, "performing". What are you going to do?'

'Easy. I'll call him and tell him I can't go.'

'Hmm.'

'What?'

'I'm just wondering. He's obviously a wealthy guy from what you've told me and there might be other people in his position there. Could be a good networking opportunity.'

'Hang on. Are you expecting me to swan up to porn central and start handing out my business card? I don't think that will end well. They'll probably think I'm touting for a completely different sort of business!'

'That's not what I'm suggesting at all. All I'm thinking is that, should some of these people decide that they like the area, knowing a friendly estate agent is going to be a bonus. You could take Ashleigh with you.'

'Definitely not. Gary would take one look at her and try to sign her up, the same as he did me. No, if I'm going to do this at all, which I'm not at all sure I am, I'll take Callum.'

'Your nerdy flatmate? Would he be up for it?'

'My boyfriend, and probably not.'

'Hold on. When did this happen?'

'Over the weekend, actually. Someone tried to mug me on Friday evening and he came to my rescue. Things kind of went from there.'

'Oh, Alex. I'm so sorry. Are you OK?'

'Yeah, I think so.'

'And this... thing you've started with your flatmate. Is it a good idea, particularly on the back of a trauma like that?'

I smile at her. 'Don't worry. I know what I'm doing, and I actually think it's one of the best ideas I've ever had.'

* * *

'You want me to do what?' Callum's face is a mask of horror.

'I want you to come with me to the launch party of a porno movie,' I tell him, handing him the invitation.

'I don't do parties at the best of times, you know that. And this... this is next level stuff.'

'You'll be fine, just ask questions like you've been practising. They're just ordinary people with an unusual job, that's all.'

'But that's exactly my worry. "So, tell me more about your work" is not a question I want to be asking a porn star.'

'Hm. I get your point. Sarah was kind of keen for me to go though, so I don't think she'll be best pleased if I back out.'

'What's it got to do with her?'

'She's got it into her head that it's a good opportunity for me to play the friendly estate agent card in the hope that it might bring in extra business.'

'That's not really how it works though, is it. Most people don't buy a house because they like the agent. They buy the house because they like the house, regardless of who's selling it.'

'Indeed, but if they're buying a house, the chances are they're selling a house, and that's where we come in with our new online model.'

'Seems tenuous, and I doubt that Gary and Gail, whoever they are, are going to welcome you touting for business at their party. You'd do better sponsoring something.'

'I'm not sure sponsoring a porn film is the way to launch a business, and Gary and Gail are the people behind Goldenschafft. They're nice, in a bonkers kind of way.'

'You're really not selling it.'

I sigh. 'I know. I don't really want to do it either, but maybe we can go, show our faces for ten minutes or so and then make an excuse to leave. That way, everybody's happy.'

'Ten minutes?'

'Well, half an hour, tops. You can do half an hour, can't you?'

'You won't leave me?'

'I'll be right by your side throughout.'

'We won't have to watch the film, will we?' he asks after a pause.

'I don't think so. It doesn't say anything about that on the invitation.'

'What am I supposed to say if someone asks me what I do?' he asks suddenly, concern back on his face.

'Sorry, why is that a problem?'

'If I tell a porn star that I'm a penetration tester, they're bound to get the wrong impression.'

'I hadn't thought of that,' I giggle. 'What would that involve, I wonder?'

'I dread to think.'

'Cut!' I yell in what I assume is the tone a film director would use. 'We need to get the penetration tester in to check how much penetration has occurred.'

'Argh, make it stop.' He covers his ears.

'I don't remember you being so squeamish last night,' I tease him.

'That's different and you know it is. I've had an idea. Why don't you ask Emma to go with you to this thing instead of me?'

'Would you prefer that?'

'I think I would. I hate letting you down, but I think this needs someone much more socially skilled than I am.'

'You're not letting me down,' I reassure him. 'It was a big ask and I totally understand why you don't want to do it.' I get up and cross the room to my phone.

'No, sod it,' he declares forcefully just as I'm about to press the call button. 'I need to stop being such a snowflake about these things. I'll come with you. As you say, they're just ordinary people with unusual jobs. And, if I can pull this off, then other social situations are going to be a walk in the park.'

'Are you sure? I'm happy to call Emma.'

'Of course I'm not sure, but I know I'll feel like I've fallen at the first hurdle if I don't do it. You've asked me to come with you to something that's important for you, and what kind of man would I be if I said no simply because I'm squeamish?'

'Do you know what kind of man you are?' I ask him as I rejoin him on the sofa and wrap my arms around him.

'I like to hope I'm one of the good guys,' he murmurs as our lips come together.

'You are. You're good and kind and brave and also incredibly sexy right now.'

'I am?'

I slip my hands under his top and run them over his chest. 'Oh yes. In fact, there's one more thing I need to ask you to do, Mr Penetration Tester,' I tell him as I start to unbutton my shirt.

He smiles. 'I'm sure I can help with that.'

32

'Are you sure you're OK? You haven't said a word since we left home,' I ask Callum as I slot my car into a vacant space in the parking area outside Gary and Gail's house. It's the day of the party and I can see guests milling about inside through the open curtains. After Callum agreed to come with me, we both kind of forgot about it in the excitement of our new relationship, so it's crept up on us somewhat. Callum has 'officially' moved into my bedroom now, although he's kept his room as a study and we still sit in there sometimes, listening to music in the dark together. I am, not to put too fine a point on it, idiotically happy, and my heart fills with love as I glance across at him now. I can see the discomfort on his face but he's doing it anyway. For me.

'I'm nervous,' he replies, 'but I'm also trying to think about questions I can ask that will keep me out of trouble.'

'I'll be right next to you, don't worry. And remember, it may be hard work but we've only got to keep it up for half an hour.'

'Don't do that!' he exclaims.

'What?'

'Talk about "hard work" and "keeping it up". That's the problem with this kind of thing. Everything is innuendo.'

'I think you're reading too much into it.'

'Hm. We'll see. Shall we go then?'

Callum holds my hand tightly as we ring the doorbell. After a moment, the door is flung open and I come face to face with Gail, dressed in a tight-fitting glittery dress that leaves pretty much nothing to the imagination. Behind her, I spot the most enormous Christmas tree, sagging under the weight of all the baubles and lights.

'You're here!' she beams, pulling us inside and enveloping us in a bosomy hug that's heavily scented with some kind of floral perfume. 'Gary will be so pleased. He's been telling everyone you're his muse, did you know that? Let's get a drink from the bar and then I'll introduce you to some people.'

'Muse?' Callum mouths at me, and I shrug my shoulders.

'Here,' she says, proffering two glasses. 'Champagne. Nothing but the best for our Alex. I'm sorry, love, I didn't catch your name,' she says to Callum.

'This is Callum, my boyfriend,' I tell her. 'Also, I hate to be rude, but I'm driving. Do you have anything soft?'

Gail looks Callum up and down, clearly appraising him, before gripping his arm and squeezing it through his shirt.

'Hm. Nothing soft about you,' she remarks as Callum begins to flush scarlet. 'You've got yourself a good one here, I reckon,' she tells me before turning back to the man standing behind the bar. 'Dave, what have we got that's soft?'

'I could whip you up a virgin Bloody Mary if you like?' Dave offers.

'That sounds lovely, thank you, Dave,' I reply.

'Gary's just finishing setting everything up,' Gail tells me as Dave adds tomato juice and lemon juice to a glass filled with ice.

'Do you like it spicy?' Dave asks, causing Callum to snort next to me.

'Umm, medium spicy please,' I reply, taking great care not to look at Callum because I can feel him shaking and I just know we're going to have an unforgivable attack of church giggles if we're not careful.

'Right,' Gail announces once I've got my drink. 'Let's meet some people.' She drags us over to a couple chatting by the fireplace. 'Ryan, Lynsey, this is Alex and Callum. Ryan plays the abbot in the film, and Lynsey is one of the girls who gets lost in the enchanted forest.'

'The muse?' Ryan asks, and Gail nods.

'Delighted to meet you,' Ryan says as he holds out his hand for me to shake. 'Gary says he couldn't have done it without your inspiration.'

'I'm sure he could,' I reply. 'All I did was reel off some Jane Austen titles.'

'That's not how he tells it and, if I were you, I'd take the credit. Rumour is we could be up for the cock door.'

'Cock door?' For some reason, an image of a cuckoo clock striking the hour comes into my head, only there's a penis popping in and out instead of the cuckoo.

'Yes, it's French for golden cock,' Lynsey explains. 'It's our industry's equivalent of the *Palme d'Or* at the Cannes Film Festival. If Gary wins it with *Big Wanger Abbey*, that firmly establishes him as one of the greats.'

'Ah, OK. *Coq d'Or*. Sorry, I was thinking of something else.'

Before either of them can reply, we're distracted by the sound of someone tapping a glass.

'Where's my muse?' Gary's voice calls as people fall silent. 'I know you're in here, Alex. Come and join me up at the front.'

'Go!' Lynsey practically shoves me in Gary's direction.

'Ah, there you are.' Gary smiles as his eyes land on me. He's wearing black jeans and another white shirt open too far down his chest, but that's not what stands out about him. His jacket is obviously made from the same material as Gail's dress, and it's sparkling in the lights, giving him a slightly camp air. He places his arm proprietorially round my shoulder when I reach him and turns me to face the room. I'm deeply uncomfortable and lock my eyes onto Callum, who looks exactly how I feel.

'Ladies and gentlemen,' Gary begins. 'A lot of you will know that I've wanted to make a feature length film for ages, but I was lacking the vision, the little spark that would give me the plot. And then I met Alex here. She'll tell you that she had nothing to do with it because she's modest, but I firmly believe that we wouldn't have the film we're about to see without her inspiration. Not only that, but she's also opened my eyes to a whole genre of historical novels that we can repurpose, and I'm looking forward to starting shooting the next film in this series, *Count Fuckula,* soon. So, please put your hands together for Alex!'

I don't think I've ever been so embarrassed. I can feel waves of heat coming off my face as the room erupts with applause. I want to run away, but Gary's grip is firm around my shoulders.

'Right, everyone, grab a seat,' Gary announces as Gail points a remote control at a receiver in the corner of the room. Instantly, people start locating chairs and sitting down as the curtains close, the lights dim and a large screen descends from the ceiling.

'Umm, Gary,' I murmur. 'I'm sorry to do this, but I need to find my boyfriend and slip away.'

'Nonsense!' he replies, completely unaware of my discomfort. 'You've only just arrived, and you must be curious to see what I've done with your idea. I've saved you a seat with Gail and me, up front.'

I can honestly say that the next hour is the most surreal of my life. The film starts innocuously enough, with four young women on some sort of car journey, chatting happily. The camera angles are a little more risqué than you'd get in mainstream cinema and their clothes are almost uncomfortably tight, but it's all pretty tame so far. The road gets darker as they enter some woodland, and then the car breaks down. Inevitably, there is no mobile phone signal, and a rather stilted debate follows where the camera focuses on them chewing their lips coquettishly while trying to decide what to do, before they conclude their best bet is to stick together and go to look for help. The camera follows closely as they go further into the forest, until they evidently pass through some sort of invisible barrier. The tight shorts and crop tops of earlier disappear, replaced by rather cheap looking imitation Regency wear.

'It's a magic forest, see?' Gary whispers to me. 'They've been transported back in time.'

'Ah,' I reply.

The girls are understandably perturbed by this turn of events, but when they turn to go back the way they came, they find their path blocked by the invisible barrier. Suddenly, a figure dressed in a monk's habit comes out of the undergrowth and the audience erupts in rapturous applause and whooping.

'Greetings, fair maidens,' he says woodenly. 'What bringest thou unto the enchanted forest?'

'Umm, yeah, hi,' the girl I know as Lynsey replies. 'We were, like, driving through the forest and our car broke down. On top of that, there's no bloody mobile signal. Have you got a phone we can use?'

'What language is this that thou speakest?' the monk replies. The Royal Shakespeare Company are not going to have any sleepless nights over this drivel, and I'm struggling to contain my giggles. 'Dost thou sayest unto me that there is a problem with thy carriage?'

'I wanted to get a remark about undercarriage in there,' Gary whispers. 'But I couldn't make it fit.'

I'm biting my lip now, trying desperately not to laugh.

'Noble monk,' one of the other girls pipes up. 'We, umm, are in great need of succour.' The audience titters predictably at this point. 'Thou art correct about our carriage, and we need a man with the right tool to help us.' She runs her tongue over her top lip suggestively, and I'm very glad the audience chooses that moment to erupt in applause again, as I can't stop a snort of laughter escaping. I wonder how Callum is coping with this?

'Also,' the third girl says, pressing unconvincingly against the invisible barrier, 'we appear to be trapped.'

'Once inside the enchanted forest, thou canst not leave without the permission of the abbot,' the monk intones woodenly. 'And he only granteth his permission to those who please him and obey his will.'

Dear God, this is awful.

'We are thine humble servants. Tell us the will of the abbot and we will doest everything to please him,' Lynsey says, now running her tongue over her lip as well.

If I thought the dialogue was bad so far, most of what follows is excruciating, and there are several points where I have to avert my eyes, while trying to block out the soundtrack of moans and grunts. Every so often there's a whoop or a cheer from the audience as a scene concludes, new characters appear, or the actors contort into a new position.

'We're close to the grand finale,' Gary tells me after what feels like an age. 'Massive gang bang with all the cast, and then the women will be magically spirited back to their working car with only a vague memory of what happened.'

When the lights finally come up at the end, I cast around the room looking for Callum, eventually finding him sitting at the back with Lynsey and Ryan. He looks as shell-shocked as I feel, and I want nothing more than to get him out of here now. Sarah and Roxanne will have to go without their networking.

Gary is being mobbed by his cast, so I sidle over to Callum, grab his hand and whisper 'Come on.' Thankfully, nobody seems to notice as we make our way over to the door and slip out into the night.

'That was…' Callum begins as we turn out onto the road. I wait for him to continue, but he seems to have run out of words.

'I am so sorry. Are you OK?'

'I'm not going to be able to look anyone wearing a habit in the eye for quite a long time, that's for certain. Also, sitting next to Lynsey and Ryan while watching them, well, that was a frankly bizarre experience. When it got to the end of their scene, they actually high-fived each other.'

'I had Gary giving me plot updates all the way through. He genuinely believes he's made a masterpiece.'

'Time and the *Coq d'Or* will tell, I suppose.'

'Do you know, when Ryan first said it, I didn't realise it was French.'

'Me neither. I was trying very hard not to imagine what it was while all sorts of unsavoury images came into my mind.'

'I know exactly what you mean. Mine was a kind of penis cuckoo clock.'

He chuckles softly in the darkness. 'I'll tell you one thing, Alex Griffiths. Being around you is never dull.'

I take my hand off the steering wheel and squeeze his thigh briefly. 'Thank you.'

'What for?'

'For everything. For putting up with shit like this so calmly. For moving in with me. For being there when I needed you. For being so much more than I ever imagined. For making me feel like the luckiest girl in the world when I'm with you.'

There's a long pause, and for a moment I worry that I've embarrassed him, but then he speaks.

'I was talking to Mum the other day. They're getting very excited about meeting you, but she said something interesting.'

'Oh yes?' My chest tightens. We're travelling up to Scotland to spend a long weekend with his parents in a couple of weeks, and I'm very nervous about making a good impression.

'She said, "The most important barometer of a relationship is whether the other person brings out the best in you. I can tell, just by looking at you and listening to you, that Alex is doing that."'

'Wow. No pressure then.'

'It's true though. I thought I was happy enough as I was. I certainly wasn't unhappy. But, since I've met you, it's like you've brought a part of me to life that I didn't even know existed. I know it's a cliché, but I feel like you've completed me. You've made me whole, and I can't imagine life without you in it now. Sorry, that sounds needier than I meant it to. The point is that you make me want to be better.'

'It doesn't sound needy at all,' I tell him. 'Because I feel exactly the same.'

He reaches across in the darkness and places his hand on my thigh. The warmth of it through my dress makes me tingle. I glance across at him and smile.

'You're enough as you are,' I tell him. 'You'll always be enough.'

EPILOGUE

EIGHTEEN MONTHS LATER

'It's really strange being just the two of us in this flat again,' Emma remarks. We're sitting in the kitchen, sipping coffee and picking listlessly at the croissants I bought in the supermarket yesterday.

'It is, isn't it?' I agree. 'It feels like a lifetime ago that we first moved in here. Are you excited?'

'I don't know if excited is the word. I'm not having doubts or anything, it's just surreal that this day is finally here. What do you think the boys will be doing right now?'

'Probably much the same as us. Mark will be contemplating his upcoming marriage to the love of his life—'

'Scrolling social media on his phone, more like,' she interrupts.

'Yes, or that. Callum will be fretting about his best man's speech. I've lost count of how many versions we're up to now. He really wants to do his best for Mark, but public speaking is not his forte.'

'Aww, bless him. It's good practice though, isn't it. Only a month to go and it'll be your turn. I'll be an old hand by then, so I'll be able to give you all the lowdown.'

I glance down at the engagement ring on my finger and smile.

We chose it together, but every time I look at it, it reminds me of Callum. Like him, it's gently understated; a solitaire diamond on a simple band. It's completely different to the massive rock on Emma's finger, but I know which one I prefer.

'Do you think he would ever have plucked up the courage to ask you?' Emma asks.

'It wasn't that he lacked courage, but he wanted it to be perfect and I think it all got away from him a bit. Did I tell you how I found out what he was up to?'

'No.'

I smile at the memory. 'He left his notebook of ideas open on his desk. I wasn't snooping, but I happened to glance at it and it was obvious what it was.'

'That's not very Callum. I'd see him more as a password protected spreadsheet sort of guy.'

'That's what I said, but he told me some things have to be analogue and his love life is one of them.'

'Bless him. Wasn't he annoyed that you rumbled him?'

'I didn't tell him until afterwards, and he was so happy when I proposed to him that it was almost better than if we'd done it the traditional way round.'

'It's so typical of you. Where most of us would be sitting around waiting for the man to propose and getting steadily more pissed off, you just threw caution to the wind and went for it.'

'You make me sound reckless. It was obvious from the list that he would say yes, and he did get down on one knee and ask me after we bought the ring.'

'Did he? You never told me that.'

'Didn't I? I'm sure I did. He did it right in the middle of the shop. The assistants gave us a round of applause.'

'I think I'd remember a detail like that.'

'Evidently not. You've been a bit busy, so it's not surprising you don't remember everything.'

Emma and Mark appear to have been competing with each other to see who can come up with the most lavish idea. Where Callum and I have opted for a church wedding with a simple buffet afterwards, they have gone to town. Their ceremony and reception are both being held at Hever Castle and, while it will look stunning in the photographs, I'm sure the cost must be eyewatering. Just to make things more complicated, they decided to buy a house at the same time, which they moved into a couple of weeks ago. They're evidently not planning on hanging around where starting a family is concerned either, as the smallest bedroom has already been set aside as a nursery. Callum and I have looked at a couple of properties (I am an estate agent, after all), but we've decided to stay put in the flat until we can afford somewhere detached where Callum can play his music at the volume he likes without the neighbours complaining.

'Michelle will be here in a minute. Have you finished with this stuff?' I ask, indicating the remnants of breakfast.

'Yeah. I'm not really hungry.'

As if on cue, the buzzer goes and I cross the room to press the button that opens the downstairs door.

'Where's my blushing bride?' Michelle sings as she drags her bags of equipment over the threshold.

'Hi, Michelle,' Emma answers.

'You don't sound very excited. It's your wedding day!'

'I was just saying to Alex, I think I'm a bit nervous.'

'That's normal, love. Come and take a seat for me. I'll make you so fabulous you won't be able to be nervous. What time are the other bridesmaids arriving?'

'I told them to come at eleven, to give you a chance to get Emma and me out of the way,' I tell her.

'Great. Let's get cracking then.' She starts running her hands through Emma's auburn locks appraisingly. 'Any chance of a coffee?'

'Absolutely.'

'Thomas says hi, by the way,' she calls as I make my way into the kitchen and start filling the kettle.

'Oh yes? How is he?'

'Loving York. He says the job is challenging but he's really enjoying it, and he and Caroline think they'll probably stay up there for the foreseeable future. Jack and I are thinking of going up to visit in a month or two.'

'I'm glad he's happy.'

'Yeah. He's settled at last, and he and Jack are getting on better than I've ever known. I think Caroline is a good influence on him, not that you weren't, obviously.'

I smile. 'Relax. You can be nice about her. I'm not going to get offended.'

'I should hope not,' she retorts. 'Talking of which, how is lovely Callum?'

'He's fine.' I hand her a coffee and retreat to the sofa to watch her work her magic.

'Trust her,' I tell a terrified-looking Emma. 'You are going to look stunning.'

* * *

It's a beautiful summer day as I follow Emma and her father through the Italian garden at Hever Castle towards the Loggia, where the ceremony is being held. The garden is in full bloom, but I barely notice because I'm concentrating so hard on making sure I don't trip over my dress or get a heel wedged in a crack. Michelle has done a fantastic job on Emma, who now sports a half up, half down hairstyle that complements her dress and veil beautifully. The other bridesmaids and I have our hair down and side swept in contrast.

Emma's nerves have obviously dissipated on the journey over, if the beam on her face as her father helped her out of the car is anything to go by. I'm also excited, but for different reasons. As we pass through the guests, my eyes alight on Callum, who is looking absolutely gorgeous in his morning suit. He blows me a surreptitious kiss as I approach, and I grin at him.

The ceremony itself is brief, much shorter than ours will be, I think. We've chosen a couple of hymns that we both remember from school days and a reading from Corinthians that Morag told us afterwards was 'the one *every* wedding couple has'. I like her, but she is very different from Callum and sometimes verges on the rude side of direct. While we're waiting for the photographer to get himself organised after we've filed back out into the sunshine, I feel a hand slip around my waist.

'You look incredible,' Callum murmurs, leaning in to give me a kiss on the exposed side of my neck.

'Thanks. You don't look too bad yourself. Did you get your speech sorted?'

'Yeah. I took out the story about the ladyboy incident in Thailand in the end.'

'Really? It wasn't that risqué.'

'Maybe not, but he's going to be returning the favour in a few weeks and I don't want to give him any ammunition.'

'Ah yes. Good point.'

It's immensely frustrating being forced to sit at the opposite end of the top table during the wedding breakfast, because I know Callum will be getting more and more anxious as the moment for his speech draws closer and I want to be there for him, but in the end my fears are unfounded. He stands and delivers it flawlessly, with dry humour that the audience obviously loves if the ripples of laughter and applause are anything to go by. As soon as the speeches are done and people start moving around, I slip round the table to find him.

'That was brilliant!' I tell him as I wrap my arms around him and kiss him. 'You literally had them eating out of the palm of your hand.'

'I was so nervous. I was shaking like a leaf,' he tells me.

'You wouldn't have known, honestly. I'm so proud of you. In fact, do you know what?'

'What?'

I smile. 'I reckon you're a keeper.'

ACKNOWLEDGEMENTS

Thank you so much for reading this book. Once again, I need to say a massive thank you to the Boldwood team, who do so much to turn my scrappy manuscripts into a finished book. Particular thanks go to my editor, Rachel. I can't tell you how much I appreciate your calm wisdom, particularly when I get stuck on a plot point or go spinning off on a dead-end tangent. Thank you also to Rose for your copy editing, and Jennifer for proof reading. Of course, getting the story as good as it can be is just the beginning, and I want to say thank you also to Amanda, Nia, Jenna and all the team for the incredible work you do connecting my books with readers.

If you've read acknowledgements of my previous books, you'll know that this is the point where I usually thank Mandy and Robyn, my alpha and beta readers. Robyn is busy with her baby daughter so hasn't been able to help this time, but Mandy has bravely stepped up again. Thank you!

Final thank yous, as always, go to my family, who could not be more supportive. And where would I be without my dog walks where I do most of my plotting, so thank you to Bertie.

ABOUT THE AUTHOR

Phoebe MacLeod is the author of several popular romantic comedies. She lives in Kent with her partner, grown up children and disobedient dog. Her love for her home county is apparent in her books, which have either been set in Kent or have a Kentish connection.

Sign up to Phoebe MacLeod's mailing list here for news, competitions and updates on future books.

Follow Phoebe on social media:

𝕏 x.com/macleod_phoebe
◼ facebook.com/PhoebeMacleodAuthor
◻ instagram.com/phoebemacleod21

ALSO BY PHOEBE MACLEOD

Someone Else's Honeymoon

Not The Man I Thought He Was

Fred and Breakfast

Let's Not Be Friends

An (Un)Romantic Comedy

Love at First Site

Never Ever Getting Back Together

The Fixer Upper

WHERE ALL YOUR ROMANCE
DREAMS COME TRUE!

THE HOME OF BESTSELLING
ROMANCE AND WOMEN'S
FICTION

 WARNING:
MAY CONTAIN SPICE

SIGN UP TO OUR
NEWSLETTER

https://bit.ly/Lovenotesnews

Boldwood

Boldwood Books is an award-winning fiction publishing company seeking out the best stories from around the world.

Find out more at www.boldwoodbooks.com

Join our reader community for brilliant books, competitions and offers!

Follow us

@BoldwoodBooks

@TheBoldBookClub

Sign up to our weekly
deals newsletter

https://bit.ly/BoldwoodBNewsletter

Printed in Great Britain
by Amazon